Saved by the Pack

A Hidden Preternaturals Novel

ADDISON NORRIS

Table of Contents

Dedication

This book is dedicated to my younger brother, Daniel…who demanded that my first book be dedicated to him.

Hope you enjoy the romance and smut, Dan.

Content Warnings

Please note that this book is intended for mature (18+) audiences and contains the following content and trigger warnings:

- Family member death/murder
- Occult/Supernatural themes
- Stalking
- Kidnapping
- Graphic depictions of violence and gore
- Sexually explicit scenes

If any of these topics are potentially triggering for you, either don't read this book or read with extreme care.

Prologue

Loretta Ramos carefully wedged the phone between her shoulder and ear as she portioned out her leftovers from the batch of pork al pastor she had made for dinner into individual containers. Her daughter, Cordelia, was filling her in on the latest from her externship that she had nearly completed but was currently complaining about one of the other girls in the hospital that she was at trying to have her take the blame for something she didn't do.

"*Mija*, you need to tell your supervisor," she chided her daughter gently, "Don't try to deal with it yourself. Don't resort to petty comebacks, either. That will only get you in trouble."

"*Mama*, you know I would never do that," Cordelia replied innocently. Loretta stopped what she was doing and glared like her daughter was standing right in front of her and put one hand on her hip.

"Cordelia, I know you better than anyone in the world. So cut the innocent act with me. I know you already have something planned and that it's only going to cause you trouble," she scolded. Cordelia sighed.

"But she deserves it," Cordelia retorted, "She's doing it on purpose and if Courtney was telling me the truth today, she was using slurs to refer to me." Loretta sighed and went back to portioning the leftovers.

She tended to make way more food than she needed for a woman living by herself, mostly because she packed an extra lunch or two with her for one of the men that she worked for. While her official job title was housekeeper for the security company, Volsung Security Services, which ran out of a massive five-story estate outside of Coeur d'Alene, she had become more than that. Over the twenty-five years that she had worked there she had somehow become a surrogate mother for the fifteen men that lived and worked there. Inevitably, when she reheated her lunch one of the men would follow their nose into the kitchen and ask if she had brought extra.

"Then you need to go to HR and report it, Cordi, Have Courtney go with you and share what she heard too."

"That's not nearly as satisfying," Cordelia muttered.

"*Dios* save me from a temperamental daughter," Loretta muttered back at her, "I swear you got your temper from that rotten father of yours." Cordelia laughed over the line and Loretta smiled, pleased that her tactic to distract her daughter worked.

"*Mama*, you are just as temperamental as I am."

"See, the daughter I raised would not be so bold as to point out her mother's failings!" Loretta lamented with an exaggerated gasp and Cordelia giggled again.

"You've been watching too many *telanovellas* again, mama."

Loretta clucked her tongue at her daughter as she started putting lids on the various containers and transferring them to the fridge.

"There is no such thing as too many *telanovella, mija*," Loretta retorted, "Besides, I've now got Daniel and Ephraim hooked on them too." Cordelia groaned.

"How did you get guys at work to put up with that nonsense? Aren't they these big, bad security guards? I can't imagine them sitting down to watch with you. Actually, I would pay to see that. Maybe after graduation when I come home to pack up my stuff to move, I'll spend a couple days at work with you so I can witness the hilarity. God, it's been ages since I've gotten to go to work with you."

Loretta paused. She knew exactly how many years it had been, fifteen, since Cordelia had been to the Volsung estate. She shuddered at the memory of seeing a massive wolf pinning her daughter to the ground, teeth at her neck. That was when she discovered who she really worked for. Cordelia wouldn't remember. Liam Benson, her boss and owner of Volsung, had assured her that her daughter would have no memory of the incident, but recommended that Cordelia not come to the estate anymore. He even paid for her to attend camps and for sitter services every summer after Cordelia had nearly been injured.

After the incident, Liam had pulled her aside and offered her an ultimatum, take a huge amount of hush money, resign, never speak of the incident to anyone, and leave town or stay, continue to work for Volsung at an increased rate, learn the truth, and become a ward. At that point Loretta had moved so much already with Cordelia, getting away from her ex-husband, that she didn't want to do it again. Cordelia was getting ready to start first grade, she had friends and Loretta refused to uproot her.

She agreed to stay and she learned the truth about the men at Volsung. She had been uneasy at first. learning about their supernatural nature, but at that point she had already worked for them for a decade, and everything just made more sense about things that she had noticed during that time. Where they had tiptoed around her before, the fifteen men also became more at ease with her and it was easy to keep their secret.

"You know how Mister Benson is, Cordi," Loretta pulled the old line that she always used whenever her daughter expressed an interest in going to the estate where she worked. While she was sure that it would be fine for Cordelia to go now, she didn't want to risk putting her daughter into the same position that she was currently in. Not that it was bad, she was paid well enough and the work wasn't hard unless one of the men had gotten into a serious fight or there was a big job that had taken most of them out of town.

"I know, I know," she relented, "The man is serious about privacy for his workers and his company, blah, blah, blah."

Loretta chuckled as thunder from a spring storm rumbled in the distance. With the leftovers packed and in the fridge she started to fill the sink with hot soapy water, missing the dishwasher from the estate. She carefully dumped in the dirty cookware.

"Now what is this talk of packing up and moving, hm?" Loretta asked her daughter diverting her again, "Why do I feel like you have news to share and you've been holding back."

"I knew you'd pick up on that," the sudden excitement in her daughter's voice was palpable, "You know that I've had a ton of interviews for positions and I finally got a job offer!"

"That is wonderful! I am so proud of you, *mija*! And where is this fabulous new job?"

"Atlanta, Georgia."

Loretta felt her stomach drop. She shut of the water and braced once hand on the edge of the sink.

"*Dios mio, mija*! That's so far away. Are you sure?"

"Absolutely, *mama*, it is what I've always wanted," Cordelia gushed, "The excitement and activity of a big city. Lots of people to meet, things to do, a chance to just get out of the small towns I've been living in. Aren't you excited?"

"Of course, sweet girl, I am excited for you. But really? Atlanta, Georgia? You'll be all by yourself!"

"I mean, yeah, I would be," Cordelia said, "Unless you wanted to come with me?"

"*Mija*—"

"Wait a second just and hear me out," Cordelia interrupted, "You have spent your whole life taking care of me, *mama*. You put your whole life on hold for me and there's nothing that I could possibly do to pay you back for that. I know that you've hidden a lot of our struggles, especially with dad, but I just want to have the chance to take care of you. They're going to be paying me plenty where you don't have to lift a finger if you don't want. You could do something that you wanted to do for a change rather than something you have to do. You wouldn't have to be a housekeeper anymore if you don't want!"

"Oh, I couldn't go, *mija*," Loretta protested, "I'm far too old for a move like that and I enjoy the work that I do. Besides, the Benson estate would fall apart without me—"

"If that were the truth, then he should pay you what your worth."

"Cordelia Elena Ramos," Loretta scolded her daughter, "I did not raise you to be this disrespectful! Mister Benson has been very generous over the years, and I am paid fairly."

"Alright," Cordelia backed down, "But don't you want to get out and see more than just northern Idaho? You said you like the work, I'm sure there's plenty of work in Georgia with all of the old family plantation houses and historic landmarks."

"*Tonta gansa*, yes I'm sure there are housekeeping jobs in Atlanta, but you know how particular Volsung is! *Mija*, if this is what you want, then go for it. Just don't forget your *mama* here in Idaho when you become a big city girl…"

"Please promise me you'll at least think about it?" Cordelia begged. Loretta sighed. As much as she hated to admit it, the idea of moving did appeal to her, despite her earlier protests. But she didn't know if she could with the agreement that she had made with Liam. She would have to ask him in the morning.

"Alright, *mi querida*, I promise you I will think about it," Loretta conceded, "but I'm not inclined to uproot my entire life now. But maybe when I think about retiring." Her daughter sighed over the line and Loretta couldn't help but laugh, "I'm going to let you go, my poor put upon daughter. I have a sink full of dishes to clean. You take care and I will talk to you tomorrow."

"Alright, *mama. Te amo.*"

"*Te amo, mija.*"

Loretta disconnected the call and turned on the radio that sat on her kitchen counter. The lively strains of music filled the space as she started to scour her dishes. The storm outside started to kick up as rain started to fall and the thunder boomed again. She thought of the Volsung men again, she knew that they were supposed to be out doing a wilderness training this evening and were going to get soaked. Which meant there would be mud and the smell of wet dog to get rid of.

A pounding on her front door startled her and caused her to drop a dish on the floor. It shattered and the pieces scattered across the sandy tile. She cursed to herself and grabbed the broom and dustpan from beside the fridge and quickly swept the broken pieces into a pile. The person at the front door pounded again.

"Coming," Loretta called out as she propped the broom against the counter and set the dustpan down. She hustled from the kitchen and dining room and down the hall to the front door. Through the large oval window in the door she could see a dark shape standing there waiting. She flicked on the porch light and peered at the person, surprised.

"Oh goodness," Loretta said opening the door slightly, "What are you—"

Her question was cut off as the figure lunged forward, pushing her back and forcing their way in. Loretta stumbled and fell back, landing hard on the floor, pain shooting up her arms and back. The intruder had turned, closing and locking the front door, while they were distracted, Loretta scrambled to her feet. She immediately thought of the panic button that she had in her purse, a measure of protection that she and the Volsung men had agreed upon if she ever needed help. She turned and ran back down the hall as the intruder shouted after her.

Back in the kitchen, she lunged for her purse which was hanging off the back of a chair. She knocked it over, spilling the contents on the floor. She cursed, falling to her knees and searching desperately. Loretta had just spied the panic button and was reaching for it when a booted foot slammed down on her wrist, not only pinning it to the floor but a resounding crack filled the room as pain shot up her arm. She started to scream when another boot connected with the side of her head.

Dizzy and disoriented, she crumpled completely to the floor. Her vision swam, darkening around the edges when she saw her assailant pull a large knife from a sheathe on their belt. As they completely overtook her she prayed for Cordelia's safety and prayed that Liam and the pack wouldn't blame themselves for this.

Chapter 1

Cordelia

The jolt from the plane harshly touching down on the tarmac jostled me awake. I couldn't remember falling asleep during the short flight from Bend, Oregon to Spokane, Washington, but I was certain that it had been the only sleep I'd been able to get during the last seventy-two hours. I rubbed my eyes as the plane taxied towards the terminal while everyone around me had already started to unbuckle their and gather their personal belongings. Groggily, I pulled out my cell phone and turned it off airplane mode. Instantly it lit up with alerts and e-mails. Dozens of social media alerts from friends writing to offer their condolences. I swiped the notifications away and felt the familiar prickle of tears in the corners of my eyes. I wanted desperately to be done with crying, my eyes stung, my chest hurt, and my throat was raw. I wasn't done mourning my mother's sudden and unexpected death, but I certainly wanted to be over crying.

I couldn't believe that just a couple of days ago I had been telling her about the job offer I had received from a hospital in Atlanta and trying to convince her to move with me once my externship was up in a month. I was so excited to, finally, be moving on from small, podunk towns like Klamath Falls, Coeur d'Alene, and even Bend. I had always had a big city mindset, even as a kid, when I hung postcards and cut outs from magazines that featured big city skylines: New York, Chicago, San Francisco, Los Angeles. I had wanted to share and experience them all with my mother. Now, instead, I had to plan her funeral.

"Ma'am are you alright?" the soft voice of the stewardess made me jump as I looked around the small aircraft, it was empty except for the two of us, the cleaning crew, and the pilots up front, who were both wearing matching concerned looks. I immediately started to scramble for my carry-ons.

"Yes, I'm so sorry," I stammered and floundered, "It's been a long couple of days. I just lost track of myself for the moment—"

"Are you driving?" I could hear the note of concern in her voice and once again I felt hot tears spring to my eyes.

"No, no, I have a friend picking me up, I'm not going to be driving."

"Alright then, don't rush, I don't want you to forget anything."

"I'm sure I've got it all, thank you." I said, feeling flushed from embarrassment, before slinging my backpack onto my back. When I looked up at her she was holding out a small package of tissues and giving me a pitying look. She made a pointed look at my cheeks and I realized that I was crying once again, this time silent tears that spilled over. With a shaky breath I took the tissues and nodded my thanks to the stewardess. I kept my head down as I exited the plane.

With only small concourses in the airport, it was a short walk from my gate to the baggage claim, but I ducked into the restroom before leaving the secured part of the airport. I just needed a moment to gather myself. Standing in the stark gray bathroom with my bag at my feet, I ran my wrists under cold water, attempting to cool the flush that had risen again and to calm me down. When I looked up into the mirror, I could see why the stewardess had been so startled. My long dark hair was frizzy and coming out of the braid it was in, which accented the dark circles under my red, bloodshot hazel eyes and my normally dusky, Hispanic complexion was the palest I had ever seen it.

With a sigh, I started to put myself back together as some semblance of a human being. I splashed cold water on my face, rubbing my cheeks to be rid of the tracks my tears had left, before undoing my braid and raking my fingers through my hair, smoothing it out. I settled on putting it up in a quick bun instead of another braid. Nothing much could be done about the eyes now, so they would just have to stay bloodshot and puffy. Satisfied, I left the restroom and prepared for the onslaught that waited for me at baggage claim.

When I exited the secured part of the airport, I saw two familiar faces: my childhood best friend Hannah and her high school sweetheart, now husband, Shane.

Hannah was the day to my night: pale, nearly platinum blonde hair, bright blue eyes, and a complexion somewhere between milky white and porcelain. When it came to our personalities, though, we could have been identical twins. In fact, several of our teachers in high school had nicknamed us the Hellfire Twins, for our short tempers and 'take no bullshit' attitudes. Usually, I cut to the quick with overly apparent sarcasm and snark, while Hannah disguised her viciousness with a bubbly personality and over the top sweetness that left people wondering. Hannah had aways been the more fashionable one of us, which was apparent even now, dressed in stylish jeans that fit her perfectly, ankle boots, and a baby blue wrap top that accentuated her slight frame.

Her husband, Shane, was an avid outdoorsman and helped out with his family's guide and rental business. He had similar features to Hannah, namely the blonde hair and blue eyes, but he looked like he had been left out in the sun for a couple of months with his tanned skin and perpetual scruff. He was dressed as he always was in boots, worn jeans, and a flannel button down with the sleeves rolled to his elbow. Hannah had always joked that he was ahead of the 'lumberjack chic' trend that had taken over, and Shane would just nod his head and say 'Yes, dear.'

I noticed that Hannah's face lit up when she spotted me in the thinning crowd, however I also couldn't help but notice that her smile didn't go all the way up to her eyes.

"Cordi," she greeted me, arms open wide. I felt my lower lip start to quiver, and before I knew it, I felt her arms around me, squeezing me tightly, Hannah's familiar floral perfume surrounding me. It was the same perfume that she had been wearing since high school and there was a comfort in something so familiar when everything else felt wrong. I hugged my friend back, squeezing her tightly. "I'm so sorry, hun. I am so, so sorry." Hannah's voice was soft, cracking over the words and I knew now that I wasn't alone anymore. Still, my stomach dropped to my feet like a lead weight. Reality was sinking in now and seeing and hearing Hannah made everything come crashing down on me.

Now, it was real.

Now, I knew I wouldn't see my mother's smile again.

Now, my world was breaking.

Somehow, someway we managed to grab my bags and the two whisked me off to Shane's truck. I sat in the back of the extended cab, staring out the window as the landscape flew by. Hannah was talking, but I was only hearing about half of it. Hannah was talking about everything. From the latest gossip about people we had known in high school to her courses she was taking at the cosmetology college and how things were going with Shane's family business, but I was only head about half of it. Hannah mentioned something about going with me to see the funeral home to make arrangements and about staying at their place.

"I want to go home."

As soon as the request was out of my mouth, I knew it was a bad idea. I knew I couldn't go yet. The crime scene hadn't been released yet. 'Mi mama's house' and 'crime scene' should have never been in the same sentence, but that was the reality of it all. My mother hadn't just died suddenly but peacefully in her sleep.

My mother had been murdered in cold blood.

Chapter 2

Liam

Are you even paying attention?" My brother's snarl snapped me out of the floating void of thoughts I had been content to sit in for the last half hour as he droned on. The pack was gathered around the large conference table that we used for pack and business meetings. I had been drumming my fingers on the glossy cherry wood surface, which had apparently annoyed Franklin enough to snap at me. I sat at the head of the massive oval table and along each side were seven occupied chairs, except Franklin's which was empty as he was standing opposite of me at a small podium going over information for the pack. Behind him were several large screens which usually worked in concert to present one large image, but were now working independently to show a myriad of information about our local fae court.

"Of course," I said not missing a beat and sitting up straighter in my chair. Nobody was dumb enough to snicker out loud at their Alpha and pack leader, but I could sense their disbelief. The urge to sigh and pinch the bridge of my nose overwhelming – a classic sign of mine that indicated that I was frustrated that everyone in the room was familiar with. To give in would be unbecoming. I held myself to a high standard that the others were expected to match. Lead by example, my father had always told me, and it was one of his many teachings that I always adhered to.

"Alright then," my brother said, the challenge in his voice plainly evident, "Repeat back to me what I've been talking about for the last five minutes." I growled at Franklin, I hated when he played these types of games. He wasn't outwardly challenging my authority and place as leader, but he was dancing on the line and he knew it. I knew that if I didn't want to, I didn't have to, and I could override him as his superior. But honestly, I just wanted to put him in his place.

"You were talking about the final details of my arranged marriage to Lord Alderkin's daughter—"

"Lorelei," Jason, the youngest, newest member of the pack chimed in. Franklin shot him a glare, and the young man shrunk into his seat.

"Yes, once Lorelei and I are wed, we will solidify our position here as defenders of the Ley while also renewing the contract that we have with his court to support us in our efforts. We will have the added benefit of continuing to live in peace with the Sidhe, the use of Lorelei's unique finding ability, a skill that they still haven't explained exactly how it works, and we will be able to continue keeping the mortals safe from the covens and coteries.

You were also discussing the return to normal business immediately following the wedding. You've reviewed half a dozen contracts and are ready to forward them to Rich and I for review for approval and execution."

Franklin groaned, knowing that I was technically correct, which was the best kind of correct. As the pack's lawyer, he often danced and dallied with technicalities to skirt trouble, the mortal law, and the absurdities of paranormal law. The latter was by far what he dealt with the most and was the most convoluted. Not just because magic was involved, but because supernatural law hinged on ancient treaties and accords that could be interpreted no less than a dozen different ways.

"Yes, you seem to have an excellent understanding of the matter at hand," he replied curtly, flipping the page of his legal pad up. "That appears to be all of the pack business for the moment—"

"What about Missus Ramos?" This time it was Noah, the pack's most adept tracker and investigator, that spoke up. A hush fell over the room and I could feel the pack all turn their gazes toward me. I took a slow deep breath because this was a delicate situation.

Loretta Ramos had, up until three days ago, been the housekeeper for the pack's estate. She was motherly, discreet, and a ward of the Coeur d'Alene Pack for fifteen years. She hadn't showed up to work nor answered the pack's calls that day. Worried that she might be injured or sick, I had sent Jason to check on her. I had been shocked when Jason had called me shortly after leaving, completely beside himself and barely keeping a leash on his wolf, to inform me that he had found Loretta dead.

The mortal authorities had to be called in, and the pack had no choice but to let them lead the investigation. It didn't matter that the pack's business had triple the resources the city police did, they couldn't get involved without definitive proof that it was related to something from the supernatural world.

From Jason's description and the initial crime scene reports that Fletcher had 'procured' from the department there was no reason for them to intervene according to the council of wolves. It rankled the pack because every single man in this room respected Loretta, would bleed for her, and (if Liam were to let go of the reins) hunt down and slaughter her killer. However, that was too risky. The preternatural community at large frowned on high profile, high exposure actions.

Sending a pack of werewolves after a mortal murderer was a perfect example of this.

Even though the pack wanted blood, I knew the call that I had to make.

"Dealing out justice is currently in the hands of the mortal authorities," my words were met by a chorus of growls. I held up my hand and they immediately silenced. "However, I am keeping a close eye on their investigation. If I am not satisfied with their conclusion, we will conduct our own investigation and, if needed, serve as judge, jury, and executioner."

While there were still a few that I could feel through pack bonds that didn't want to wait for bloodshed, most of the pack found my resolution agreeable. I would reach out to the individuals after the meeting concluded to make certain that they did nothing stupid, presupposing Frank didn't corner me in my office to reprimand me in private. "As a final note on the matter, I have arranged for all of her funeral costs to be paid for by Volsung and pack accounts…so long as there are no objections?" All the men shook their heads.

"Is there someone to make the arrangements? Or do we need to intervene?" Silas, my second in command, asked. He was a details man, which came from years working in international logistics, nothing ever seemed to escape his notice.

"There is," I replied haltingly, "Most of the pack should remember that Loretta has a daughter." I watched with satisfaction as Edgar and Augustus, two of the pack that were constantly jockeying for position, looked ashamed. The girl had stumbled into the middle of one of their many dominance fights. I was forced to intervene, pulling Augustus in wolf form off her, and used the limited magic of the pack and my position as Alpha to suppress her memories. It had directly led to Loretta becoming our ward. I had not been pleased with either of them after the incident and they had both been punished for their behavior. "She is supposed to be arriving back in town today."

"Were you ever able to get a hold of her and let her know about the payment arrangement you made?" Silas asked, curiosity evident on his face.

"Ah, no." I admitted sheepishly, "I am hoping it will be a pleasant surprise for her to not have to deal with that burden. Now, the meeting is adjourned, you can carry on with your normal day." My dismissal was firm, and nearly all the pack left.

Except Silas and Franklin. I suspected I was in trouble and I appreciated that they at least waited until the other members of the pack were out of ear shot before laying into me.

"William, this treaty isn't a fucking joke, I cannot fathom why you continue to treat it like it is one. We are just over two weeks out from the wedding date, now is not the time to start checking out." Franklin snapped as he sat down harshly in his chair to my left. I was shocked as he was never prone to swearing. I contemplated my brother for a moment. The familial resemblance between my brother and I was abundantly apparent. We shared the same hard jaw, roman nose, fair-skinned complexion, and deep-set eyes: his a startling shade of green, mine a golden-green hazel.

Where we differed was our physicality. We were both tall, but he was lean like a swimmer or runner where I was broader in the shoulders and torso like a wrestler. I kept my sandy blonde hair longer and a bit unruly, but not so long that it couldn't be easily tamed for business meetings or ruin my professional appearance, and it could be styled if I felt like it. Frank's hair was darker, closer to brown than blonde, and he kept short on the sides, with only a enough length on top to be parted on the side and gelled into place. He looked like a stereotypical lawyer, a fact that I had teased him about over our long lives.

"I've never been a fan of political marriages," I groaned rubbing my temples, "and I've never understood why some nations are so willing to send their daughters off for the sake of keeping the peace. I mean Lord Alderkin doesn't even really know me, he doesn't know the pack and hasn't even bothered to try in the half century we've been here. But it doesn't faze him, he's ready to send his daughter off to a pack of wolves. We could be psychopaths!"

"Luckily most of us aren't. I'm beginning to have doubts about our fearless leader though," Silas quipped.

If I were to be considered 'tall and broad', Silas made me appear scrawny. He was close to seven feet in height and pushing three hundred pounds of solid muscle. His head was shaved bald, but he often sported a few day's growth on his chin, never fully committing to a beard. He cut an intimidating picture with his perpetual scowl, dark skin, and narrowed eyes, and everyone assumed he was just an enforcer and muscle, which was the furthest thing from the truth. He was incredibly intelligent, an intelligence you could see in his brown eyes whenever he worked on a problem. He ran logistics for security jobs and when we needed to transport or protect discovered artifacts. While not entirely tactical, his plans often accounted for out of the box complications that had saved us on jobs more than once.

With regards to his comment, however, I swiped a hand down my face, hiding the fact that I was childishly rolling my eyes.

"Har. Har. You're too damn funny," I sneered back at him.

"Well then look at it this way," Franklin said leaning forward and tapping his index finger on the tabletop, "Blood ties, in the form of a child, will be stronger than any written treaty. Not to mention you're getting up there in years—"

"What the hell is that supposed to mean?" I snarled, letting my power as pack Alpha drip off each word. Franklin and Silas both winced.

"What your brother means," Silas interjected, "Is that you're quickly approaching two hundred and fifty years old and haven't found your mate yet. Perhaps it is time to consider that isn't going to happen and you need to keep the pack from being stymied." I grunted, hating when the two of them teamed up and used logic on me.

Goddamn Universal Pack Laws.

Back when civilizations were being founded and growing like weeds, the original council of werewolves had decided on a series of laws to govern all packs. While they weren't hard and fast rules, the trend over the centuries was rather simple: Packs that adhered to the Laws had a better longevity than those that didn't.

And the number two rule was that no member of a pack could find a mate until the Alpha had claimed one. Werewolves were, by nature, incredibly jealous and potentially violent creatures, and for a wolf to find a mate before his Alpha…well it didn't usually sit well with the Alpha and typically led to lots of bloodshed and the pack dynamics changing.

I pinched the bridge of my nose, a migraine starting to settle in behind my eyes.

"Alright, alright," I conceded, "I will take my marriage to Lorelei more seriously and treat it with the proper respect it deserves. I will not shirk my duties any further as Alpha. I have been selfish for far too long."

"Damn straight," Silas growled. Both Franklin and I looked at him with open shock. My second in command winced and mumbled something about needing to check in with some business or other and stormed out of the meeting room. I looked to Franklin, hoping for some explanation, but he looked just as dumbfounded as I did.

"Has he found his mate?" I asked, shocked by the potential revelation.

"Not to my knowledge, but he does leave the estate grounds more than anyone for business." Our pack, in addition to being united as a single group of werewolves, also worked together under the banner of a security company that provided an array of services to the preternatural and mortal communities. Silas oversaw any jobs that had to do with transportation which let to him spending a good deal of time away from the pack's estate. As my second in command, I trusted him implicitly, however if he was hiding something from me, it could be cause for concern.

"I'm sure we'll find out what's been eating him once the wedding is over," I say, cautiously dismissing it for the moment. "But I will try to talk to him and see what is going on." The last thing I needed was a fissure within the pack, if we didn't present a unified front to the fae we were going to be seriously screwed.

Chapter 3

Cordelia

I never liked funeral homes. They always gave me the creeps and Gates' Funeral Home was no different. The building had once been a large family home, but the main floor had been converted into several large parlors to hold multiple viewings, the upstairs served as the administrative offices where Hannah and I were meeting with Mister Gates, and the basement, I assumed, was retrofitted for embalming. But that wasn't what bothered me the most, although it was creepy to think of how kids, at one point, were raised here.

It was the smell.

The smell turned my stomach the most: musty with an old overpowering floral scent and something astringent that ran underneath it all. Combine that with the too spongy flooring, the drab floral wallpaper with a unsettling pattern and it was a recipe for nausea. I could feel the few bites of breakfast that I had shared with Hannah starting to fight its way back up.

"Miss Ramos, let me just start off by saying that I am so sorry for your loss," Mister Gates' demeanor wasn't helping my upset stomach. I smiled tightly at him and gave a curt nod. I felt Hannah's foot nudge mine and when I looked at her, she was giving me a supportive but distinct 'play nice' look. I was certain that she was going to be a great mom, which was going to happen sooner rather than later. Hannah had broken the news to me the previous night and I had been over the moon for her and Shane. It was something positive for me to focus on in the ocean of sorrow I had found myself in. Shaking my head, I looked back at the funeral director.

"Yes, thank you," I say haltingly, "It's just been all so overwhelming and I'm having a hard time just processing it all."

The elder man nodded knowingly; he was used to this type of thing. I took a deep breath as he prepared to speak.

"The loss of a loved one is always very difficult, even when one has the time to mentally and emotionally prepare." He paused a moment, allowing me to absorb his words, as he searched for the next ones, "When we lose someone, violently and without warning, the hurt and pain that we feel seems to run deeper and people are often left holding this emotional baggage. It could be anything from things left unsaid to just being robbed of the opportunity to say goodbye; or telling someone how much you love them and hearing someone say those words in return. That baggage becomes a struggle to hold onto and causes us to feel overwhelmed which directly causes us the inability to cope.

"Our aim is to give you, your family, and everyone that was friends of your mother the closure that they need. It is rough to hear but the fact is, the dead are gone and funerals afford the living one last chance to say goodbye." He then transitioned into the various service types that the home offered along with service options through the Catholic church that my mother belonged to.

All the options and choices made my head buzz.

They all also sounded expensive.

Sitting there listening, I wrung my hands as he talked about casket types and funeral plots. My mind, sadly, had finally found a focal point aside from my mother's murder to fixate on.

How on earth was I going to pay for all of this?

My mom had some savings, I knew that for sure, and I had a little saved up, but I had student loans that were looming large in my future and this funeral would easily match one year of those loans, and then some.

I must have been staring at the financing brochure that was on his desk a little too long, because Mister Gates cleared his throat causing me to shift my gaze back to him. He gave me a generous, kindly smile, like he knew where my thoughts had drifted to.

"Now, normally, we would be discussing financing and down payments, which is something I absolutely detest. However, Miss Ramos, you have a benefactor."

"I'm sorry, a what?"

"I was contacted by a third party, and they let me know that they would be footing the bill for all of the costs of your mother's service."

"I…I don't know anything about this," I stammered looking at Hannah, who looked as confused as I felt, "I didn't ask for or want this. Who would do something like this?"

"Well, the person didn't specify that they wanted to be anonymous so, I suppose there's no harm in telling you," he stated simply as he flipped through a small notebook, "Volsung Security Services, their CEO reached out to me—"

"Liam Benson," I said without even thinking. Gates and Hannah both looked surprised. "He was my mother's employer." I said by way of explanation.

All I could see was red. I had never met the man personally, and my mother always spoke so highly of him. I did not feel the same. I had a problem with the fact that my mother worked her hands to the bone for him as his housekeeper at his estate for twenty-five years and not once did he offer her any increase to her pay beyond a flat annual increase and only gave her the most basic of benefits. And here he was, deciding now to chip in and help.

I wished he was here now because I'd love to give that jackass a piece of my mind.

"I don't see what the big deal is," Hannah said as we turned on to the street where she lived. I watched the cookie cutter houses pass by, thinking hard before I answered her.

"My mom and I always only had each other. If we needed anything, we were a team working together to get it. We were partners in crime and didn't rely on anyone else to give us a helping hand. She took care of me, and now it's my responsibility to take care of her and return the favor, and some suit, who never bothered to give my mother a real pay raise, has the audacity to waltz in and just pay for everything. It's insulting."

"I hate to break it to you, but maybe he's just trying to be nice. Maybe there is no motive behind it other than generosity. Your mother did work for his family and for his company a long, long time," Hannah reasoned, and I shook my head at her, I couldn't help thinking that there was some ulterior motive that I didn't know about yet. Knowing what I did about Benson and my mother's employment, it boggled my mind that suddenly now he was stepping up. Seeing my expression, Hannah frowned. "Also, I don't want to sound rude, but you're a mostly broke college student. Not having to take on more debt may not be the worst thing."

She had me there, and as much as I wanted to agree with her, my pride just wouldn't let me. Nobody I had ever met just gave away that much money without a hook or catch attached to it. There was no such thing as a free lunch after all. If you wanted something, you worked for it and earned it, that was something my mother had ingrained in me. It was something that had never failed me, at least not yet.

Approaching Hannah's house, I could see that there were more cars than normal in the drive. It took me a moment, but I was shocked to realize that one of them was my mother's silver Toyota Camry, but the other one was a massive Ford pick-up truck with the Coeur d'Alene Police logo on it. I immediately wrung my hands and swallowed hard. When I first had gotten the call about my mother, Detective Riley, who was in charge of the case, had grilled me pretty hard asking me questions that I wasn't in the mental state to answer and could barely wrap my head around. I wasn't prepared for another round of that.

Hannah parked on the street next to the driveway before giving my shoulder a supportive squeeze. When we got out of the car, Shane and a uniformed officer exited the house. They appeared to be joking and laughing, which chased away most of the anxiety that was churning in my gut. Surely it couldn't be bad news, right?

As we approached the porch, I recognized the officer.

"Well, well! Look at you, Officer Miller!" I said teasingly. The officer tried to seem unaffected, but I could see the faintest hint of a blush creep up his neck. I immediately stepped up to hug him, and he returned the hug tightly.

"I am so, so sorry, Cordi," his voice hadn't changed one bit since high school, "We're going to find him." I stepped back from the hug, reeling a little bit from his words as reality settled back on me, one of his hands lingered on my shoulder.

Despite belonging to different social groups in high school, Jackson Miller and I had been friends for a long time, our families had been neighbors for most of elementary school. His family moved away to Idaho Falls for a short time before they moved back as we were beginning high school. During that time, he had gone from a timid, kind of athletic kid to a golden boy quarterback. We had reconnected through volunteer work at the hospital the summer after our freshman year.

He hadn't changed much during the five years since graduating high school, except maybe looking a little tired. He was still taller than me by a few inches with broad shoulders that were barely contained by his dark colored uniform. His blonde hair was a little closer cut, way less boy band than it had been, and the beginnings of a five 'o clock shadow along his jaw. His blue eyes still held some youthful glimmer, but he looked painfully serious right now.

I regretted for a moment falling out of touch with him, because we really had been thick as thieves. He had stayed here, determined to make it onto the police force, while I had gone away to school to study medical imaging.

I realized I was just standing there staring at him while my mind wandered. I took another step back, breaking contact with him, as I floundered for a response.

"Thank you…I know." Both seemed stupid, but it was all that I had. Jack nodded understandingly and then started patting his pockets.

"I'm actually, uh, here on semi-official business," he said producing a set of familiar looking keys from his pocket, "I've got good news and bad news. Good news is that your mother's car has been released, so you can get around town now. I had the guys down at the car wash detail it for you and everything." He held out the keys to me.

"Thanks, Jack. You didn't really have to go through all of that trouble."

"You didn't see it after the techs were done with it," he said attempting to lighten the mood. I smiled, but it was fake. I didn't want to think about some stranger combing through my mother's car with luminol and fingerprint powder. Jack must have sensed that because he quickly dropped his half smile and continued with business.

"Unfortunately, it's looking like it might be the end of the week before her house will be released." That was something of a relief for me. However, I started to imagine the clean-up that would need to be done and I felt my stomach flip. That was another problem for another day. For now, I wasn't going to think about it.

"Thanks, Jack," I repeated taking the offered keys. "Again, I appreciate it all."

"Yeah, no problem—" he was cut off by his radio crackling to life. "Excuse me." He took a few steps away from Shane, Hannah, and I to respond to the call. I looked down at the keys in my hand, and I noticed an extra keyring and set that was marked with a gold tag that said, 'Benson Estate' and an idea immediately came to mind. It was probably terrible, but I quickly resolved myself to follow through with it by the time Jack came back.

"Well, I've got to go, but maybe we can grab lunch or dinner later this week? Catch up a bit?" Jack asked. I nodded, but my thoughts were elsewhere.

"Yeah, that sounds great," I smiled. He pulled a card out of his chest pocket and quickly wrote on the back of it before handing it to me.

"Duty calls," he said before saying goodbye to Hannah and Shane. He climbed into the police truck and backed out of the drive, waving before he took off. Once he was off, Hannah and Shane headed towards the house, I headed towards the car.

"Where are you off to?" asked Hannah with a suspicious glare.

"I've got an errand I need to run real quick," I responded, trying not to give anything away, "And just want some time to clear my head."

"Uh-huh," she said disbelievingly, "If you're not back by sundown and I haven't heard from you, I'm sending Shane and Jack to that estate after you."

"Fine," I replied and unlocked the sedan and climbed in. I had driven my mother to work plenty of times over the years, when I needed the car when we had needed to share the car when I was in high school. I was sure that I could still find my way to the Benson Estate.

Chapter 4

Liam

I was reviewing prospective jobs and other business requests in my office when I felt a ripple of worry and excitement work its way through the pack bonds. Something was happening, and everyone was taking notice. Before I could figure it out, there was a sharp knock on my office door, judging from the scent it was Franklin again. I didn't want to delve into the minutiae of the agreement with the fae for the fifth time today, and I certainly didn't want to talk about marriage or the wedding again.

"Go away, Frank," I shouted, "I'm busy doing actual work." The door opened, and my brother brazenly popped his head into my office around the door.

"Like you're the only one that works around here," he scoffed, using the door as a barrier between him and I.

"It feels like it more and more," I responded, turning away from the computer to stare directly at him, "If you're here to ram more wedding business down my throat, I might have to consider killing you."

"Actually," he hesitated fingertips drumming on the oak door, "this is more of an…immediate problem."

"I don't have time for the dramatics, what is it?"

"Miss Ramos has just pulled through the gate, she informed Gus over the intercom that she wants to talk with you. He also said that she sounded…angry." He looked at me with an arched brow, silently asking if this was a problem he should deal with. While I was certain Franklin could have her spinning and running in circles without giving her any real answers or insight, it felt cheap and underhanded to me. If she wanted to talk to me, then I would talk to her. I flicked off my computer screen and pushed my chair back from my desk.

"No," I replied standing and grabbing my suit jacket from the back of my chair and sliding it on, "I will talk to her. I owe her that much." Franklin stepped further into the room.

"You say that like it's our fault her mother was killed. Is there something you know that I don't?"

"No," I responded tersely coming around my desk and buttoning my jacket, "However, Fletcher made a rather convincing argument that has me thinking." I moved past Franklin and exited my office. Franklin quickly caught up and matched my pace as we went down the wood paneled hall.

This wing of the estate housed our business offices and featured a lot more polish and professional décor than the upper floors where our various personal suites were housed. Every fifteen feet or so there was a solid, oak door behind each was a personal office for each of the pack members who required them for their position with Volsung. As we walked past some of the doors were open, members of the pack meeting and preparing for a return to business as normal after the wedding, but I also got the sense they were all waiting to see how this interaction with Loretta's daughter was going to play out.

"What did Fletcher say?" Franklin pressed.

Fletcher was our pack's lone Beta wolf, meaning he was more mild-mannered and less aggressive than the rest of the members of the pack. He and his wolf just didn't compete for pack standing, meaning that he was about the only person that could really speak freely to me and the others, because we wouldn't take it as a challenge or threat. When I had gone to him after the meeting the other day to ask why he wasn't content with my ruling on investigating Ms. Ramos' murder, he laid out a very logical, convincing argument.

"He thinks someone might be attempting to sabotage or interrupt the uniting of us and the fae. Which makes sense, with us in agreement with the fae, the Ley here will be one of the most well-guarded in the states, if not the world. There's no doubt in my mind that the Covens and Coteries would like to see this treaty fail."

"Do you want me to contact the Council?" Franklin asked, referring to the governing body of werewolves as we passed one of the sets of stairs that led to the upper three floors, "We can have an independent investigator sent out and have them look at the case."

"No," I responded immediately, "You know just as well as I that they'll investigate us as well to ensure that we're still fit enough to defend the Ley. That's an added stress we don't need right now."

"Well, what is your plan then?" Franklin asked as we reached the top of the main hall staircase. The space was grandiose with a single sweeping, wooden staircase took up the right side of the room and a lofted walkway that led to eastern wing of the estate which housed more offices on the second floor and more living spaces on the third, fourth, and fifth levels. The floors of the entry were dark hardwood, polished to a high shine, and the walls were a pale, blue-gray color and peppered with curated art that an interior designer had suggested when we updated the space about five years ago. The lower half of the walls had wainscoting that matched the floors.

To right of the stairs the hall opened to a 'formal' living room, typically the space was used to meet with clients during initial consultations. To the left was the dining room, large enough to host all fifteen members of the pack. Opposite of the main doors was another hallway that lead to the back of the house and a windowed corridor that looked over the acreage behind the estate. That corridor housed Ephraim's small clinic, Fletcher's lab and workspace, and the stairs leading to the basement.

The only other major features were the massive chandelier that hung from the ceiling and the large wooden double front doors that were about ten feet tall and works of art in and of themselves dark wood with scrolling, ornate ironwork.

I remember how Loretta complained that it looked like a showroom and was missing personality and heart. I had always countered that it was just a space that we needed to move through and needed to look professional when we had clients show up for meetings. Loretta would shake her head and mutter something about 'stupid men.' With a sigh, I turned to Franklin.

"We're going beyond monitoring it in the local news. I've given Fletcher permission to hack the local police department's system and monitor the case."

"You WHAT?!"

Franklin's tirade was cut off by the resonant chimes of the doorbell. I shrugged at him before heading down the curving steps at a light jog.

"He's an adept hacker, already had a backdoor into their system, and knows not to get caught. He's also been specifically told not to interfere." I could feel my brother glaring daggers at me as the doorbell sounded again.

"This conversation isn't over—"

"It is for the moment," I countered, interrupting his tirade. I rested my hand on the knob of the door and looked back at him with a stern, commanding look. He threw his hands up in the air in frustration and with a harumph, Franklin stormed off in the direction of his office. I turned back to the solid wood door and took a moment to breathe and calm myself. On the other side of this door was a reeling, hurting young girl that demanded all my attentions at the moment. I needed to drop my normal aggressive nature and focus on helping this Loretta's poor daughter out.

I raked a hand through my hair, straightened my lapels, and opened the door. I opened my mouth to greet her and froze. In my mind, I had imagined the gangly, young girl that had accompanied her mother to work when she had been seven. The girl, no…*woman*…in front of me hardly reminded me of the memory in my head.

Her skin was warm, tawny color that looked like it was soft as silk to the touch. Her heart-shaped face wore an expression of slight confusion, her full pillowy lips slightly parted, like she was on the verge of saying something. Her eyes were wide, showing of their caramel brown color. She wore a pair of dark wash jeans that flared at the bottom of the leg, and hugged her hips, and her off the shoulder blouse was a deep maroon color with bell sleeves and all kinds of lace and ties that I wanted to peel off of her. She possessed all those qualities that appealed to the baser side of my wolf and I: she was shorter than me by a head, her body was that appealing hourglass shape – full breasts, narrow waist, and flared hips that I knew instinctively would be perfect to grab onto as I fucked her from behind, rough and fast. My pulse raced as I felt my body react embarrassingly quickly to her presence.

"Mister Benson? Liam Benson?" She asked with a silken voice that sent a thrill through my body. What was this reaction I was having to her? I could feel my wolf clawing and scraping at me to take and protect the woman in front of me. She was the only thing he wanted, and he wasn't afraid to fight me for control. As I mentally wrestled my wolf back down, I managed to maintain my control and my composure, but only just. I hadn't had this much trouble reigning in my wolf since it awoke when I was a teenager.

The worst part of this mental struggle and surge of animalistic desire was that I was sure the rest of the pack could feel it too.

"Miss Ramos," I managed to finally cough out in a strained voice, my hand bending and crushing the door handle that was out of her sight with my superhuman strength.

"Are…you alright?" she asked with a hand extended like she was torn between touching me and keeping me at arm's length. If she made contact, I was certain that I would literally lose control and my wolf would take over. Based on my wolf's thoughts that were bubbling to the surface, it would mean rutting right here on the doorstep. Very consciously I leaned back from her hand, avoiding contact but instead catching her scent as the breeze caught her long, onyx colored hair. She smelled of woman, anger, sorrow, and arousal. I homed in on that middle scent, the sour mix of salt and pain. It angered my wolf for a variety of reasons but cleared the hormonal haze that had taken over my thoughts.

"Sorry, yes, I am fine," I replied putting on my business voice, "Although I should be the one asking you that, Miss Ramos." I opened the door further and motioned for her to step inside. She didn't at first and seemed to be considering her options of entering or running back to her car. I prayed for her sake that she didn't run, my wolf loved to chase anything, especially prey. Her running would trigger that instinctual response and this interaction would not end well. Thankfully for both of use, she relented and stepped into the pack's home. My wolf howled for joy.

"It's been pretty miserable," she replied after looking around the foyer, all hesitation now seemingly gone as she took in the space, frowning at the opulent chandelier hanging in the space, "It's the most horrid experience I could ever possibly imagine." Even though her voice was soft and quiet, not carrying through the massive foyer, the undercurrent of anger, frustration, and sorrow was beyond evident. I felt very exposed in my own den. I was supposed to be its master, but something about her was enchanting and completely disarming. Thinking about her words and tone, I didn't know how to respond immediately. However, my voice made its return when I sensed that all the pack members were focused on me through the pack bonds.

"You have our deepest and most sincere condolences. Loretta, your mother, was more than just a housekeeper to us. If there's anything I can do—"

"Actually, that's why I'm here." She fiddled with her hands, keys jingling. I quickly surmised it to be nerves.

"We can speak in my office then," I reply gesturing towards the stairs, "Follow me." As I turned to go up the stairs, I fought hard to suppress a groan and a growl. My brother stood there waiting, for the most part looking nonchalant, but I knew better. He was tensed and on guard.

"Miss Ramos, this is my brother Franklin. He serves as our company's legal counsel," I introduced him as we made it to the top of the stairs. Franklin smiled winningly and extended a hand to her, and I immediately had to fight to keep my hackles from raising. How dare he try to touch her! Couldn't he see that she was mine?

I felt a whirling tug on the bond between Frank and I, he was attempting to get my attention…not that he didn't already have it. I locked eyes with him, challenging him to try anything.

She is your guest, brother, your visitor. You do not have a claim on her. Rein in that possessiveness or the pack will do it for you. My brother's thoughts echoed through my head, loud and clear. Once again, I felt completely disoriented and set back on my heels.

"Miss Ramos," Franklin's real voice snapped me back into reality, "I'm sure William has already told you, but you have our deepest sympathies on the loss of your mother."

"Yes, he did, thank you?" she fumbled over the words, getting flustered for a moment before returning to a stoic mask. It was endearing to see that moment of weakness.

Franklin shook her hand, covering it with his other for just a moment before releasing it. My wolf relaxed immediately, of course he wasn't making a move on her. He was just being friendly; he wasn't trying to have his throat ripped out. *Come on, Liam, you are better than this!* I chided myself.

"If you need my assistance, page me," my brother's voice carried a very distinct tone of warning. He knew that I was barely in control, which meant Miss Ramos could be in trouble. If I lost control, Franklin and Silas were about the only members of the pack that could stand up to me and that was only if they presented a united front. Individually, I could put each of them down without breaking a sweat.

"I assure you everything will be fine. Please, this way Miss Ramos." I gestured down the hall towards my office door and she walked beside me. With every oaken door we passed, I could feel the attentions of the present pack members perk up and take notice. The walk past the seven doors to my office at the end of the hall seemed to take forever as we walked in silence, the only sound being our muffled steps on the runner covering the wood floors.

I wanted to reach out to Cordelia but instead settled with clenching and unclenching my hand. When we finally reached my door, I opened it for her and she moved into the room stiffly. I scented the air left in her wake: worry, unease. I shot a look back at my brother who was still watching us from the stairs for provoking these feelings from my guest, never considering for a moment that I could be the cause. I turned my back on him, entered the office and closed the door with a sharp click.

My office wasn't an overly large space as I typically only used it for one-on-one meetings with the pack members. One wall was lined with bookshelves, filled with trinkets and mementos from my past alongside my modest personal collection of books and a several binders related to Volsung's business operations as well as a few bound tomes related to the werewolf council. My desk took up a good portion of the space, as well as the two wingback chairs that were positioned in front of it.

Under normal circumstances, my office always felt plenty large enough, but as I stood at the closed door, breathing slowly, I decided it was entirely too small. I focused on the familiar scents of old paper, leather, and the sharp evergreen scent of the air freshener Loretta used in our house. But all those scents paled in comparison to hers. I refused to linger on it and looked at her instead.

She was watching me with open concern on her face as she continued to fiddle with the keys she had in her hand, especially a pink canister looking charm. That gave me pause: werewolf or not getting maced was a terrible experience. She was smart, prepared, and could certainly read a situation. I would have to work to put her at ease.

If you want her so badly, let me take the lead. I shamed my wolf, who growled but curled up and relented in response. He knew I was right, and he must have wanted her bad if he was willing to give up the fight so easily.

"Please have a seat," I gestured to one of the chairs in front of my desk. I very purposefully walked around the desk and sat in my normal, executive desk chair. This meant the desk was between her and I, a show to prove that she was safe here and that I had no problem putting space between us.

My wolf hated it.

I ignored the temperamental bastard.

I was surprised when she didn't hesitate and gracefully took a seat. I also noticed that she kept that pink canister in her hand, at the ready.

"Thank you for seeing me, Mister Benson. I apologize for showing up out of the blue."

"No problem at all, and please, call me Liam." I watched carefully as her cheeks darkened for a fraction of a second with a flush. My wolf howled inside my head, seemingly pleased.

"Yes, um, well Mister Benson, I'm actually here for a couple of reasons. First," she reached into her purse and pulled out a second set of keys and placed them on my desk. I picked them up, looked at them, and then looked at her.

"My mother's car was released to me today and there were those extra keys attached to her car keys. I presumed, based on the key chain tag, that they were for your home. I figured you would want them back."

Mate keep. Enter den.

My wolf decided to chime in as I put the keys away in one of my desk drawers. Normally he didn't try to vocalize his desires with actual words, so the fact he wanted her to keep them to have access to the estate was unsettling. I was trying hard not to focus on the word he used to describe the woman in front of me: mate.

"Thank you, Miss Ramos. I had forgotten that your mother had a set, but you didn't have to drive all this way to return them."

"I know," she replied and then sat up a little bit straighter in the wingback chair, "But I'm really here to talk to you about the funeral arrangements."

"Ah, I see that Mr. Gates wasn't clear. I don't want or need to be a part of the planning—"

"I'm not here to discuss plans," she interrupted, her words sharp and curt, which made me sit up in my seat, "While your offer of assistance is appreciated and more than generous – I cannot accept it."

Chapter 5

Liam

Beg pardon?" I was blindsided, my wolf was just as equally perplexed. "You don't want help?" I watched her closely and could see her thinking hard and choosing her words carefully.

"It's my mom, *mi mama*," she said as if that was enough of an explanation. I must have looked lost because she continued. "It was always just her and I…and I don't want your help."

My eyebrows shot up and she flushed. I didn't know if I should be insulted or laugh. Before I opened my mouth and made an ass of myself, I looked at her and really considered her. Her gaze was unwavering, and she held her head high and almost defiant. It was strange for me, as I had become used to throwing my weight around with the pack like a brute and having them obey my every instruction. She was different. If I threw my weight around and insisted that I pay for the funeral it would only anger her. This was going to take some finesse.

"I meant no offense to you, Miss Ramos," I replied holding my hands up in a disarming fashion, "I had a great amount of respect for your mother and wished to help in the primary way that I could." Her face darkened and there was spark in her eyes. My words didn't placate her at all. In fact, I was certain that I had just awakened that which I was trying to avoid.

"I'm sorry but I have a hard time buying that. She worked for your family, first your father and then you, for almost three decades and yet we were always fighting to make ends meet." Her words were clipped and terse before she cut herself off. She clearly wanted to say more and speak her mind, but something was keeping her from doing so. I suspected it was her pride.

"Your mother had a very…set…idea in her mind about what she should be making in my family's employ for the work she was doing. She would not take a pay raise from us if there wasn't some additional responsibility that we gave to her. She always thought she was taking advantage of us, I think. Which is why my father and, eventually, I gave up."

I spoke mostly the truth, except the part about my father as Loretta had only ever worked for me. Her knowledge and belief about my father stemmed entirely from the slight memory alterations that I had to do after she had stumbled into a dominance fight when she was young. As an Alpha of a pack, I was charged with keeping its secret saft. Knowing that I would have to tell Loretta about us and swear her to secrecy, I took extra precautions with Cordelia so she wouldn't immediately realize that the men her mother worked for never aged, including making her believe that I was my father. Eventually she might realize or remember truly occurred when she was a child. But for now, the altered memory was more of a help than a problem.

"Really?" she asked, disbelievingly. I wasn't lying about trying to give her mother a raise. I had tried, nearly yearly in fact, to give Loretta significant raises and she often refused or negotiated me down to a smaller amount.

"Really," I echoed, "Besides, you take a mop to the face once from your mother and you have no choice but to comply with whatever she wants." I was surprised when Cordelia let out a sharp, watery laugh.

"Oh God, she didn't," she replied burying her face in her hands, "What happened?"

"One year, I just gave her a raise," I started, relaxing into my chair, remembering the situation well, "I didn't mention it, I didn't say anything about it, just gave her the increase. I didn't even think about it until I was walking through the kitchen to grab a glass of water when she wacked me across the face with the mop."

"At least tell me it was the handle," Cordelia groaned running a hand down her face seemingly embarrassed but not surprised by her mother's action. I couldn't help the smile as I remembered Loretta's stern expression as she scolded me like I was a child.

"No," I said laughing, "I got a face full of dirty mop water and I had been in the middle of asking a question to boot, so I had all the yarn from the mop in my mouth too. God, I will never forget that taste as long as I live: mud and Pinesol." Cordelia winced and shivered.

"I'm sure the talking to was just as bad."

"I have a strict father, served in the military, and had never been dressed down so completely as Loretta did that day. The rest of the guys gave me flack for months because everyone could hear her."

"Just be thankful she never came at you with a *chancla*," Cordelia laughed, her eyes crinkling at the corners, "Her aim was deadly. There was this once time when I was a teenager, I gave her crap about wanting the car to go hang out with Hannah. She had told me no over and over but I just kept pushing and being a bratty teenager. From two rooms away and around the corner this *chancla* comes whipping around and smacked me in the back of the head hard enough that I swear I saw stars."

"Had I known that, I probably would have hired her on as a security specialist," I teased, "Although I don't know what Gus, our rangemaster, would have said about having flip-flops as part of our weapons training." Cordelia burst out laughing, throwing her head back while full on, out of control gut laughing. For a moment she was entirely carefree and the burden of sadness had been lifted from her shoulders. This was the way this woman was meant to be, and I was overcome with the urge to make sure that she never felt sadness again. With one hand she wiped tears from her eyes and with the other she waved her hand.

"Dios, all I can imagine now is a bunch of burly security guys hurling *chanclas* at targets or bad guys," she wheezed. I gave in to the urge and started laughing as well. When she finally settled she spoke again, "I did not realize that my mother could be so difficult to work with."

I quickly shook my head.

"Your mother was not difficult, she was particular. I know that it might seem similar to you, but we absolutely respected and adored your mother and everything she did for us. Which is why, whenever she turned down a raise, I added the annual amount of her raise to a retirement fund for her."

"Really?" she asked, disbelief in her tone. It wasn't the truth, but it did sound good. I nodded, avoiding the outright lie. My wolf didn't like lying to her, but he wasn't the one in control.

"Oh," she said. In that one syllable I could hear that all the relief in the world.

"So, rest assured all of what I'm 'paying,'" I replied using air quotes, "your mother earned from her diligent and excellent work."

She didn't say anything immediately. She sat rigid -- fists clenched, head bowed. Then her shoulders started to shake and I was hit with a wet, salty scent. I gulped and cursed myself silently. I had made her cry. My wolf rose in a panic. There was nothing for him to kill to make her feel better and he didn't know what to do. His demanding desire was for me to fix this. Immediately.

Cautiously, I stood and walked around the desk. My intent was to take a seat next to her, but that wasn't close enough for my other half. Before I knew it, I was on one knee in front of her, holding her hands. The significance of this was not lost on me: As an Alpha, I lowered myself to no one. Ever.

The look on her face reflected the shock that I felt at my actions, but for different reasons. The remaining tears rolled down her cheeks, her makeup was beginning to streak, and I could feel my heart clench in my chest. My grip on her hands tightened and all the words I wanted to say got stuck in my throat. I wanted to tell her that she wasn't alone in her mourning, I would mourn with her. I wanted to say that I would find the person who caused her this heartache, rip their head off, and present it to her on a silver platter. I wanted to say that I would protect her from ever feeling like this again. I wanted to tell her that I would give my last breath to keep her safe. All I was able to manage was a soft: "I'm so sorry, Cordelia."

I came crashing back to reality when she pulled her hands from mine.

"Thank you for everything, Liam," her voice was filled with pain, the joy and humor now completely gone from her tone. Her tone also sounded suspiciously like she was saying goodbye and I wasn't about to let that happen. I felt like a bastard when a thrill ran down my spine at the sound of her saying my name. It was a strange combination of pleasure and shame.

"Of course," I said, standing and moving out of her personal space. "I presume that this puts an end to your protests about the financial assistance?" I didn't want her to leave, I wanted to draw out our interaction, just to be in her presence for a minute more. I would take every stolen moment that I could get, but when she stood, I knew I my time was up.

As we moved to my office door, my wolf wanted to revolt, take control and hold her close, but I tuned him out. I was blindsided a second time by the layers of her scent, and I wanted so badly to reach out and take her hand again, just so I could pull her close and breathe her in deep. I, instead, settled for clenching my fists and walking to the door. I could hear her soft steps as she slowed next to me, and I fought back a groan as I opened the door. She had stopped so close to me that I could feel her body heat along my side. I exhaled harshly through my nose and wrenched the door open. I stood back and motioned for her to go first. I realized my mistake when she walked past and her scent wrapped around me like the embrace of a lover. It was agony not to caress her long, dark hair. We were both silent walking down the hall to the stairs.

Rounding the corner, we both stopped short. Filling the entry from wall to wall, were the other fourteen members of my pack – all waiting, all expectant. Once we came into view, they each placed a hand over their hearts and bowed their heads in unison. I felt a know of emotion in my throat, suddenly realizing the gravity of what they were doing, what they were signaling. She looked at me questioningly, and I did my best to not let any emotion slip.

"What…" her question trailed off.

"They all wished to pay their respects," I croaked out after attempting to clear the lump that had lodged itself in my throat spinning the white lie as quickly as I could. She didn't need to know that this was a show of respect within the pack. That it was their acknowledgement of her as my mate. She nodded once and headed down the stairs. I followed closely behind her. Her steps were smooth except as we got towards the bottom of the staircase. She faltered, losing her balance. I kept her upright by circling my arm around her waist, catching her, and righting her. She looked up at me and her face had turned bright red when she realized her hands were braced on my chest. I could feel her heart rate pick up, and once again I could smell her attraction, her arousal.

"I need to go," she insisted, her voice low. She pulled away and made for the door, running away from me. I wanted to chase her, *needed* to chase her. My wolf lived for the thrill of the chase; Cordelia had no clue what her hasty retreat had awakened. She looked questioningly at the bent and misshapen door handle before looking back at me.

"Thank you, Mister Benson."

"It's Liam," I corrected her again, my voice sounding more like a growl than my normal voice. She smiled, her face flushing again.

"Thank you, Liam." And just as quickly as she had arrived, she was gone. I felt a loss strike me deep in my soul. The last things I heard before I involuntarily began to shift into a wolf were my brother and Silas.

"Hold him boys, don't let him chase her!"

"Well, I guess we're going to have to cancel the wedding."

Chapter 6

Cordelia

I didn't immediately drive back to Hannah's home when I left the sprawling, five-story estate that Volsung operated out of. Something was nagging me about everything that had just happened there. I gripped the wheel tighter as I drove aimlessly. There was something about that place, something about Liam and the others that was hiding on the edge of my memory. Something big. Something important. And try though I may, I just couldn't get it to come into focus.

The only thing that was occupying my thoughts was Liam.

My face felt like it was on fire at the thought of him. There was something about him that was so unlike the guys I had dated when I had been on campus: a junior engineer that drank like a frat boy (even though there were no real fraternities on campus) during my freshman year and a member of the basketball team who had probably been my first real relationship.

Like me, he had grown up in a small town but, unlike me, he wanted to stay in Klamath Falls and be a big fish in a small pond. I just couldn't commit to that life though; I had spent my life in small towns, and I wanted something more than that. Specifically, the excitement, adventure, and energy that big, metropolitan cities had to offer. My thoughts circled back around to Liam as I pulled my car into the lot of a strip mall. I parked and cranked up the air conditioning to try and cool myself off.

Just from our short conversation, I got the sense that Liam was so much more worldly, mature, and experienced. He spoke with knowledge and confidence that made me want to simultaneously listen and roll my eyes. It didn't hurt that he looked like he had just stepped off the cover of a romance novel: he was tall, broad, and brooding with a jaw that could probably cut glass and tousled dark blonde hair. But there was something else about him that drew me in.

He had a commanding presence that made you sit up and take notice. He was certainly confident, but not cocky. He definitely expected his words to be followed, that much was certain when I had told him that I didn't want his help paying for my mother's funeral. I squeezed the steering wheel with my hands and clenched my thighs together, trying to ignore the rush of heat I felt flare through me. Everything about his brooding looks screamed command and danger but the look in his bright hazel-green eyes as he knelt in front of me begged me to trust him.

I tried not to think too hard about it, but there was part of me that delighted in the fact that I had told him no. I didn't think of myself as a troublemaker, per say, but I couldn't help but get a kick out of ruffling feathers. My mother always told me I had too much fire in my blood because I undermined authority in my own way. I just thought of it as keeping people on their toes. Liam's reactions made me think that maybe he wasn't as unflappable as he wanted to seem. Of course, the "No" I had given him hadn't lasted very long before I caved.

As I leaned closer to the air vents blowing out cool air, I reviewed everything that happened at the Benson estate. Liam was completely zoned out after he opened the door, and then snapped on the commanding mask. During our conversation in his office, he certainly seemed to be in control. Dios, when he told me that story about mi mama hitting him in the face with a mop, I wanted to die from embarrassment and laughter. It was just so her, and from the way he laughed I knew that he got her, got us. Then the thought of him on bended knee in front of me, pleading and sincere, he seemed to swing his emotions on a pendulum, back and forth between extremes. That was too much drama for one person to deal with, but it didn't make him less attractive. It made him a puzzle, and I loved solving riddles and puzzles.

There was only one thing that sent a chill down my spine: the reaction of his . . . associates. . . or employees . . . I wasn't sure what they qualified as. My mother had told me that the Benson family ran a specialty security business out of their estate, so it would make sense that they were employees. But it was kind of weird that they all lived together. It was also weird how they reacted to seeing me. They moved as one when they bowed their heads to 'pay their respects.' If I was being completely honest, it seemed a little 'culty' to me. I had practically raced out of there, especially once I saw them: two angry looking men that sent a chill up my spine.

There was something about them, a memory in my mind that swirled around like fog. It was there, but it dissipated any time I tried to grab on to it. There was something about the two men that I didn't trust, that was unsettling to me.

Something dangerous that I couldn't quite remember.

My thoughts were invaded by my cell phone ringing loudly, making me jump. I rummaged through my purse and pulled it out. Of course, it was Hannah calling me.

"Hey," I answered the call.

"Your time is up, where are you?"

"Pioneer Village, next to the World Gym."

"Why are you at the gym?"

"I'm not in the gym, just in the parking lot. I needed some time to sit and think. I'll be back at the house soon enough."

"Good, then you can tell me about everything that happened."

"Nothing happened," I lied. Hannah sighed into the phone.

"Cordi, if nothing happened, you would be home by now and not sitting outside of World Gym."

She had me there.

"Fine," I agreed, "I'll tell you all of the details when I get back. See you in a few." Hannah gave me a sickly sweet and energetic goodbye and I ended the call. My phone vibrated in my hand nearly the instant that I hung up and I read the notification: an e-mail from my program advisor. I took a slow breath and opened it.

Cordelia,

Let me start off by saying how sorry we all are to hear about your mother. Carrie and I are available if you need to talk, we have both gone through dealing with the loss of a parent and if you need anything, and I mean ANYTHING, at all please, please, please do not hesitate to reach out.

With regards to your concerns about completing your externship: do not worry! We are currently working with your site admin to get details worked out. We do not want you to stress it, especially with graduation a month away, and we will get it sorted for you. The number one priority is taking care of yourself. Right now, we're looking at having you return to Bend and finishing making up your last month whenever you feel able to return, even if it is post-graduation.

I don't want to get your hopes up, but we have had a site at Kootenai Medical Center in Coeur d'Alene in previous years, they were just off the rotation this school year. If we can convince them, you could potentially finish up the last month there as you handle any family business.

I will touch base once I have more concrete details.

Rhonda

I exhaled once I finished the e-mail. I had been dreading that I was going to be kicked out of my program, but of course there was nothing for me to worry about. There was part of me that had hoped that they would just hand wave me through, I had completed all but the last handful of competency evaluations, but the program was strict when it came to completing all of the course work. It didn't matter that I had already scheduled my board exams, they would turn me away if I didn't get my degree.

I looked long and hard at the third paragraph; I didn't know how I felt about completing my externship in town. I knew I was still planning to move to Atlanta after graduation but that I would need to sort out my mother's estate. The thought of that seemed incredibly daunting to manage on my own in a month, and I could only imagine it would be more difficult if I weren't here in town. I would probably have to contact a lawyer, which I didn't know any. My mind flashed back to Liam; he had mentioned in passing that his brother was their company's legal counsel. I would hate to lean on them, but they already knew my mother and I had the feeling that I could trust them. I decided to keep that thought in my back pocket for now.

I responded to my advisor, thanking her for her help and understanding, and letting her know that I would keep in contact with her about how I was doing. Once I had sent off that e-mail, I shook out my hands and backed my car out of the gym lot and headed towards Hannah's house.

"Took you long enough!" Hannah exclaimed as she opened the door. She had clearly been waiting for me to return. I shook my head at her as I walked across the threshold of the house. The whole house smelled like fresh Italian herbs and garlic bread. My stomach gave a loud grumble. I hadn't been eating much, but apparently it demanded to be fed.

"Shane went out with some of the guys," Hannah said ushering me to the table and politely forcing me to sit, "So you can speak freely." She loaded up my plate with a heaping pile of spaghetti, meatballs, and a large chunk of garlic bread. And though she set it in front of me, there was a certain level of expectation in her eyes, which caused me to roll mine.

"There's nothing to talk about," I muttered before digging into the delicious looking plate in front of me. Hannah snorted and started another plate for herself.

"Yeah, because nothing happening explains the nearly two-hour detour to make it back."

I felt my face get hot and jammed a forkful of pasta into my mouth, pointedly ignoring her triumphant look.

"This is really good," I said with a full mouth.

"I'll give you the recipe once you tell me what happened."

"Fine," I swallowed hard deciding to go with the cliff notes version of what happened, "I went out, gave Liam his key back, told him I didn't want his money, he made a convincing argument, and I left."

"Liar."

I scowled at my friend, who took a big bite of sauce covered bread. Her haughty look told me that she already knew what happened, even though she didn't. And I was sure whatever her imagination had come up with was infinitely worse than what happened.

"I hate you so much right now. My mom's boss is hot, alright!"

"I knew it!" She said slapping her hand on the table. "Did he sweep you off your feet, promise you a better life?"

"What? No. This is real life, Hannah, not one of your stupid romance novels."

"First off, my romance novels are not stupid. They are escapism at its finest. Secondly, he must have been smoking hot, I haven't seen you this flustered since Casey Graham in sixth grade."

"Ugh, seriously, Hannah?"

"Well go on, details Cordi, details!" I took another bite before laying everything out for her. The strange behavior at the door, our conversation in his office and sharing memories about my mom, and the weird salute thing that happened right before I left.

"You're sure this Liam isn't some kind of cult leader?"

"Yes, I'm sure," I replied, using my bread to sop up the last bit of sauce on my plate, "Because I would think that my devoutly Catholic mother would have objected working for a cult."

"This Liam guy was your mom's boss the whole time? Isn't he a bit old for you then?"

"No! He's only recently taken over from his dad, I think. If he's a day over thirty I would be shocked."

"So, what are we talking about here. Tall, dark, and handsome? Fit and athletic? You're being cagey."

"He is my mom's boss! I'm not looking to get in his pants!"

"*Was* your mom's boss. *Maybe* you should. Plus you said he was hot."

"Hannah!"

"What?" She asked before getting a serious look on her face, "You've literally been to hell and back in the course of the last week. But," she pointed to my cleared plate, "you realize that this is the first time that you've eaten a real meal since coming home, right? We're worried about you, Cordi. I know that none of us can even begin to understand what you're going through. All I am saying is that you don't have to go all emotionless robot on us. You're still human, you're going to feel mad and sad, and that's okay." She scooped another pile of spaghetti onto my plate. "It's also okay for you to work through some of those feelings in the sack with a handsome, local entrepreneur."

I couldn't suppress my sudden, rough bark of laughter.

"Alright, alright," I said, holding my hands up in mock surrender, "I'm sorry I've been keeping everything in and worrying you. I will try to be a little bit better about not bottling everything up. I'm just...I'm tired of crying, of being sad. I feel like I have no tears left to cry for my mom, which makes me feel like a terrible daughter."

Hannah placed her hand on mine and gave it a squeeze.

"You and I both know that's not true. Your mom was a hell of a woman, and you are too. I know she was proud of you and that she would never think that you were a terrible daughter."

"I know," I said, blinking my not so dry eyes.

"Now, back to our distraction for the evening: What size were Liam's shoes?"

Hannah and I talked well into the night: she tried to focus the conversation on my sex life and what part Liam should play in it while I attempted to steer the conversation in any other direction. We only stopped when Shane got home. I left the two of them at the dinner table and headed to the guest room of their house. I did feel much better after my talk with Hannah, I felt more like myself than I had in the past couple of days. Her cooking had certainly helped with that.

I collapsed on the bed, kicking off my shoes and groaning at how it cradled me. I didn't realize just how tired I was until that moment. I should have gotten up and changed into pajamas but sleep quickly carried me off.

When I woke up the next morning, I was still dressed, in the same position I had fallen into, and the bedroom light was still on. Shaking the cobwebs from my head, I chased after the remnants of my dreams. They had been incredibly vivid but were quickly fading as I became more alert. Soon the only remnants that lingered were images of Liam that had been conjured up from my conversation with Hannah the night before.

I prayed that a cold shower would get rid of the uncomfortable heat I felt surging through my body.

Chapter 7

Liam

The three days after Cordelia's visit were fucking excruciating.

I was testier, moodier, even though I wouldn't admit it out loud. I had problems controlling my wolf, he was lurking and finding opportunities to pounce and take control. There were a couple of moments when I went from sitting in my office to being in the driver's seat of my Lexus without any clue how I had gotten there. I knew the pack was aware of these lapses, because I could sense their unease through our bonds. I was also irritable because Franklin and I were still having to go through the motions of the agreement with the fae and the wedding plans because Franklin hadn't found an out for me yet.

It also didn't help that I knew Cordelia was dreaming about me.

There wasn't a handbook for werewolves on how to deal with the discovery of their mates and mate bonds because every relationship was different and unique to the couple. One thing I knew for sure was that, more often than not, aspects of the bond settled in for the werewolf first. The case was certainly true for me. There had been something in the conversation I had with her, or possibly even just the contact from holding her hands, that had established a type of connection between us that my wolf had latched onto. Right now, that connection only seemed to open-up when she slept and relaxed to the point of letting her guard down. And when it was open, it was like a dam had burst.

Every night I was witness to her dreams, without getting to be a participant. It was like I was trapped behind a window, watching with no sound, no context. However, it didn't take a genius to figure out context. Her dreams were almost entirely focused on the two of us as lovers. Images of the two of us in bed, her face in the throes of orgasm teased me every night. And every morning I would use those images to chase after my own release in the shower. Then later in my office, where her scent still lingered. And again, in my bed before falling asleep, where I could use my silk sheets to imagine what her tender flesh might feel like.

But not today.

Today was her mother's funeral, and there was something unsavory about the thought of pleasuring myself to her subconscious thoughts.

After a frigid shower, I spent the next twenty minutes staring at my collection of suits. This was, perhaps, the only time in my life where I was worried about what to wear. I wanted to impress, but not go completely over the top. Something that will catch her attention but not make me look like a rich asshole. I'm ashamed to say that I spent most of my time trying to decide between a black dress shirt and a white oxford.

"I'm being ridiculous," I snarled to myself and grabbed the white shirt. I opted for a classic looking tailored black suit with a single breasted, two-button jacket. It carried an air of sophistication and command that was a comfortable skin for me. I skipped selecting a tie because I refused to agonize any more over my appearance.

Leaving my suite, I was immediately greeted by the sight of our Beta wolf leaning against the wall, patiently waiting. The first word that always came to mind when I looked at Fletcher was gangly. He bore a remarkably similar resemblance to Shaggy from the Scooby Doo cartoons – tall and lanky with a soft face and relaxed posture. His hair went down to his shoulders, but was well kempt and sand colored, and even though his eyesight was perfect, he had a pair of tinted glasses that partially obscured his blue eyes. Knowing him for as long as I had, I knew that, even though he was the resident techie and computer expert, he was no slump and was built like a runner with mostly lean muscle.

I hadn't seen him since our talk after the pack meeting, when he suggested that Loretta's death was just suspicious enough and rather conveniently timed with the impending contract with the fae. In addition to the extra work of looking into her death and his independent contracts that he had for himself, I knew that he had been busy with various research assignments for our security firm. I had let him work and didn't pester him, because I knew that he would reach out if he had found something. I caught sight of his tablet and beckoned him to walk with me.

"Did something get flagged in the investigation?"

"Yes and no. Something did come up but I thought I would run it past you," Fletcher explained before unlocking the tablet and handing it to me. "I noticed a strange coincidence in the reporting. All of the officer reports and the detective report use much of the same phrasing."

"It's a small department," I reasoned looking at the text on the screen, "It doesn't surprise me that the language is similar."

"It's more than just similar though. It's practically identical. All someone did was copy the text and used the thesaurus tool to change key words." I read through the statements more closely. Had Fletcher not told me, it wouldn't have been immediately apparent. I doubt that the police chief would notice.

"What do you make of it?" I asked before handing the tablet back to him. He scratched at his beard and thought a moment before speaking.

"Could be nothing but the side effect of a small police force," he said as he snapped the tablet case shut, "The fact that they were all entered by the same user makes it just a little bit more suspicious. It could be that a single person was tasked with doing data entry, but…"

But it was still suspicious. The hair on the back of my neck stood on end.

"What course are you wanting to take?" Fletcher hesitated for a beat before clearing his throat.

"I need to pull the information on the user, however, shortly after accessing the reports, the normal means that I use to view data on the force's system was…terminated. When I tried to get back in, I realized that they implemented security updates, a lot of them, and I won't be able to get back in without direct access to the system," he tried to sound nonchalant, but there was tension that lurked beneath the surface.

He knew that what he was asking to do was violating the council's policy on dealing with mortal officials. He knew that werewolves were told not to interfere or get involved with any mortal governing body, especially one the size of the state of Idaho.

"I know it's the last thing you want me to do, but it would be easy to pull the user information locally. So, I want to head in to get it and also see if I can get my hands on the written reports to compare them to the digital versions."

"You want to break into the police station?" I asked disbelievingly. Fletcher's brow furrowed.

"When you put it like that and 'break in' is such a strong phrase…"

"Fletcher," I growled warningly.

"Fine! Yes, I want to break into the police station. I won't be taking anything, just looking at the case file and snagging some user data and putting a backdoor into the system again. I can be in and out in the blink of an eye."

I could hear the ring of truth and confidence in his words, and I believed him. But allowing him to follow through with this plan would violate one of the Universal Pack Laws: Don't fuck with mortal affairs. But if my mate was in danger, it meant that the Council could jam their laws up their asses.

"Do it, but take Dave with you." David was another specialized member of our pack. Before coming to my pack, he had been near savage and a lone wolf. We were originally under orders to kill him, I wound up making him part of the pack instead. His past was … troubled to say the least. But because of his troubled past, he had picked up on a number of useful infiltration skills and knowledge. I knew that between the two of them, there was little chance of there ever being a trace that they had been there. We reached the top of the staircase and I saw that everyone else had gathered in the foyer. I was suddenly filled with a profound sense of gratitude as they stood around talking.

I watched them unaware of my presence, their murmurs filling the air with a comforting level of noise. Some Alphas might have been angered by the fact that they were acting casually and hadn't immediately acknowledged my presence, especially considering that we were about to go to my mate's mother's funeral. But seeing them at ease and ready to support me in whatever I needed meant more to me than words, especially after my erratic behavior over the last few days. Alphas more and more were commanding their packs with a ruthlessness that was unbefitting for our kind.

Because of this tight grip, most packs had turned into cutthroat battles for dominance, with the members waiting for the Alpha to slip up so he could be replaced. I would argue that because of that, most packs had forgotten what our purpose in life was. I stood on the side of tradition, our pack was dedicated to being protectors, the bulwarks shielding the weak from the monsters that lurked in the darkness. God knew that I had slipped up more than enough for the pack to overthrow me and challenge me for control. Planning to violate and upset the treaty with the fae was only just my most recent faux pas.

To see that they trusted me and were ready to rally behind me, despite all my mistakes, made me realize just how lucky I was to lead this pack. I felt a tug on my mental bonds with the pack, and I looked down to seek Franklin looking up at me. He rolled his eyes in an exaggerated way.

"Had I known that finding your true mate would make you wax poetic for an hour, I would have suggested against it." His snarky words drew the attention of everyone and they looked up at me, waiting for my response.

"Ass," I smirked and started down the stairs with Fletcher two steps behind me. "We're going to attend the funeral and not cause any kind of ruckus." The skepticism in the room was palpable. No one wanted to be the one that asked what they were supposed to do if I lost control of my wolf being around Cordelia.

"Franklin, you'll be with me. If I start to lose myself the warning word is 'rain,' understood?" Everyone nodded.

"May I make a request, sir?" Fletcher asked as he kept his head angled down as dictated by pack etiquette. I gave an affirmative grunt and he lifted his gaze to the rest of the pack. "There is a strong possibility that whoever or whatever killed Loretta Ramos will be at the funeral today. We should probably be on the lookout for anyone attempting to get close to her daughter or her body. I know that we're still allowing the mortal authorities their chance, but they tend to miss things." Everyone nodded their heads in agreement. I let out a long slow breath.

"Let's go then."

The funeral home parking lot only had a handful of cars in it when we pulled up with our caravan of SUVs. We were there an hour in advance of the funeral, but I had figured more people would have been in attendance by now. However, it didn't escape my notice that there was a truck with the city police's decal parked next to Cordelia's sedan.

"So much for keeping a low profile," Silas grumped as he parked the car. I grunted in agreement as he killed the engine and we climbed out of the lead car.

When the pack went out in public in any group larger than two, we had to be incredibly aware of our movements. There was a natural order in how we moved as a group usually with me in the front and the rest of the pack flanking or behind me. It should come as no surprise that when we moved like that, we looked incredibly predatory and attracted unwanted attention.

To combat this, we walked in a reverse order, with the lowest ranking members in front, followed by Silas and Franklin who were my second and third, and then the rest of the pack in descending order with me bringing up the rear. I'm not sure how or why it worked but moving in that manner seemed to put normal mortals at ease around us. So, I waited patiently for everyone else to enter the funeral home before me. It rankled at my wolf that I would be the last one to Cordelia, but secrecy demanded it.

Walking into Gates' funeral home, I was immediately hit by the overwhelming scent of flowers, especially roses and lilies. I could hear Franklin sneeze ahead of me and I couldn't help but smile. He hated flowers so this was sure to be torture for him. Following my pack into the parlor I was struck by a few things.

The first was Cordelia. Even through all the flowers, I was able to catch her unique scent. She was wearing a dark gray dress that hugged her curves with black tights encasing her shapely legs. Her long dark hair was contained in a loose braid that hung over her left shoulder, the end of it curling around the shape of her breast.

"Did you check the weather report?" My brother asked, causing me to jump. I hadn't heard him approach. I took a moment to gather myself.

"I believe that it's supposed to be sunny all week," I replied, letting him know that I was still in control of myself. He nodded and went to take a seat with the rest of the pack. I took a moment to take in my surroundings aside from my mate. On her left was an older woman who bore a striking resemblance to Loretta. Loretta had mentioned a younger sister who lived in New Mexico a few times while in my employ, I presumed this was her. Which meant she was Cordelia's aunt. The two of them were currently engaged in a quiet conversation.

To her right was a young, blonde woman whose belly looked to be just barely swollen with a child. She must have been two or three months along. Behind her was a lanky young man who was speaking with a uniformed officer. The two men weren't greeting people, rather they seemed to be there to scare off anyone that might be looking to cause trouble, including me and my pack.

Part of me wanted to accept that challenge for dominance, but I did not want to upset Cordelia. As I approached, her blonde friend made a strange, strangled noise which caused Cordelia to look up at me. The blush that crept up her neck to flush her cheeks was an instant turn on and I had to focus hard on my breathing.

"Liam – Mister Benson," she corrected herself, "I didn't know that you would come." She approached me and there was a moment of hesitation where she was torn between a handshake and a hug. I made the decision for her as I cautiously and carefully embraced her. Our embrace was the closest that I had ever been to heaven in a single moment.

"Of course, I – we came," I murmured in her ear, "Your mother was more than just an employee. She was and will always be family." As much as I didn't want to, I released her from my embrace. I missed her warmth and her scent immediately. Looking down at her I could see the color rising in her cheeks, and I wondered if it was from embarrassment or arousal. I swallowed hard as she unconsciously bit her lip and looked up at me through her dark lashes. She had no idea that she looked like pure sex in that instant. I wanted to reach out and caress her cheek, run my thumb across her plump lips. I wanted to convey to her that she was my everything and treat her the way that she deserved to be treated.

Before I could do any of that, a man cleared his throat loudly, making Cordelia jump. I looked to the source and the cop was looking at me like he wanted to rip my throat out. I settled my sights on him and straightened my posture.

Did the kid think he could intimidate me away from my mate? It wasn't going to happen, but he was welcome to try.

Chapter 8
Cordelia

I huffed out an angry breath at Jack as he glared at Liam. He was on duty, technically, but had insisted on being here. He said it was because he didn't want anyone to cause trouble. I was beginning to think that he watched far too many crime shows and thought my mother's killer would turn up at her funeral. I didn't think he was entirely wrong, but my mother's circle of acquaintances was so small that it seemed improbable that some stranger would show up.

It just reaffirmed, for me at least, that my mother knew the person that had taken her life.

I shook off the dark thoughts and elbowed Jack, but it didn't seem to faze him. When the string of guys from Volsung entered the parlor and greeted me by name, he started to get a little stand-offish. Shane had pulled him into a conversation as a distraction, but Jack's big brother, overprotective streak had reared its head when Liam hugged me.

"Jack, Hannah, Shane, *Tia* Rosa," I spoke up trying to break the tension, "This is Liam Benson, my mother worked for his family's company."

"A pleasure to meet you all," Liam said, never taking his eyes off Jack. I hoped that they would stand down. Jack was my friend and Liam…well he wasn't quite anything to me yet, but I was beginning to hope that maybe he might be. After three nights of dreaming about him, I had finally come to terms with my infatuation with him. He checked the boxes of everything that I was looking for in a man and I decided that if something developed between us naturally, I wasn't going to try to fight it.

Just when I thought I was going to have to separate the two of them, Jack's radio crackled to life. He hesitated, but broke eye contact with Liam as he stepped away to respond. With the staring contest done, the tension in the room completely evaporated.

"It's nice to meet you," Hannah chimed in and extended a hand to Liam. Hannah, who had decided to live vicariously through me, of course thought that Liam was the cure for all my ailments and wanted to know every single detail. Being pregnant, I began to suspect that Shane was treating her with kid gloves causing her to be sex starved. Add in the pregnancy hormones and I wouldn't be surprised if she had been driven insane.

"A pleasure to meet you," Liam replied taking her hand. I swear I could see her eyes glaze over at the sound of his voice. Shane looked panicked until their handshake was over, and I had to fight not to laugh out loud.

"Thank you for coming," I said, and Liam turned his full attention back to me.

"Of course," he replied, "How are you doing, Cordelia? Do you need anything?" The concern in his voice was very real and there was just that touch of commanding, imploring me to be honest.

"As well as possible, for now. Thank you for asking." He gave me a nod of understanding. I saw his eyes flick to something over my shoulder and I turned to see that Jack had come back to our group from the radio call.

"Hey, I have to head out. A couple of big rigs got tangled out on highway twenty," he was speaking to me but staring at Liam, "I'll be back as quick as I can."

"Thanks for coming out while you could." He broke from staring at Liam to nod at me and squeeze me on the shoulder before leaving the parlor. As he left, another wave of people entered the parlor. I took a deep breath and tried to steel myself, but I already felt exhausted. I felt a squeeze on my hand and immediately looked down to see Liam's large hand wrapped around mine. I looked up at him.

"What are—" but I couldn't finish. Looking into his eyes I felt a shift in me, like someone had lifted a great weight off my shoulders. The weariness that had been draped around me like a wet blanket was gone and I felt lighter, stronger. I wanted to ask him if he had felt it too, but the new group of mourners had reached us, and I immediately went to greet them and accept their condolences and Liam went to join the rest of his group.

Aside from the standoff before the funeral, things went smoothly. It was agony for me that we had to have a closed casket funeral. I had wanted to see my mother one last time, but everyone from the detective to the Gates' mortician had cautioned me not to, that it was better for me to remember her as she was. Which meant to me that the injuries she had suffered were much worse than people were letting on.

I tried hard not to focus on those dark thoughts as the chaplain read passages from the Bible that were meant to comfort me, but they didn't. He delivered a canned eulogy that was nice but was more about justice and didn't truly capture the spirit of mi madre. My tia held my hand the whole time, I could feel her tremble and I knew that I needed to be strong for her. I didn't know how or if I would be able to be that for her because I knew that I would need someone to support me and I didn't have that. But—I did.

As the chaplain spoke, I cried, wept openly even, but I never felt weak or out of control. I didn't understand why. While we were at the cemetery, I bawled like I had never cried before, but still felt a great strength inside myself. When we moved from the cemetery to the reception at Hannah's parent's house, I tried to look for the explanation. As I listened to conversations, spoke with people, and shared stories with everyone gathered, it dawned on me.

Liam.

As I walked towards the kitchen to grab a drink, I could feel his eyes follow me, and I somehow knew that he had watched me the entire time. Observant but not overbearing. It seemed like he understood that I needed to cry, to mourn, but he was at the ready if it seemed like I was going to fall.

Christ, I had only talked to him twice and I felt like he knew me better than I did.

I looked back before entering the kitchen, to see if I was right. His group was lounging mostly in the living room and spilled out onto the porch, mingling with others and providing a relaxed atmosphere. Liam sat at the center of it all, his posture relaxed but he was as still as a statue.

His eyes on me.

I felt a hot shiver race up my spine as I darted into the kitchen. I moved to the sink and turned on the cold water. I held my wrists under the water and breathed in and out slowly. Why was he having such a profound effect on me? Why was I acting like a horny high schooler? I squeezed my thighs together, attempting to stop the tingling heat that settled there whenever I thought of him. When the cold water didn't help, I went for the fridge and grabbed a beer.

I twisted off the top and dropped it on the counter, letting it bounce across the granite surface. I took a long pull from the bottle, washing my tongue with the bitter taste of hops, hoping that it would help with a mental palate cleanser as well.

"Cordelia?" Liam's voice sliced through me like a hot knife through butter, I melted at the sound of it. I lifted the bottle to my lips again, but before I could drink, he had one hand wrapped around the neck of the beer bottle, keeping me from tipping it up and the other around my waist. I could feel the hard planes of his body against my back, his warm breath along my ear and neck. "Is this necessary?" His voice was little more than a rumble I felt reverberate through my body.

"I'm only having the one," I tried to reason. He grunted, pulling the bottle from my grasp like it was nothing, and downing what was left in a single pull. He set the empty bottle on the counter and wrapped his now free arm around my midsection. As he held me, I felt completely overwhelmed: by my mother's death, the funeral, my college career, externship, my future job in Atlanta, everything. It all suddenly came crashing down around me and I broke down again.

Liam didn't say a word. Instead, he hugged me; his muscular arms holding me up. I felt him dip his head and rest it on my shoulder. His face was pressed against the curve of my neck and I felt an electric tingle every place that his skin touched mine. I could feel the tip of his nose and his lips brush against me, they were soft and warm sending a shiver down my spine.

I tried to calm myself, but couldn't stop the loud, hiccupping sobs. Liam murmured something in a language that I didn't understand. It was filled with hard consonants and deep vowels that were foreign sounding compared to Spanish or English. As he continued his litany, voice soft and deep, his lips brushing against my neck, he began to sway to the right and left like we were having an intimate slow dance. Liam then took a deep, slow breath, held it, and then exhaled slowly. His hot breath on my neck sent a shock directly to my core.

But after that initial surge of heat and desire, I concentrated on his breathing and began to mirror it with my own breaths. After a few rounds, I felt my muscles start to relax. I closed my eyes and just savored the feel of having another person close to me. The past year on externship had been busy and being in this position showed me just how far I had flung myself into my work. I had basically shuttered myself away forsaking everything that was akin to a social life.

I hadn't realized just how much I missed it, until this moment.

Whatever was between us was nearly tangible. My attraction to him had been instantaneous, which honestly was downright frightening. And judging how he acted today and the way that he was holding me now, I suspected that he, at least, felt that same pull. The only thing I didn't know was where to go from here. We had only met for the first time a few days ago and things were certainly progressing fast.

I had managed to force the tears away again; he had worked some kind of magic on me, and I felt that weight lift from my shoulders again. I didn't want the moment to end, but I knew that I needed to actually talk to him. I stood a little bit straighter, resisting the hypnotic swaying motion long enough for him to straighten up and relax his hold on me. I turned, lingering in his arms as they settled around my hips, his fingers interlaced as his hands rested against the small of my back. Not thinking about where his hands were at too hard, I tried to put on a stoic face.

"Mister Benson—"

"Liam," he corrected.

"Liam," I repeated slowly, my brain scattered, "I don't know—I'm just not sure what this is or how we got here." I stumbled over my words, only saying half of what I wanted to say. I wanted to say that he was the only man I had ever wanted this badly. I wanted to tell him that my attraction to him was insane. I wanted to eloquently ask him if he felt the same things that I felt, that inexplicable, magnetic pull between us. His hazel eyes seemed to glimmer behind his half-closed lids. He looked like he had been drugged or like he was high.

Was it me? Did I have that effect on him?

"I think," he started after a long pause where it seemed like he was considering his words extremely carefully, "that we are two people that just met. Two people with an incredibly strong attraction to each other. An attraction that I would like to explore if you are willing."

I felt like someone had just set my face of fire. He wasn't wrong in what he said, but, damn, is it wrong for a girl to want a little romance? Liam's eyes snapped open like his words had just registered in his own mind.

"A date. What I meant to say was that I want to take you on a date," he shook his head like he was trying to wake himself up, "I want to get to know you, Cordelia, and I want you to know me."

"I would like that, Liam," I replied as I reached up and stroked his cheek. I'm not sure what compelled me to do it, but it felt right in the moment. Liam leaned into my touch, and it strangely reminded me of a dog leaning into a good scratch.

"Good. I'm not sure what I would have done if you had said no."

"Cordelia? *Chiquita?*" My aunt called out for me, her voice coming down the hallway. Liam and I sprung apart, like two teens that had been caught making out. My aunt popped her head into the kitchen, "You have some people heading out that would like to say goodbye."

"I'll be right out," I replied, fiddling with my skirt. My aunt looked at me with a curious stare.

"*No tardes demasiado,*" she chided and disappeared from the doorway. I looked back at Liam. He stood rubbing the back of his neck with one hand and his other hand on his hip. I was once again struck by his masculine beauty. He looked like he had literally stepped out of a magazine.

"I have to—"

"Yeah, no, I've taken too much of your time. Go and see to your guests. I'm sure that my associates are wondering where I am."

I started to leave but hesitated before getting to the door. Next to the door was a mail organizer with a collection of pens and markers on it. I grabbed a black marker and turned back to Liam, who was only a few steps behind me. He looked baffled as I grabbed his hand

and pulled the cap off the marker with my teeth. On his palm I wrote my phone number and recapped the marker. I blew on the ink to dry it so it wouldn't smudge. The shock on Liam's face was the most priceless thing I had ever seen.

"Cordi!" My aunt called out.

"Coming!" I replied as I tossed the marker back into the organizer.

Before I left the kitchen, I turned back to Liam a final time. He was staring at his hand with a look of amusement on his face. Feeling bold I stepped closer to him, raising onto my toes and placing my hands on his firm chest, and kissed him on the cheek.

"Text me," I whispered into his ear, which sent a shiver through him. I was happy that I could have the same effect on him that he had on me. I quickly ducked out of the kitchen and headed to where my Aunt was sending off some of the funeral attendees from my mother's church. I wondered how long it would take before he texted me.

Chapter 9
Liam

Four hours, twenty-three minutes, and thirty-seven seconds.

That was how long I waited, in sheer agony, before I sent Cordelia a text message. It had been an incredible feat of strength on my part.

The pack had left the reception shortly after Cordelia and I had our shared moment in the kitchen. Returning to the pack's estate, I tried distracting myself by watching a movie with Ephraim, Noah, and Daniel, but I couldn't focus on the movie and began pacing which had set them all on edge. I excused myself and went to my office, hopeful that I could distract myself with work. I soon found myself staring blankly at the computer screen, not comprehending any of the security requests or documents that I clicked through.

Frustrated, I went to take a long hot shower, which quickly did nothing but aggravate my wolf because he felt like I was washing off Cordelia's scent. So, I changed into gym clothes and went for a run around the property, under the guise of checking the fence and the pack's protection wards.

And that had just been the first hour.

I eventually settled for running my frustrations out on the treadmill in the gym. Both my wolf and I loved to run. He had objected to the treadmill at first, wanting me to full shift and run through the woods and acreage of the estate, but I reminded him that wolf paws weren't the most effective for using a cell phone, which we needed to contact Cordelia. He relented begrudgingly. But I could understand why he wanted to change.

For him, I knew that there was a sense of freedom to go anywhere, especially since I spent most of my time indoors conducting meetings or on the phone. For me, running was an escape that allowed me to shut my mind off. When I ran, nothing mattered. Pack finances, treaties, the latest schemes of witches or vampires, security contracts. There was just the mechanics of the body, feeling the muscles, lungs, and heart working in concert to keep churning and moving forward.

After two and a half hours, I returned to my room, sweaty and exhausted, and collapsed onto bed to look at my phone. The next fifty-three minutes and thirty-seven seconds I spent starting and erasing more than a dozen messages, concerned about tone, word choice, and emojis. The latter of which I hated more than anything. Language could convey so much more than the little, inelegant cartoon images, but I would use them if that was what Cordelia used. I had tried to keep my message casual, but concerned:

> **Cordelia, it's Liam. I wanted to send you a quick message so you would have my number in the event you needed anything. How are you feeling?**

I was worried that it was too wordy, but it was true to who I was and how I spoke and wrote. As I waited for her response, I looked at the smudged ink that was still on my palm. I hadn't been able to bring myself to wash it off. I smiled, thinking about the way that she had hastily scrawled her number there. I don't think that she realized that I already had her number from her mother's emergency contact information and that I had programmed it into my phone the day that she had turned my world upside down.

The thought of her mother made me frown. My instincts were telling me that something was off about the whole situation. While Cordelia took the time to mourn her mother, I had kept my eyes and ears open to everything else that had occurred during the funeral. I had been glad that Cordelia had been preoccupied because it seemed like everyone had a theory about what might have happened to her mother. Plausible suspicions such as Loretta catching her ex-husband attempting to steal from her to the outlandish accusations of her being involved with a cartel. Which was frankly ludicrous and insulting to the woman's memory.

The other thing that hadn't set well with me or my wolf had been the young cop that tried to challenge me. My wolf viewed him as a rival, which meant he wanted to rip his throat out to establish my dominance and position as Cordelia's mate. While I had been inclined to agree with my wolf's desire, that wasn't the biggest thing about the young human that had stuck with me. I immediately noticed how possessive of Cordelia he had been and how she seemed to be oblivious to it. It appeared like a typical case of unrequited infatuation.

If I had to guess, Jack was very much in the 'friendzone' and Cordelia had no clue as to how he felt because he had never manned up and told her. While I was still concerned about her emotional and mental state, I was damned and determined to make absolutely clear to her about how I felt. Judging from how Cordelia unconsciously reacted when we were in the kitchen together, she was certainly attracted to me. She had even tried to communicate how our mate bond made her feel. Considering that it was currently one sided, it had surprised me that she could feel it that strongly.

A chirp from my phone immediately derailed my thoughts. I eagerly snatched the device up and unlocked it.

Hey thnx for the message. I'm exhausted tbh but feeling ok...kinda dreading tomorrow

What is tomorrow?

The police are releasing mom's house in the morning and I'm supposed to meet with a rep from the hospital about my externship. I'm stressed about it all

There was good and bad in her message and I took my time unpacking it. First, and most obviously was the fact that she was going to be getting access to her mother's house the next morning. I was sure that Jack had been the one to proudly tell her, which rankled me. Judging from the timeframe and how underfunded the department was, I seriously doubted that they had done any restoration or remediation of the home. There was no way I was about to allow her to clean up her mother's crime scene. I knew in an instant that the pack would all chip in to make sure that she didn't have to deal with it. I would be lying to myself if I didn't also think it would be an opportunity to check and see if the police missed anything.

I quickly switched messages to create a chat group with Fletcher, Joshua, and Silas, telling them about the situation and what I wanted to do. Fletcher and Josh both quickly agreed, with the former suggesting that we install a security system for her and the latter letting me know he'd pack an SUV with everything he would need to get started on remediation first thing in the morning. Silas left the message read but didn't respond – his typical response.

Secondly, there was the mention of her externship. Her mother had recounted on several occasions, proudly, about how successfully Cordelia had been performing in a difficult medical program at her college. If I remembered correctly, it was something to do with x-rays or ultrasound. I cursed myself, wishing I had paid more attention to what her mother had gone on about. I sent a separate message to Ephraim telling him I wanted to talk to him in an hour or so. I knew he and Loretta had talked quite a bit about what Cordelia's studies. He also had contacts at the hospital, but I wouldn't call in any favors just yet.

If I may, myself and some of my associates could assist with the house. I'm not sure what condition it's in, but it's not something that you should have to deal with on your own. If you wish, we can work on it while you meet the rep at the hospital.

You've already done so much tho. I feel like I'm taking advantage of you.

You're not taking advantage of me if I am freely offering to help. I appreciate it, Liam. I appreciate everything you've done for me and my family. I just want you to know that :-) I'm supposed to meet the detective at the house at 9am

and I'm scared of what's happened to
the house. But you'll be there, right?

Of course, Cordelia.

You can call me Cordi, everybody else
does ;-)

I found myself stupidly smiling at the phone screen, running my fingertips along her messages. Her messages were sincere and relaxed, completely different from the tone and demeanor she had when she had first visited my home, and even different still than when she was at the funeral. She was a confident individual but knew her limits and knew when to reach out for help…even if she didn't ask for help directly. I found my Alpha instincts kicking in and I wanted to protect and provide for her in every way I could. But I suspected if I did that, I would only drive her away. I had to admit that I was lucky being as forward as I was about the house, but by her own admission, she was dreading it.

As superficial as it was, if she wanted and needed a man to help her with it, I had no qualms about stepping into that role.

Alright Cordi, I will meet you at your
mother's house in the morning.

Thank you, Liam.

As I relaxed, sinking further into my bed, I could feel the newly familiar tug at the back of my mind. An interesting aspect of being a werewolf were the mental bonds that were shared with the pack, as an Alpha I had bonds with each of the members of my pack and I could feel their ties to each other, at least on the surface. I knew when two of the pack were at odds or when they were joking around. I knew roughly what they were thinking. Depending on how close I was with the pack member, I could see through their eyes on occasion. As Alpha, I could also interact with them and vice versa, communicating through thoughts mostly. I thought I had known everything about the way bonds worked.

Mate bonds were on a completely different level.

There were many things that were the same. I could feel Cordelia's emotions. I could sense her surface thoughts. But there was something much more visceral about it all. I didn't just sense how she was feeling; I felt her emotions like they were my own. I couldn't just sense her thoughts; they had started to creep into mine. During the day when she was awake, the flow was stemmed and I received only her strongest emotions or thoughts, but at night, in the evenings, when she relaxed, I got everything. It was like there was no filter between us when it came to her thoughts. I was just receiving everything at the rawest it could be. But without her accepting it, I could only take, I couldn't give.

I closed my eyes and followed the tug.

The biggest difference between my connection with Cordelia and my connection with the pack was that I couldn't see through her eyes. When I tried, I instead found myself standing near her, as if I was in the room with her. I also found that I couldn't really interact or communicate with her like I could with the others. It was frustrating that our connection was only working in the one direction. I could have forced my way in and activated our bond, but that felt wrong and like a violation of her. When she had talked in the kitchen, I had thought that for sure, the bond would have lit up for her.

That thought made me frown, wondering if I had picked the right course on dealing with this special connection. But I refused to second guess myself. For now, I was trapped behind a two-way mirror, I could only look and take.

I hoped that this would change with time, but I wasn't sure. It made me yearn for help, but when I had asked my father and uncle about it the day prior, their responses were in the form of raucous laughter. My father was particularly amused by the whole situation, laughing for a solid twenty minutes before he was able to speak. I had growled at him, complaining about how someone should really make a frequently asked questions guide or something. But though I wished for it, there was no guide, no handbook, nor tutorial about mate bonds.

Focusing back on Cordelia and her surroundings, I could see that she was in a bedroom that was familiar to her. From her thoughts, I knew this was a guest room at her friend Hannah's home. She had been staying there for the last week as she waited for her mother's home to be released by the police. She had shed the gray and black clothing and was now dressed in a red tank top and white shorts. I admired the colors on her as they went well with her skin tone. I watched as she sat on the bed, a laptop to her left and a collection of thick books on her right. I looked at the titles.

Textbook of Diagnostic Medical Sonography
Ultrasound Physics Exam Prep Guide

I decided that would have to look those titles up later, I was now even more curious about her course of study. I could also tell that she was using studying as a tool to distract herself. I felt for her. I had lost many friends and family throughout the last two centuries. Grief was never easy. The only thing that had ever helped was time.

Cordelia fidgeted on the bed, flipping through the books. The way that her fingers danced along the page, caressing them as she turned them, caused my thoughts to take a carnal turn. I imagined what it would feel like if her fingers were to dance like that on my skin. If I didn't know any better, I would have sworn that she was teasing me. She looked over to her phone, drumming her fingers on the textbook. She put down the book and picked up the laptop. I watched as she clicked through a few pages of social media before going to what looked like e-mail. She very rapidly typed and e-mail and sent it off. She then looked back at her phone.

In a huff, she picked it up and tapped the screen, scrolling through various alerts before putting it face down on the bed. She went back to the textbook and pulled it into her lap. She began twirling a pen between her fingers. Initially I thought she was reviewing something. I quickly realized that she wasn't paying attention at the book at all. She was looking at her phone. Out of curiosity, I reached out and looked at her surface thoughts.

"Maybe he fell asleep? I'm sure he's probably busy."

It dawned on me, she was waiting for a response from me! I pulled back from my mental trip and stared at the phone in my hand. I gathered my thoughts and typed out a message.

You're welcome, Cordelia. What are you up to now?

A moment after I hit the send button, I could feel her excitement.

I wound up texting with Cordelia until two in the morning. I admit that it wasn't my preferred method of communication with her. I would have much rather heard her soft voice, but through the messages, she opened up and shared parts of herself that it seemed she didn't normally share. We talked about superficial subjects – favorite movies, music, and books – but we started to touch on deeper topics – goals she had and what she was planning on doing after college. She was planning on relocating but she didn't say where, which had caused my wolf to panic. I quieted him with a sharp thought.

We would not overpower our mate's desires. We were there to build her up and support her. If she wanted to move, we would make it happen. The pack's business was mobile and versatile, we could literally run it from anywhere in the world.

I had lost track of time as we texted back and forth, ultimately not ending the conversation until the wee hours of the morning with her agreeing to go out with me in the evening once she had finished orientation at the hospital. Even though I was used to late nights, I still felt sluggish the next morning. Climbing into the SUV that Josh had loaded the night before, I let him drive as I dozed in the passenger seat. Josh was a lower ranking pack member who had experience in remediation of violent crime scenes and disposal of remains, human and otherwise (a necessity for a pack like ours). I woke up to his sharp voice.

"What the hell is he doing here?"

He was also fiercely loyal to the pack. And there was only one person that the pack had taken a sudden and immediate dislike of in recent days.

I opened my eyes and immediately saw that Cordelia was standing beside her car, arms crossed, scowl on her face as Jack talked at her. I saw red.

"Is this going to be a problem?" Silas asked me. I looked in the sideview mirror and could feel my wolf rising to the surface. I tried to put the reigns on him, but he felt like our mate was in danger.

"As long as he doesn't make it one."

Chapter 10

Cordelia

hy are you so mad, Cordi? We can go in and start cleaning." Jack asked as I waited for Liam, making no move towards the house.

I was attempting to hide my anger at Jack, but his remark let me know that I wasn't doing a good job. I had been more than a little flustered by Jack's presence when I showed up to meet the detective this morning. When I had talked to Detective Riley last night, it was just going to be him to hand over the keys and talk about the investigation. He had left twenty minutes ago after having me sign some paperwork and turning over the house to me.

When I had asked about the investigation, he staunchly informed me that he couldn't talk much since it was an active investigation, but he did inform me that they were working on a lead. He also quietly advised me to reach out to Jack or himself if my father reached out to me in the coming weeks. His words sat like a lead weight in my stomach. Before he left, he recommended a couple of local attorneys to help settle my mother's estate. He then left me and Jack to our own devices.

Normally I would welcome Jack's presence but knowing that Liam would be showing up at any moment, had caused me to be angry with him. It began to feel like he didn't think I could handle things by myself, that he was my only resource. In fact, as I listened to what he wanted to do and his plans, I realized that since I had come back to town, Jack had been constantly hovering and injecting himself into any situation that I encountered. He was prepared to swoop in at any moment. And, if I were being honest with myself, the overbearing, older brother act was getting old really quick. In the past, I might have appreciated the white knight routine when we were teenagers, but now, as an adult the routine was starting to wear a little thin on my nerves.

"Did it ever cross your mind that it might be a little much for me to clean up my mother's crime scene?" I snapped at him, "That this is going to be an incredibly difficult experience for me?"

Jack looked like I had slapped him, a look of surprise that quickly morphed into a stone-faced façade.

"I'm only trying to help, Cordi. Your mom was like family to me, too."

I wanted to correct him. My mother was family to me, whatever connection he felt to her and suffered from her death was a blip on the radar compared to what I was feeling. I opened my mouth to tell him off when a welcome voice made us both jump.

"Good Morning Cordelia. Officer." Liam's voice went from warm to cold in an instant between greeting myself and Jack. Jack glowered at him. I smiled before relaxing my crossed arms. Liam and two other men were walking away from an SUV that I hadn't noticed pulled up during my spat with Jack. One of the men was perfectly average. In the back of my mind, I knew there was more to him than being average, but between Liam and the other man he just faded into the background. The third man, however, captured my attention more than even Liam did.

He was massive, practically towering over Liam and the other man, and he was probably as wide as the two of them put together. His size along with his shaved head, dark skin, and piercing brown eyes struck quite the imposing and memorable figure. I remembered him from the funeral but in the funeral home he hadn't seemed as big or intimidating. Maybe it was the fact that we were outside that made him seem like a looming skyscraper of a human, or it was the tightly controlled murderous look on his face. There was no denying that his presence was intimidating and formidable. From the corner of my eye, I saw Jack take a step back.

"Benson, what are you doing here?" Jack asked, tugging on my arm to pull me back and position himself between me and Liam. I rolled my eyes and pulled my arm from his grasp. I stood between Jack and Liam's group, facing Jack.

"I invited him," I snapped harshly, putting my hands on my hips. I was tired and Jack's attitude was the last thing I wanted to deal with today. "I think you should go, Jack." I watched as Jack clenched his jaw and I saw the hurt in his eyes. I almost opened my mouth to try and smooth things over, I felt guilty for taking my frustration out on my friend, but he didn't give me a chance. With a nasty scowl on his face, he turned on his heel and stalked off to his truck without saying anything more to me. I winced as he slammed the door and peeled out. But once he was gone, I felt my insides unclench and I was able to immediately relax. I turned to face Liam and his associates.

"Sorry about him," I said avoiding eye contact with them.

"You don't need to apologize for someone else's behavior," the big man grumbled, which sounded more like a growl with his deep bass voice, "His actions are his own." I looked up at him and he was intently staring after Jack's car. There was something a little unnerving about his intensity and his forward leaning stance. It looked like he was about to take off after Jack. Liam cleared his throat drawing my attention and his associates.

"Cordi, I'd like for you to meet two of my pac-partners," he stumbled over the last word like he had meant to say something else. "This is Silas," he gestured to the large man before gesturing to the man who was slightly shorter than himself who had white-blonde hair, a round, friendly face, and ice blue eyes, "And this is Joshua." It shouldn't have surprised me that Liam had someone like Silas on the payroll. He did run a security company after all. If he sent out Silas as any kind of guard, anyone would think two or three times about messing with him. I held out my hand to Joshua first, who looked horrified that I had done so and gave a wary glance to Silas, who smiled and shook his head.

"She doesn't know any better, Joshua," Silas chuckled. His soft laugh swept away the angry look and he didn't seem as intimidating. But his words confused me.

"Know what?" I asked. Silas didn't respond and just shook his head. Casting him a side eye I looked back at Joshua. "Well, it's nice to meet you."

Joshua shook my hand, the look of horror completely wiped from his face and replaced by a sympathetic smile.

"You as well," he said with a nervous nod, "Wish it was under better circumstances, all things considered."

"Josh has worked in remediation for decades," Liam explained, "He will take care of your home as if it were his own." Josh paled a little and looked like he was now shouldering the weight of the world, but Liam's words rang in my ears.

"Decades?" I asked. Josh looked like he was perhaps two or three years older than me which would put him in his late twenties at most. All three of the men exchanged a look that they thought was too subtle for me to notice. "How--?"

"Seems like it, anyways," Silas said smoothly interrupting me before nodding towards the house, "Have you been inside yet?"

Immediately my stomach started to churn at the thought.

"No, I—" The words stuck in my throat. I wanted to explain that seeing where my mother had bled, had died would shatter my soul into a fine powder that could never be made whole again. That being in the house where someone had stolen her life away for some selfish reason was too much for me to handle. But even though the words stuck, I could tell that they understood. Joshua held out his hand.

"We'll make it right." There was something about his words that carried weight. His seriousness was so earnest, like he was making a solemn vow. There was also a part of me believed that his promise went beyond just my mother's house. I dropped the house key into his outstretched hand. Just like at the funeral, I felt like a weight had been literally lifted off my shoulders.

"Thank you."

With a nod Joshua headed towards the house, Silas close on his heels. I started to take a step and fall in behind them when Liam tugged gently at my elbow.

"This may be presumptuous of me," he said, turning me gently from the house and towards my car, "but I don't think you need to be a part of this."

My knee jerk reaction was to argue with him but remembered my words to Jack. I didn't want to deal with it, I didn't even know if I could deal with it even if I had wanted to. Liam and his partners were a godsend, but there was part of me that continued to wonder at his motivations. There was another small part of me that felt like I needed to take responsibility. Most of me, however, just wanted to curl up in a ball, cry, and not have to act like an adult. I rubbed my face, suddenly tired.

"You need to quit being right," I muttered with a smile. Liam chuckled before shaking his head and hooking his thumbs through his belt loops.

"It might also be presumptuous of me to ask if you've given any thought to where you would like to go on our date." His body was relaxed, but his voice and eyes were tight. Like he was worried I would back out. It was a curious thing, seeing someone so commanding act so unsure. I wanted so badly to tease him, but it seemed the wrong.

"I'm not going to lie, it's been over a year since I've gone on a date, but the last one I went on involved reviewing film highlights of my ex's games," I admitted before matching his stance but leaning my back against my mom's -- my sedan. "So the bar's pretty low, but I think you can manage to 'wow' me." I regretted my sarcasm for a moment before Liam smiled wide.

"Oh, I'm certain I can do better than that," Liam said, his voice dropping to a rumble. He lifted a hand to caress my cheek, his work-roughened fingers trailed along my skin and up to capture my errant bangs and tuck them behind my ear. His hand then came to rest against the side of my throat, heavy, and warm. I wanted so badly for his hand to keep going down the side of my body. I gulped, trying to dismiss those thoughts, but when I looked up into his eyes, the thoughts came back tenfold. I felt like his molten golden-green eyes could see right through me and could see everything that I wanted from him. As if to confirm that he leaned in like he was going to kiss me.

And then my phone began to ring and vibrate in my back pants pocket, breaking the moment and causing Liam to take a step back from me. I angrily pulled it out but my anger evaporated when I saw it was the hospital calling. I looked back up at Liam, whose eyes still looked like molten gold.

"Hospital," I said by way of explaining and answered, "This is Cordelia Ramos."

"Cordelia, hi! This is Barbara White at Kootenai Health. I just wanted to check in and make sure that we were still on for this morning?"

"Barbara, hi and yes," I said glancing at my watch, "This morning still works for me. I was getting ready to head over. I just finished up with the police--"

"Oh dear! I forgot you mentioned that. I am so sorry for your loss. You can go ahead and take your time."

"It's alright, I'd like to get everything set up and hopefully get up and working by Monday."

"Yes absolutely! Well, you come on over whenever you're ready and head up to HR, they will page me, and we can get you all squared away. Orientation should only take a couple of hours, you'll be getting the speed version of it. See you in a little while."

"Thank you, see you soon." I replied before pulling the phone away from my ear and disconnecting the call. Liam had a sad but pleased look on his face.

"I take it you have to go."

"Yeah," I reluctantly agreed scuffing my shoe on the ground, mentally and physically dragging my feet because I didn't want to leave him. It was a strange feeling for me. Liam had been on the fringes of my life for years, and unfocused figure in the background. But now that he was in focus, I was having a hard time remembering what my life was like before I met him. Surely less complicated and confusing, but strangely enough not as full. As if sensing my uncertainty, he leaned forward and kissed my forehead.

"Go," he softly commanded, "I'll be waiting when you're done. I promise." His words were so solemn, I couldn't help but feel like there was something more that he wasn't telling me.

"It's going to be a couple of hours, if you have other things you have to do today..."

"Cordelia, nothing is more important than you are today." I felt my heart clench at his sincere words and my face felt like it was on fire. I was struck dumb and couldn't move. With a grin he opened my car door for me, motioning for me to sit. I frowned and slid into the driver's seat before reaching to shut the door. Liam caught it and I looked up at him expectantly.

"By the time you are done, I will have come up with how to 'wow' you on our date." He winked at me and shut the door. I literally felt my heart flutter and stutter in my chest. It took me several tries to slide the keys into the ignition, but I eventually succeeded and started the car. Carefully backing out of the driveway I turned the wheel to head away from my house. Once I had turned the corner and was on my way to the hospital, I let out a nervous laugh.

What had I gotten myself into by agreeing to a date with him?

Chapter 11

Liam

I stood in the driveway, watching Cordelia drive off toward the hospital. Once her car disappeared from my sight, I stalked towards the house. The Ramos house was a small two-story abode and looked like a slice of suburbia with it's cheery creamsicle color and dark brown trim and shutters. The shrubs and plants around the house were just starting to bud with new leaves and life, but their spindly, skeletal limbs created and unwelcome air of foreboding, especially considering what I knew waited for me on the inside. The welcome mat outside the door was well tread but crusted with mud from the number of people in and out of the house especially after the recent rainstorms.

My wolf and I vowed that we would find the one that had taken our mate's mother and they would suffer. I didn't hesitate at the front door and walked in as if it were my own home. I was immediately overcome with a myriad of scents and the prevailing sound of silence.

Everything about their home was the opposite of the estate. The small entry way was cluttered with shoes, bags, and jackets showing that Loretta was prepared for the temperamental spring weather of northern Idaho. To the left was a living room that was vibrantly colored, filled with plush furniture and a huge host of knickknacks and odds and ends, a large red bricked fireplace dominated the far end to the room. The walls were covered in framed pictures rather than art pieces that had been cultivated for the space.

As I looked at the pictures on the wall, I could tell that silence was not how this house was supposed to be. Every picture that I looked at screamed of music, laughter, and energetic conversation. In my gut I knew that the Ramos household had been one filled with excitement and frenetic activity. The pack would bring that back to her life, in spades. My wolf and I were both pleased at the thought of giving Cordi such an intangible gift.

"Where are you?" I asked, barely raising my voice, knowing that Silas and Josh would hear me just fine.

"Dining room," came Silas's reply from down the hall. I walked through the Ramos' home using my nose to capture every scent that came to the fore. From the familiar evergreen scent I had come to associate with Loretta, to the floral notes I had picked up from Cordelia, to the biting musk that was Jack's scent. The latter made me growl, but I knew from what digging that Fletcher had done he had been one of the responding officers after Loretta's scream had been called in.

There were other human scents, many of them faded from time or faint because the person had been a stranger to the home. There were about a half dozen that were stronger, but not nearly as strong as Loretta or Cordelia, I presumed that these were the investigators and police. But there was nothing telling in those scents, which frustrated me and my wolf. Normally my wolf was a patient hunter, but I was finding that where Cordelia was concerned, he had zero patience.

When I entered the dining room, I felt my stomach clench in disgust and a growl bubble up from my throat. Loretta's murder had been two weeks ago, the violent blood splatter had darkened nearly to a murky shade of rust tinted black. I was horrified to see that it covered the table, the carpet, and the walls. Whoever had murdered her had done so with a barbarity that made my stomach turn – which was saying a lot as a werewolf.

"Dammit," I swore harshly stepping forward into the room. My gaze swinging from Silas, who stood with arms crossed against a wall with his eyes closed and his body tensed, to Josh, who was kneeling on the floor next to the worst of the staining, a sharp knife in his gloved hands, and a small section of carpet pulled up at his fingertips.

"The carpet and pad will have to be removed," Josh said clinically, his eyes narrowed as he examined the damage, "I won't know about the subfloor for sure until I get the carpet and pad up. The dry wall is also going to have to be ripped out and replaced. I might be able to salvage the table, but it's going to take some work. Removal, deep clean, and ozone treatment should keep any smells from returning. I can get it all removed today, might take me a couple of days to get everything put back together. Cleaning the odds and ends will take longer though, up to a week, if she wants to keep everything."

"Do it. I will ask Cordelia about the table. If it is any kind of heirloom, we'll have to restore it. If not, I'm inclined to dispose of it." Joshua nodded and started to inspect and sort objects in the room: those that were fine and those that would need to be dealt with. I turned my attention to Silas, who hadn't moved an inch, his eyes still closed. He was taking slow steady breaths in through his nose and out through his mouth. I could tell he was homing in on something, so I waited patiently for him. When he opened his eyes, I could see the beast lurking in them.

"There's something, it's barely there, so I don't know if it is a natural smell of the house or something much worse." I closed my eyes and inhaled deeply, but nothing stuck out to me.

"Sage," Silas said when I opened my eyes, "but it's…old. Faint." I frowned immediately. The smell of sage in and of itself wasn't overly suspicious. Sage in conjunction with a brutal murder made me think of one thing.

"Covens," I mused out loud, "Witches." Silas nodded.

For most of recorded history, mundane mortals had speculated about the existence of others: preternaturals like witches, monsters, werewolves, vampires, fae, and the like. Overall, all literature, film, and pop culture about such beings was wrong. Vampires weren't affected by garlic or wooden stakes but were still affected by sunlight. Werewolves didn't have a weakness to silver and we didn't pass lycanthropy to unsuspecting victims through biting them, but a bullet to the brain would kill just just like anyone else. The fae weren't always kindly gnomes and nymphs, most were calculating and exacting individuals who horded power in their courts like misers. And witches weren't doddering old women cooking up potions in cauldrons – they were much worse.

Across the world were massive sources of power: natural collections of energy (spiritual, elemental, and otherwise), that preternaturals, witches being the most frequent abusers, had sought out for personal gain. These places are known as Ley Wells, or Leys for short. The denizens of the preternatural world often sought these places out to augment their own power: Vampires in control of a Ley Well were known to be able to move during the day and turn entire towns into mindless thralls. A coven's spell could be much further reaching, more potent, if the energy of a Ley Well were used to fuel it. In my experience, witches and vampires couldn't pass up the temptation of broadening their powerbase. Which wouldn't matter to me, except that both groups preyed upon normal mortals, viewing them as lambs to be sacrificed for dark rituals or cattle for slaughter.

That was where werewolves come in.

Legend has it that sometime during the beginning of the Bronze Age, preternaturals were commonplace, viewed by some as gods walking the earth and were revered, worshiped, and only sometimes feared by the mundane masses. There was a witch coven, the name of which has been lost through the centuries, that wanted more: more power, more slaves, more land and they were the first to tap into a Ley Well for a significant amount of power. Up until then, most uses of Ley Wells had been like sipping from a wine glass, careful and tiny. The coven had thrown caution into the wind and attempted to swallow all its power in one gulp. It was like trying to swallow torrents of water from a burst dam. The spell that they cast, thankfully, backfired, not only resulting in their destruction, but it also literally wiped a civilization off the map.

The normal mortals went from revering our kind, to hunting us outright.

Desperate grabs for power were made by all, attempting to gain and keep some semblance of balance and order, but thousands died in the process and our ancestors went into hiding. It was then that werewolves took up the mantle of silent defenders, seizing control of Ley Wells and keeping others from tapping into the power for two main reasons. The first: unlike the witches and vampires, werewolves drew power from their pack, whether the pack drew on the Alpha or the reverse. We didn't need an external source of power because ours came from within, from the bonds that tied a pack together. There was no temptation to control a Ley Well for power, because we couldn't use it. Second and more importantly: we needed normal mortals to reproduce, because there were no such things as female werewolves.

And so the war began: werewolves versus vampires and witches.

The Fae were a bit of a curiosity because they decided to remain neutral to it all. They could use the Leys for power, but their power more stemmed from the belief of mortals in them. Many fae had gone incognito over the millennia to ensure that there was a healthy belief in the fae – from the tales of the Brothers Grimm to the latest fantastic animation from Disney. But their involvement wasn't my concern at the moment. My concern was that we had missed a coven moving into our domain and allowed them to murder my mate's mother. My wolf growled at the thought, the primal sound rumbled from my throat.

"Have Noah start looking for the typical signs," I instructed Silas, "Missing pets or unusual adoptions from shelters, abandoned property purchases, and the like. If there are witches in Coeur d'Alene, we need to eliminate them before they can establish themselves a base here."

"Especially since we haven't rooted out the bloodsuckers yet," Silas groused. I nodded in agreement. A vampire coterie had moved in somewhere in the city limits. Missing person cases had quadrupled over the last year, indicating that we weren't dealing with a single vampire but a coterie that was at least a dozen strong. It was a nuisance, but nothing that was out of the ordinary. This wasn't the first group that thought they could take the Ley from my pack. But if there were a coven of witches in addition to a coterie, that was certainly not something we could take lightly.

"While Noah is running down leads on a coven, have August and Edgar each take a group and redouble on hunting down the vampires at their last known hunting grounds. Fletcher should have the data in his lab."

"Do you want them to pull in available hands? Contract security work is nonexistent in preparation for the wedding, which is now up in the air so most of the guys have available time."

I thought about it for a moment, weighing the pros and cons.

"Pull one of the others to help Noah. August and Edgar can split the rest. Except for Fletcher and David. They are working on a special project."

"Frank told me about it," Silas grunted, "He was incredibly pissed about the whole thing. Do you really think that with all of the plates that we have spinning that having those two get so close to the cops is the best idea, especially with you continually needling one of the officers?"

"You have a better idea?" I snarled at him, not liking the casual challenge to my decision. He immediately uncrossed his arms and held his hands up in a gesture of surrender, ever so slightly tilting his head up to expose his throat to me.

"You know I don't. I agree with your plan of action. I feel like a bastard saying this, but Loretta's murder didn't really matter before. When you realized Cordelia was your mate, everything changed. She's vulnerable outside of your protection, outside of the pack's protections. We are sworn to protect her, but it will be easier to do once you're able to bring her into the fold. Whether that means we deal with a mundane murderer, witches, or vampires, we will see it through, Liam. I've been around long enough to see what happens in packs where a wolf's mate lingers outside of the protection of the group."

"What happened?" I asked out of morbid curiosity. Silas shook his head.

"Nothing good," Silas replied his face darkening and his entire body was tensed. The thoughts or memories seemed to pass with the shake of his head and he looked up at me. "Josh and I have this, Liam. You ought to make sure that Cordelia is alright. I'm not saying she's the target, but the longer that she has no clue of what's out there, the greater risk she is at. Especially since you didn't have any of the others follow her to the hospital to keep an eye on her."

I nodded before clapping Silas on the shoulder. I was no young pup, having more than two centuries of life under my belt, but Silas was older than I. While I had spent my years shadowing my father learning to lead a pack, Silas had been more of a nomad, moving from pack to pack and even spending time as a lone wolf. His knowledge and experiences were varied from my own, so I trusted what he had to say. But that didn't mean that bringing Cordelia into the fold was going to be an easy task for me to do.

After the confrontation we had about paying for the funeral, she didn't strike me as the type of woman that wanted to be swept off her feet. Sure, she had relented, but I knew that it meant that I was going to have to get creative with ways to bring her closer. Sure, I could have read the dossier on her that existed because of her mother's employment (and Fletcher's not so innocent need to meddle in my affairs) but that felt dishonest. No, I would find a way to win her over on my own.

I *had* to find a way to win her over on my own.

I just had to hope that she wouldn't shut down on me or play off any feelings that she might have as side effects of grief and mourning after the loss of her mother.

"I'm on it," I assured Silas as I started to head towards the door, "She agreed to a date today."

"Don't be stupid," Silas jokingly commanded, "If anything comes of the searches, I will notify you. I'll make sure that everyone plays nice while you wine and dine your mate." For a moment, a wave of relief washed over me. I owed Silas big time with this and overseeing the distribution of workload.

I knew that being second in command was a hard position, all the responsibility and none of the power. I had been second in my father's pack for over fifty years, and I was always acting as a messenger, a courier, and sometimes a confidant or counsellor for the other members of the pack. Seconds had it hard because ultimately the burden that they were under, was to serve the Alpha while keeping the best interests of the pack at heart. It was literally a ball of confusion on a good day, a migraine inducing mess on the worst of days. Silas managed to balance all the aspects well. I suspected that it was only a matter of time before he went off and founded his own pack. Sensing my thoughts, he shook his head.

He headed toward the kitchen since, which was filled with dishes that had been left soaking – reports indicated she had been cleaning up after dinner when she had been attacked.

"I'm not going anywhere Liam," he said pulling the plug and draining the water before refilling the sink, "You've got a good thing going here that's about to get much better for everyone. Why would I give all that up to start over and deal with a bunch of whiny ass pups? You know I'm your man for as long as you want to tolerate me." I could tell that there was something else, a second meaning hidden behind his words, but my mind was on Cordelia and I just wanted to get to her and make her my sole focus.

"We'll talk later," I informed him and he took it in stride with a bow and a cheeky salute that made me chuckle before he turned back to the sink and started cleaning dishes. I exited the Ramos's home, hopped in the SUV and headed towards the hospital where I knew Cordelia was trying to finish her externship so that she could get her degree. The entire drive over, I was distracted, thinking about what to do and where to take her. She was stressed, so I wanted to help her blow off some of that tension before "blowing off" some tension.

A smile came to my face, even as I pushed the racy, dirty thoughts from my mind. I knew the perfect place to take Cordelia. It was a little unconventional for a first date, but I had a feeling the risk would be worth it. When I arrived at the hospital, I immediately found her vehicle and parked the SUV near it. I texted the pack with the message to pick it up sometime later. Leaving the keys in the center console, I exited the SUV and perched against Cordelia's sedan and settled in for a wait.

My wolf was a very patient hunter, indeed.

Chapter 12

Cordelia

When I came out of the hospital, I wasn't surprised to see Liam leaning against my car. There were no other vehicles near mine, so I assumed that he had been dropped off because the distance between my house and that hospital was much too far for him to have traveled on foot. He seemed relaxed but guarded. To be honest that's what I was feeling too. By some miracle and with the help of my advisors at the college, I was able to get the last month of my externship transferred over. Considering the extenuating circumstances, everyone was driven to not only see me succeed, but it seemed that they were trying to make things as smooth as possible.

As I got closer to Liam and my car, he extended out a hand to me. Not sure what I was thinking when I took it, but I quickly found myself wrapped up in his arms with his face pressed to the column of my throat, almost identical to how we had stood in the kitchen the day of my mother's funeral. I felt suddenly as if my spine had been replaced by an iron rod.

"I hope and pray that you're not thinking about bailing on our date," Liam joked, a sure attempt to relieve the tension that I was feeling.

"Not entirely," I replied speaking the truth. He spun me to look at him, his clear eyes needy and searching.

"What are you afraid of?"

Such a simple question.

Such a complicated answer.

Everything about Liam and how I was beginning to feel about him was easy and effortless. It felt like I had known him my entire life, like he was the piece that I had been missing to be complete. Whenever we were together, there was an inherent acknowledgement and deference to the other person that you would only see in couple that had twenty, thirty, or more years invested in their relationship. It wasn't something that happened overnight, which was my biggest problem. I had only really known Liam, actually known him and not just word of mouth through my mother, for less than twenty four hours. To sink into that comfort, like a worn-in armchair, right off the bat was dangerous.

I needed to finish my externship.

I needed to graduate.

I needed to follow my ambitions and go to Atlanta.

What I did not need was a complication like Liam Benson clouding my judgement about my future. No matter how easy it was to be around him. I convinced myself in that moment that there was nothing I was afraid of; I knew my own mind and I knew what I wanted. Short term, that meant Liam. Nothing long term would change for me.

There was nothing for me here anymore.

"Nothing. I'm not scared," I replied, hearing the belief and conviction in my words. Liam chuckled, the deep sound vibrating through me and straight to my core, making me squeeze my thighs together.

"Good," he replied dropping his arms from around my waist and letting me step away. I immediately missed his warmth, but I held myself back and distracted myself with looking down and fishing my car keys out of my purse.

"How's the house?" I had worried about it during my orientation and meetings. My mind conjured up terrible images that had kept me near tears all morning. When I looked up, keys in hand now, Liam was frowning and serious.

"Josh has removed the carpet and drywall that was damaged," he said haltingly as if each word was being painfully pulled from him. "The carpet and the dining room table were the —" he cut himself off and cleared his throat, "Is the table something that is important to you? An heirloom or anything like that?"

"No. My mom picked it up at a garage sale."

"I would recommend just getting rid of it then," Liam replied solemnly, his voice brokered no argument, so I nodded in agreement with him.

"That's fine then. What about—"

Liam held a finger up to my lips. His eyes were soft and concerned as he shushed me. I wanted to be mad; but I couldn't find it in me.

"I know it's your mother, your house, your life and if you want specifics, I will tell you because you deserve to know. But…" he trailed off, looking the most uncertain I had ever seen him; the uncertainty and discomfort in his eyes was more than I had ever seen in a person before. I swallowed hard, feeling bile rise in my throat.

"It's that bad?" I sounded like a child in my own ears and I hated it. I jumped a little when Liam let out a frustrated growl that sounded more like a beast than a man.

"It's that bad," he confirmed, rubbing my arms like I had just told him I was cold, "I know you hate this coddling and not knowing what's going on. But please believe me when I say your peace of mind is far more valuable than the details. Let me and mine take care of this for you. This is something that never should have been your burden."

In the back of my mind, there was something that bothered me about his last statement. I had the feeling that there was something he wasn't telling me. Something important. I opened my mouth to ask him, but I stopped. Asking the question on the tip of my tongue would only add unnecessary complications to this relationship. I had to remind myself that this was short term. Short term meant ignoring the complications. Instead, I asked the other question that had been plaguing my thoughts all morning.

"Where are you taking me on our date?" At that he smiled wide.

"It's a bit of a gamble, honestly. I'm not sure what you'll think of it, but I think it will alleviate some tension." I raised an eyebrow at him as he held out his hand, asking for my keys. "Trust me?"

It struck me as curious that the last thing he said was a question, not a statement. He was asking for my trust. If I read between the lines, I could see the unspoken promise that if I gave him my trust, he would take care of me. It was a massive, overwhelming thing right in that moment, and I focused on the here and now, choosing to ignore that promise.

Without a response, I put my car keys into his hand before walking around to the passenger side of the car. Liam was right there beside me, opening the door for me and closing it once I was in. I took a deep breath as he walked around and climbed into the driver's seat, he waited and made sure that I had fastened my seatbelt before even starting the car. The radio came to life, the pop station filling the car with a crooning ballad, and we sat unspeaking as he pulled out of the hospital parking lot. Watching him drive from the corner of my eye, I couldn't help but feel like he was being overly cautious, like I was precious cargo. I felt my face flush and I mentally chanted that Liam was short term and nothing more.

"Isn't it a little early for drinking?" I jokingly asked as he parked in front of a bar called The Snake Room. One of the first nights I was back in town, Hannah had told me that Shane was going out for drinks with his coworkers at The Snake Room. I figured it was some type of strip club. Hannah assured me that it wasn't. It was just a bar that had a unique lumberjack theme. I arched a brow at Liam and he laughed shutting off the car.

"No risk, no reward." He winked at me, "I'll explain once we get inside." Still skeptical, but curious, I got out of the car. Liam came around my side, pocketing my keys before looping my arm through his. When we entered the bar, I was expecting something like the dives my friends and I had gone to when we were on campus. A place that was dark, reeked of stale beer, with a bunch of surly men hoping to drink their woes away. That was not this bar.

The first thing that hit me was the smell, wood fire and the savory scent of a hearty meal being cooked. The inside was clean and bright and the lumberjack theme was almost painfully overdone. If the food tasted half as good as it smelled, I could forgive the obnoxious amount of red and white plaid. Classic country music played softly from hidden speakers, while the murmur of the lunch crowd filled the room but wasn't deafening. Occasionally a loud *thunk* would ring out, like something banged against the wall. A matronly looking woman behind the bar hollered out in greeting.

"Welcome back, Mister Benson! It's been too long since you've graced us with your handsome self!" I bit back a laugh as Liam exaggeratedly rolled his eyes.

"It's good to see you too, Sonya." This time I couldn't help but let out a snicker at his put-upon tone. My laughter died on my lips as the woman scrutinized me. I immediately panicked, thinking that I wasn't the first date that Liam had brought here. I followed him as he walked towards the bar and Sonya.

"Will you be needing the private room today?" she asked dropping her voice.

Liam shook his head and pulled out his wallet and a credit card with an easy smile, "I actually want one of the throwing galleries." Sonya's eyes lit up as she plucked the card from his fingers.

"I've got gallery three open right now, so it's yours. Are you wanting lunch? I can send one of the boys up to take your order. Did you and your lady want something to drink?"

"Yes, to lunch for sure. Send the waiter by in ten minutes or so. As for drink, just my usual. Cordi what would you like?"

While they were speaking, I had eyed up the impressive wall of liquor and long line of beer pulls, I was excited to see that they had one of my favorite hard ciders on tap.

"The pineapple cider," I said, "Just a sixteen and a glass of water." Sonya nodded.

"I'll send it right up. Menus are already there. Enjoy yourselves!"

Liam immediately steered me from the bar to a stairwell that I hadn't seen when we had first walked in.

"So, you come here often?" I asked as he motioned for me to go up the stairs. I held my ground waiting for an answer.

"Occasionally clients don't want to meet at the estate," Liam explained when I refused to budge, "But there are times that the meetings still need to me kept discrete. Sonya is good about letting me use one of the private party rooms if a client wants to meet in public."

"Oh," I said, losing some of my indignation. Liam put his hand on the small of my back, pushing just enough to get me moving again, but not before he dropped his lips down next to my ear.

"Feeling jealous?" He teased. I did my best to ignore how correct he was, but his low chuckle was enough to prove that he knew he was close to hitting the mark.

Going up the steps, the second floor was sectioned off into six large rooms, each with a large window showing into them. The rooms we walked past had groups of people in them and I watched with fascination as they hurled axes to the far end of the room where boards with crude targets painted on them hung on the wall. I looked at Liam and shook my head.

"Really?" With a roguish smirk, he took my hand and pulled me along. His large warm hand around mine caused my stomach to erupt with butterflies and my knees to go a little weak.

"Trust me."

Despite my earlier misgivings at the hospital and promises to myself, I did.

I was beginning to think that I was screwed.

I know that I had told him that I would be easy to 'wow' and had almost expected something crazy and over the top. Coeur d'Alene was a tourism hot spot being surrounded by incredible forests, so there was no shortage of thrilling adventures as date options, but this already was so much better. He led me into a smaller throwing gallery with only two high-top tables and one target on the opposite end of the room. Despite the dull thuds of axes hitting targets in the rooms around us, it was surprisingly intimate.

"How did your meeting go?" Liam asked as I hopped up into one of the chairs at a table and pulled a menu to look at while he took the seat across from me.

"It was alright," I replied, "Same procedures, different hospital for the most. I've been through most of it before. With only a month left on my externship I was really glad to find out that I would have to learn a new records system. Perhaps the best news was that I would be able to start on Monday. It will be nice to get back to some normalcy." Liam gave me a sad smile.

"I wish I could wave my hand and take away your pain and sorrow," he told me, his voice painfully earnest, "but time is the only thing that's going to help. Returning to normalcy will help, but don't push yourself too much. Know that it's alright to have days where you're not okay and that all you want to do is seek out comfort, whatever form it may take." He placed his hand over mine on the table, and I felt a tingle race through me making my toes curl inside my shoes.

The atmosphere shifted, filled now with something electric and expectant. When I looked up at Liam, his eyes dark with something I hadn't seen before in other guys who looked at me – hunger. I nearly opened my mouth to suggest something that I might have regretted, but the waiter, in full lumberjack uniform entered the room with our drinks and complete obliviousness. He took our orders and by the time he left, the tension had ebbed once again.

"So," I drew out the word as I sipped my cider and gestured toward the rack that held the axes, "Why don't you show me how this works." With a smirk, Liam slid out of his seat while rolling up his sleeves. He took his time examining the axes, picking them up, hefting them, gripping them, before he eventually settled on one. He approached the throwing line and, with axe in hand, he pulled his arm back. He took two long slow breaths and then I heard the crack of the axe cracking the wood and sinking into the center of the target. I blinked a couple of times, shaking my head in disbelief. His arm had moved so fast I didn't even see it. No…that couldn't be right…

"Your turn," he said with a smile before going to retrieve the axe he had just thrown. Determined to prove that I was just as good as him, I went over to the rack, selected my own axe and stepped up to the throwing line just as he returned. Trying to copy him, I held the axe in one hand and hurled it towards the target. It clattered to the ground halfway to the target. I let out a huff and stomped forward to retrieve it while Liam chuckled. When I picked it up, I spun around and pointed it at him.

"Are you laughing at me?"

"I would never dream of laughing at a woman wielding an axe."

"Smart man."

We took turns tossing axes at the target, his sinking in every time, mine barely even making it to the target. He tried very hard to give me pointers, but my competitive side reared it's ugly head and I was determined to figure it out on my own. To my surprise and delight, he didn't take offense, giving me space and time as I figured it out. By the time our lunches arrived, I was at least getting the axe almost to the target.

As we ate I found myself relaxing even further thanks to our conversation and the excellent hot, pressed sandwich. Liam was a surprisingly animated speaker using his hands to talk and over the top expressions that made me laugh out loud. Combined with his deep voice, he was absolutely magnetic and mesmerizing.

"What did you do then?" I asked, as he paused to take a sip from his pint. He was telling me a story about a prank war when he had been enlisted and I was on the edge of my seat.

"The only logical thing," he said, his eyes sparkling with mischief, "I put his car on the roof of the admin building."

"How?" I asked with a laugh and he shook his head, "What did he say?"

"I will never tell how, that is one secret I will take to my grave because even all these years later he has never figured it out," he grinned at me, "As for what he said…well I'm not going to repeat it in polite company, but let's just say it was a string of curses that has never seen its equal."

I laughed even harder, using my napkin to dab tears from the corners of my eyes. When I looked back at Liam I could see that hungry look lurking in his eyes again.

"Come on," he said standing and extending a hand to me, "One final toss and this time I'll help you with your form, Miss Competitive." I rolled my eyes but still got out of my seat and headed back to the throwing line and picked up the axe I had been using. I figured he was just going to tell me what I was doing wrong, so I was woefully unprepared when he came up behind me and put his hands on my hips.

He used his foot to widen my stance just beyond shoulder width. His hands gripped my hips, setting and straightening them. His fingertips skimmed up my sides to my shoulders, squaring them with my hips and pulling back on them straightening my posture and having me stand tall. For a moment, I couldn't help but imagine what it would feel like if he was pulling my shirt up and off me, his hands against my bare skin. I blew out a long, slow breath, suppressing a shiver as he gripped my arms, having me raise them above my head and holding the throwing axe with two hands.

"Use both hands, it will give you more control and strength as you throw," he instructed, his voice low, gruff, and (if I wasn't mistaken) wanting. I never would have guessed that fixing my throwing stance would be a turn on, but Liam's hot breath on my neck and firm body behind me had me wound so tight that I was fit to burst. He took a step back and I took a deep breath before flinging the axe forward. It hit wide of the target to the left, burying itself in the rough boards. I may have missed the mark, but at least the axe stuck this time. I excitedly turned around to share my victory with Liam and froze.

I had heard friends describe men as 'pure sex' before but hadn't comprehended it fully until I turned and saw Liam. He leaned against the high-top table, propped up on one elbow, which caused the fabric of his blue button-down shirt to strain against his muscled torso. The thumb of his other hand was hooked through one of his belt loops, tugging his dark jeans down just enough that I imagined that I could see a sliver of his tanned skin between the bottom of his shirt and the top of his pants. And his face…damn…

His eyes were half lidded, shadowed and dark with want as they wandered over me. His look made me feel like I was wearing the sexiest lingerie, even though I was in a pair of simple jeans and a worn-out shirt from my college. What sent me nearly over the edge was how he was biting his lip as he looked at me; like it was that simple action alone that allowed him to hold back from pouncing on me right then and there. I was overcome with the need to be the one biting that lip.

"Do you want to get out of here?" I hardly recognized my voice, soft with a slight rasp that betrayed just how aroused I was feeling. A shock raced through my spine, straight to my already wet core when he licked his lips in response before uttering two words that made my body tingle.

"Let's go."

Chapter 13

Cordelia

Liam settled our bill at the bar and Sonya sent us off with a cheery smile and wave, and a salacious wink. Once we were outside, I noticed that the wind had picked up a fair clip and it looked like storm clouds were moving in. I wished I had brought my jacket with me, but the morning had been so nice, a taste of true spring. When we were back in my car, Liam quickly checked his phone with a frown, before shooting off a message with a grumble that wasn't words.

"Everything alright?"

"Fine," he replied with a frustrated sigh, "I had hoped they would be done with the first phase of clean up by now." He hesitated, and I knew that he didn't want to give more details. I gave a commiserating grunt and squeezed my thighs together. Nothing was quite a mood killer like the remediation happening at the house. I tried to think of alternatives, but there was no way that I was even going to consider taking Liam to Hannah and Shane's house for whatever we were about to get into.

God, I sincerely hoped that it involved a bed and Liam sans clothing. Liam let out a sputtering cough as he started the car. We were silent the whole drive to my mother's home. I couldn't stop myself from fidgeting, half veiled attempts to find some kind of pressure or relief for that need in my core. Every time I moved, Liam would inhale sharply and grip the steering wheel tighter. The tension in the car built in the silence until I was ready to burst by the time we made it back to my house. I felt the swell of defeat when I saw that there were a couple of trucks still in the driveway. Liam parked my car on the street before getting out and heading around the front to my door. He helped me out of the car, and his touch was hot, it was nearly singing my skin.

Liam and I walked up to the porch, and from inside the house I could hear several voices as well as the sound of a couple of machines or power tools.

"Just a second, Cordelia," Liam said, clearly agitated. I nodded and he darted into the house. I sat on the porch swing, every nerve ending of mine felt like it was on overload. While he was in my house, I tried to get my head on straight. I tried to think about anything that would calm me down so I wouldn't immediately jump Liam when he came out of the house. Puppies and kittens usually worked.

But then I thought about Liam holding adorable little puppies or fuzz ball kittens and I felt flush.

Then I imagined the same scenario, but now he was shirtless.

"Fuck," I swore to myself and buried my face in my hands, convinced that I was losing my ever-loving mind. It was at that moment Liam stepped back out of my house.

"They'll be about ten minutes," he growled, his eyes hazy with need.

"There's a park a few blocks away—" His raised eyebrow made me stumble over my words, "It takes about ten minutes to go there and come back. We can kill the time." He didn't seriously think I was suggesting that we go to the park and...

I mean I was adventurous, but I didn't want to get arrested for lewd conduct.

Liam extended a hand to me.

"Shall we?"

We never made it to the park. We were almost there, when the heavens opened up and began to pour cold rain down on us. We sprinted through the rain, holding hands and laughing like kids. Liam had attempted to seek some shelter for us under trees along the sidewalk back, but we were completely soaked by the time we made it to the porch of my house.

"Are you alright?" Liam asked, raking a hand through his damp, sandy blonde hair, attempting to rid it of the water that clung.

"Yes," I said breathlessly, "I would have suggested just waiting it out here and starting a movie if I had known it was going to rain this hard—" I was going to crack a joke, tell him that I wouldn't melt in the rain. But when I looked up at him, the words got stuck in my throat. The rain had soaked through his blue button down which caused it to become nearly transparent and was plastered to his torso. I had dreamt about him night after night, haunting my dreams from the moment we met. I had imagined his body a dozen different ways but seeing him in the flesh made me realize: My dreams hadn't done him justice.

Liam was an imposing figure, tall and broad, and his chest and abs looked as if the muscles were chiseled from stone. Running my hands along his abs, I marveled at every defined ridge and groove. His body firm and so incredibly warm beneath my palms. My mind finally caught up to what my body was doing, and I belatedly realized that at some point I had closed the gap between us. I was touching him and not thinking about it, caressing his body with the touch of a lover.

I immediately tried to pull my hands back, but he caught me by the wrists. I could feel the heat rising in my cheeks and the embarrassment burning in my chest. I looked down at our feet like they were the most interesting things I had ever seen, mine in worn sneakers, his in a designer brand.

"I'm sorry," I choked out, "I don't know what I was thinking." That wasn't entirely the truth. My thoughts were scattered to the wind, but they were on him. I wanted him so much, and I had my plan of this being a short-term relationship, but I was suddenly overcome with uncertainty.

It was one thing to fantasize about him and think that a short-term fling could work between us, but it was another thing to be facing it head on. Now that I was here and about to take the next step, engaging in those fantasies suddenly struck me as foolish. I was determined to not stay in Coeur d'Alene and up until recently I had been (as far as Liam was concerned) the help's daughter. I was not ashamed or embarrassed about what my mother did, but in my experience, my mother's occupation was an easy cause for others to see us as lesser than them. Liam released one of my hands and held my chin, forcing me to look up at him.

"Cordelia, you have nothing to apologize for," he spoke in earnest before suddenly leaning down and kissing me. The kiss was soft, fleeting. A gentle caress of his lips against mine before he pulled back. When it happened, I made a pained, needy noise, something more feminine than a grunt and more dignified than a squeak. Liam's response was a chuckle that was husky and deep. His hand shifted from holding my chin to cupping my cheek, the look in his eyes was hot and needy, mirroring the same look he had given me before we left the bar. His body, however, was tensed, thrumming with energy and desire that he was keeping a tight leash on.

"Cordi, I've wanted you since the moment you stormed up to my house. I have never felt this way about anyone or anything. It's frightening how you consume my every waking moment, but I find myself not caring and not wanting things any other way. And if you want me, I will be yours, and yours alone. I promise you. I just need to know if you will have me."

His words were so heavy: promises of commitment and need. That didn't work with 'short-term'. That didn't work with moving to Atlanta.

I should have run into the house.

I should have slammed the door in his face and packed my bags.

But I didn't.

I ran my hands up his chest, watching his eyelids flutter shut in ecstasy, before burying my hands in his hair and pulling his lips down to mine. Where our first kiss was a light caress, our second was needy and hungry. Liam swiped his tongue across the seam of my lips, and I opened to him. He teased my tongue with his, darting it in and out of my mouth, as if he were simulating what he hoped to be doing very soon. I leaned back against the front door, catching the handle and opening it. Liam picked me up, wrapping my legs around his midsection, and carried me over the threshold, kicking the door shut behind him.

For a moment I wondered if the others were still in the house. Then I realized that I didn't care. Liam, I presumed, had warned them to get out of the house.

We continued our kiss as he carried me up the stairs, stopping the war between our tongues long enough to ask: "Bedroom?"

"Second door, right," I moaned. Liam moved at a double time pace. Once again, a door was opened and then kicked shut by him. He placed me on my feet near the end the bed. His hands went to the button at the top of my jeans, his frenetic movement slowed way the hell down, crawling and creeping forward. Every touch was specific and calculated, like he was carefully unwrapping a present and was trying to savor every moment of revealing my body to him. All I wanted him to do was to rip the damn fabric off my body. As each article was removed, he would pepper my exposed skin with those soft feathery kisses and a gentle caress of his fingertips.

He leaned forward kissing along my neck before guiding me back onto the bed, sitting me down near the edge before laying me flat on my back, with my legs around his waist. He was above me, his hands on either side of my body, caging me in. He moved his hips against mine and when I felt the rigid length of him behind the zipper the rough material of his jeans rubbing against my exposed skin. I couldn't hold back the keening moan that worked its way up from my throat. He continued the slow, torturous swirl of his hips as he buried his face in the crook of my neck, nipping at the skin with his teeth before soothing the sharp pain with a gentle kiss.

"Liam," I panted, "Clothes. Off. Now."

With a grunt, he pulled away before quickly divesting himself of his soaked shirt, pants, and boxers. He looked down at me, pausing again with a look that was both savage and reverent.

"My god, you're exquisite," Liam's tone was reverent as he stroked himself and licked his lips. The combination of his worshipful tone and vulgar actions, had me squirming under his gaze. My own gaze fell to where his hand was, stroking himself for me. I gulped and wondered if I was going to be able to handle the full, thick length of his dick. I couldn't wait to find out.

"I'm on the pill," I blurted out. It was easily the least sexy thing to ever say as a hot guy strokes himself and stares at your body. "Thought you should know." Liam's smirk would light my panties on fire if I was still wearing them. He stroked himself a couple more times before bending over and snatching up his pants.

"Good to know, love," his voice was thick and rough with need, "But we should still exercise some caution." He fished out his wallet and pulled out a small, square silver packet. I'm sure I was insane for thinking it, but even through my hazy lust filled mind, there was something incredibly sexy about his caution. Liam ripped open the packet and carefully rolled it onto himself. He put his left knee up on the bed, heat rolling off his body as he closed the distance between us. I looked down, to see his hand wrapped around the base of his shaft. When he began to tease my core with the thick head of his erection, I couldn't hold back the wanting cry.

"Liam!"

"I'm here, Cordi, I'm here. I just want to make sure you're ready for me," he paused, panting, and poised at the entrance of my slick channel, "Is this your first time?"

His question caught me off guard, and I shook my head no. Suddenly embarrassed that I was admitting to the man who was about to rail me (complete with his cock at the gates) that he wasn't my first. "But," the word came out strangled and pleading, "It's been over a year since the last time I had sex." I failed at fighting back the giggle, "You are much—"

"Bigger?" Liam's amusement should have been annoying, but instead it sent a shiver through my body as I realized what he was saying.

"In every way."

Liam's chuckle was deep. I wondered what it would feel like if he had done that while buried to the hilt inside me.

"We'll take it slow, love," Liam said as he dipped into me shallowly, stretching me, and retreated. All amusement now gone from both of us. I swore, digging my fingers into the comforter and mattress. Liam lifted my right leg, placing it on his shoulder and wrapped my left around his hips. He leaned forward, pushing himself further into me. I bit my lip and closed my eyes. Good God, he hadn't looked that big. I felt like I was going to be split in two starting in between my legs.

"Cordelia, look at me." Liam's voice commanded, and my eyes immediately flew open. The first thing I noticed were that his eyes were dark, pupils dilated, the blackness swallowing up the hazel and green color of his eyes. His jaw was clenched and he was breathing harshly through his nose, like he was doing everything within his power to hold himself back, to be a gentleman. "If it's too much we can stop. I'll take care of you, we don't have to rush this." I considered his words for a moment and appreciated him allowing me the option of backing out.

But honestly: fuck that.

Instead of answering, I dug the heel of my left foot into his rear, causing his cock to push deeper into my sex.

Chapter 14

Liam

Christ, if Cordelia kept this up, I was going to climax before she had had the opportunity to find her own release. I grazed my fingertips against her leg that was propped up on my shoulder and grabbed her hip with the other. I felt like a goddamn teenager again, barely able to control myself and sharply heading towards orgasm. And if the tightness in my groin was any indication, I would be coming harder than I had in years. Feeling her heel dig into my ass, I surged forward, burying myself to the hilt in her slick heat. Her sharp inhale let me know that she hadn't been prepared for my intrusion even though she wanted it, but the way she ground herself against me let me know that she was fine with it and adjusting.

"Cordi, dammit," I swore, my voice guttural. This woman completely undid me. Her body was an instrument of pleasure and she had my number. I slid my hand along her hip, savoring the feeling of her smooth, tanned skin beneath my fingertips, stopping when I grazed against the delicate bundle of nerves hidden beneath coarse hair at the apex of her legs. The keening noise that came from her throat and the clench of her already tight channel had me practically gnawing on the inside of my cheek to maintain control, forcing myself to use the pain and coppery tang of blood to keep me focused.

"More, oh God, Liam," she begged panting and started to writhe on the bed. Every movement sent an electric jolt of pleasure straight to my cock. I stayed unmoving inside her, teasing her pearl, until she climbed higher and higher towards a climax. When I was convinced that she was just about as far gone as I was, I began to move.

The first time I pulled back, her whimper damn near ripped my heart out of my chest, but when I thrust back into her, she screamed my name, which filled my chest with a primal warmth. I picked up the pace of my thrusts, slowly beginning to piston in and out of her tight warmth. God, how had she gone more than a year without anyone? My wolf growled inside my head, pleased that there were no others in recent memory for her to compare us to. Of course my wolf was also less than pleased that we were being cautious. He wanted to fill Cordelia's womb with cum, have her bear our pups, and become den mother of the pack.

I could feel his want coursing through me, a live and visceral thing, and I did my best to tamp him down. He didn't understand human nature: if we forced her into being ours, that would only make her run from us faster. Humans, people, individuals had this habit of running away from things that are good for them because they inspire too much fear within their hearts. I wasn't about to let that happen with Cordelia.

"Liam, I'm going to…I'm so close," Cordelia's words were barely above the sound of a whisper and I could feel the telltale rhythmic fluttering of her walls. I increased the pace of my thrusts, strumming her swollen clit harder with my thumb, trying to meet her at the edge so that we could fall together.

"That's it, Cordi, mate mine, come for me," the words left my mouth sounding feral and completely unlike myself. Cordelia let out a throaty cry as she found release, I pumped into her a few more times before I felt the familiar jerk of my cock as I came, spilling my seed into the condom. Our ragged breathing was the only sound in the room as we both came down from the incredible high that only comes from sex. I eased her leg from my shoulder before leaning forward and planting my hands on either side of her body, before kissing her forehead, each of her closed eyes, the tip of her nose, and then her lips.

"Are you alright, Cordi?" I was concerned, she lay unmoving, taking large gulping breaths.

"Uh-huh," she said, answering in a familiar affirmative tone. I kissed her lips once again, before delicately extracting myself from her to deal with cleaning us up. I slipped into the hall and found the bathroom. I dealt with my own mess in the most perfunctory manner as I waited for the water to warm up. Once it was the perfect temperature, I grabbed a washcloth from where they were neatly folded on a shelf and ran it under the tap. Back in the bedroom I found Cordelia exactly where she had been when I left, body exhausted and spent, languidly laying across the deep plum colored comforter. Warning her about what I was going to do, I then tended to her, wiping and cleaning her up before heading back to rinse the cloth. By the time I had gotten back into the room, her breathing had become steady, and I chuckled as I realized that she had fallen asleep.

I pulled down the covers before picking her up and moving her so that I could tuck her in. Watching her burrow into her pillow I wanted nothing more than for that to be my chest, but I couldn't. Not just yet. I quickly pulled on my boxers and wet shirt for some modesty before exiting the room with my cell phone. I dialed my brother as I walked through the house, checking doors and windows, making sure that they were all secure.

"Dear brother!" Franklin's tone was way too bright and chipper, "And how are you faring this afternoon?" I quickly looked at my watch and saw that it was barely five o clock. With everything that had happened today, I figured it would be much later than that.

"Fine," I replied latching the deadbolt on the front door, "I don't anticipate that I will be back to the estate tonight. Can you reschedule my morning meetings for tomorrow afternoon?"

"Already done," came Franklin's mirth filled reply, "Joshua called on his way back to let me know that you, and I quote, 'busted up into the house like his dick was on fire.' Further he said, 'His mate's legs were wrapped around him like—'"

"I don't need the specifics, Frank, I was there," I said, just the thought of Cordelia clinging to me like a second skin and crazed with need was stirring my desire back up for her. Not that I could do anything about the stirring in my boxers since Cordelia was asleep. Franklin paused and it was so unlike my brother to not be rambling or inserting his opinion into every conversation. "Frank, did I lose you."

"No, I'm still here," his voice sounded different, less flippant. I could hear his footsteps on the wood floor and then a door close, "Look, I know we don't do a whole lot of emotion talks since you feel everything we are feeling, but I just wanted to say that I am so happy for you."

I stopped going up the stairs mid-step.

"Frank—"

"No let me get this out because I need to say it," Franklin interrupted me, "The whole pack has been worried about you since the proposal came to the pack for a political union with the fae, but me more so than everyone else. You've been different over the last couple of decades, ever since you became Alpha and the council assigned us to defend this Ley."

"Yeah, the council," I snorted, "Their decision had dad written all over it."

"You're probably not wrong," Frank mused, I could tell he was thinking about our father, "I still remember how he blew a gasket when you told him I was coming with you."

Gerald Benson, our father, sat on the council that governed werewolves, served as the prime example of a 'good and old school' Alpha, but could be a temperamental asshole behind closed doors. Franklin and I had a whole host of half-brothers from our father's previous couplings, most of them far older than us, but we were the closest in age and we were (as far as we knew) the only ones with the same mother.

Carmen, our mother, had been father's true mate and was an incredible woman. Though true mates share in a werewolf's longevity and immunity to time and aging, it didn't protect her from human ailments. Ovarian cancer had taken her from us and when she died about seventy-five years ago, a part of our father died as well: his empathy. Which had caused him to turn into an insufferable bastard, most of his anger had been taken out on Franklin.

While the rest of his sons had proven to be Alpha material, Franklin not as much. It's not that he couldn't handle all that came with leading and caring for a pack, it was just that he didn't want to. He much preferred working in support of a pack and working behind the scenes rather than in the limelight. He also wasn't a Beta, so his lack of 'gumption' had frustrated and angered our father to no end. The wounds from the beatings that Frank had endured to 'toughen him up' still haunted me because there was nothing I could have done. They had been severe leaving visible and invisible scars, but Dad was careful to never make them life threatening. The only way then to save him would have been to challenge my father for dominance and the role as Alpha. I was confident in my ability to fight, however as a realist, I knew my father could still whoop my ass into next century.

I was glad when the council had appointed me as Alpha and protector of the Ley in Coeur d'Alene when the last pack needed to move out, because the first thing I did was claim Franklin as part of my pack. Dad had not been pleased. Time had mellowed out Dad's anger and I had reconciled my relationship with him. But I knew that there was still some resentment between the two of them.

"He thought that I would be so distracted with everything that I would forget you," I said taking a seat on the staircase, "Thankfully for us he underestimated our bond." Frank let out an indignant snort.

"You do realize that I was perfectly capable of handling the old man."

"I know, but you were going to be dead well before you got mad enough to do anything about it." Silence hung on the line, we both knew I was right, he just didn't want to admit it.

"Regardless," Frank said clearing his throat suspiciously like he was trying to mask frustrated tears, "Between defending the Ley, running the business, and the pack you've lost some of you along the way. You were so busy putting everyone else first, it was like you forgot about yourself. You weren't giving any consideration for your needs nor were you really caring for yourself and it made the pack restless. Silas and I understood what was happening, but none of the others have known you as long or as well as I have to know how much you have changed."

"Duty and pack above all," I muttered quoting the phrase our father had beat into our skulls.

"It's your duty to care for yourself because without you, Alpha, there is no pack," Frank countered with the words our mother had always said. "She completes you, Liam, in a way that I don't think you can fully see yet. Plus, all of the others are excited that they can start their hunts for mates as well."

"They would have gotten that with or without Cordelia," I said, a bitter note sneaking into my voice. Not for the first time, I cursed the universal pack laws. Rule number two: no wolf can claim a mate until their Alpha had claimed theirs. There had been too many lost lives because a jealous Alpha couldn't keep it in their pants, so it became universal law. Franklin hummed thoughtfully.

"I owe it to you, for everything you've done, to find you a way out of the damn contract. I've started combing through it, but it is over a thousand pages long. I'm going through it as quickly as I can, but I'm also making sure I don't miss anything. Not to mention the fae write in the most archaic and over complicated manner that I've ever seen."

"That's why I pay you as much as I do to be the pack's lawyer," I tease, "I don't have the patience for that level of detail."

"You don't pay me nearly enough," Franklin retorted without any malice in his voice and a long-suffering sigh. There was something off, I could hear it in his words and feel it through our pack bonds.

"Frank?"

"Yeah?"

"You said that all of the others are excited to find their mates...are you not?" The line was silent except for Franklin's quick, anxious breathing. "It's...complicated..."

I waited for him to elaborate, but when he didn't, I knew he would only get angry if I were to push.

"I'm here."

"I know," he said and I could hear him shift uncomfortably on the other end of the line, "we can unpack all of my mental and emotional baggage later. Right now, we both have more pressing things to tend to. You need to tend to your mate, and I need to find a way to not piss off the fae. I will see you tomorrow." The line clicked off. I sat there for a moment staring at my phone screen running my hand over my face.

"Liam?" Cordelia's soft voice reached me from where she was waking up in her bedroom. I scrubbed my face one more time before standing and heading back to her. I met her as she was coming out of her bedroom, clad in a pair of hot pink shorts that clung to her curves in a most appealing way and a worn thin, half shirt that allowed me to see the delicious skin of her stomach. In her arms was the sopping wet mound of our clothing. When she saw me, a mischievous smile blossomed on her face. "I figured you couldn't have gone far. Especially considering I have your pants."

"I had thought about leaving, because someone fell asleep on me after round one. I almost couldn't handle the blow to my ego," I teased her, loving how deep red color flooded her cheeks. "Where are you going with that?"

"Oh, I was going to toss this in the dryer," she replied pushing past me to hide her embarrassment. I followed her down the stairs to the laundry room that was just past the kitchen on the back of the house. As she tossed our wet clothes into the dryer, I slipped off my wet shirt and boxers and threw them in as well. After she had started the dryer, she turned to me and her hungry eyes roamed over me, but I could hardly concentrate on that. The water from the clothes had completely soaked through the front of her shirt, turning the thin material transparent and exposing her full, pert breasts.

With a growl, I scooped her up and deposited her on top of the dryer, jerking down her shorts in the process. I was pleased that she was wearing nothing underneath. With one hand I began to tease her as I stroked my swelling cock with the other. I kissed her relentlessly, trailing my kisses to her ear.

"Round two," I rumbled before dropping my head to her breast and making her scream my name.

Chapter 15

Cordelia

My second week at home was a significant improvement upon my first. Liam and I spoke and saw each other every day after I wrapped up my shift at the hospital and he wrapped up his work for the day. The time that we spent together was easy and pressure free. We would have dinner together before some other activity, sometimes watching a movie or television but usually falling into bed together. The sorrow and pain I had experienced during that first week with dealing with my mother's funeral and murder was slowly being erased away by my time with Liam. It was incredible. He was incredible.

We spent our first night alternating between some of the hottest sex of my life and quiet moments of us talking, touching, or that fuzzy space between being awake and asleep. We spoke at length about movies, music, and food but also about family, friends, and life in general. I told him about my time at school, the rigors of my program and their high expectations for students and about my externship in Bend. He told me about taking over his family's business when his father retired, the unique personalities of his team of employees, and trying to live up to the legacy his father had left behind.

The entire night, as we talked, I could sense that there was something more, something that he was holding back from me.

"You know I think it's weird that I don't remember you," I commented as he told me of some of the antics he and his brother Franklin had gotten into when they were young. We were laying in bed, he was on his back his hands propped behind his head, I was on my side, my body tucked against his as I trailed my fingers over his bare chest. He looked at me, his brow furrowed.

"What do you mean?"

"Well, there were times growing up that my mother took me to your family's estate when my sitter had been sick," I explained, *"I don't remember any other kids or teens around. Actually, I don't remember much of anyone being around. I was always curious why it was such a big house if there was never anyone in it."*

"My brother and I spent a lot of time away," he replied. From some of the stories he told and the description of his father, I wouldn't have been surprised if he had spent some time at a boarding school or military academy. But I could tell he didn't want to talk about it, so I didn't push. There were plenty of subjects I didn't want to talk about either.

"Does your company still train guard dogs?" I asked shivering. I felt his body tense under my fingers.

"Why?" His voice was overly cautious.

"Just curious," I said trying to downplay the fear I felt, "There was this one time, I might have been seven or eight, and I had gone with my mom to work. She had set me up in the kitchen and I had a couple of books with me, but I had finished reading them and I was bored. She had mentioned that there was a library so I decided to find it and see if I could find new books to read." I swallowed hard and closed my eyes.

"I remember walking through these massive empty hallways, scared to check any of the rooms because my mom had told me not to snoop, but I didn't want to wait for her to show me where the library was. I was walking past this one room when I heard a yelp, like a dog had gotten hurt. I liked dogs and wanted to help it if it had been hurt bad." Liam wrapped his arms around me and pulled me close. He stroked my hair, whispering soothing words to me that were too quiet for me to understand. I realized that I had started to tremble uncontrollably.

"I don't…the things that happened after I opened the door are a little fuzzy." I say softly, unable to stop the words now that they had started. "I remember something big slamming into me, knocking me to the floor. There was a bunch of guys shouting and I remember this snarling mouth filled with sharp teeth going for my throat," I gulped, "But then your father was there, yanking the dog off of me, shouting at the others to chain him up."

"I remember," Liam said softly. I turned and looked at him, startled.

"What do you mean you remember?"

"I remember him telling me about it," he amended, "He was scared shitless that you had been hurt, that your mother was going to be furious with him. She was, just so you know."

I couldn't help the nervous chuckle that bubbled up. Liam's large warm hand cupped my cheek, tilting my face up to his and we locked eyes.

"I promise nothing like that will ever happen again," his voice somber, "I'm sorry that you had to endure that." As he spoke, his eyes boring into mine, a realization hit me. His eyes were identical to his father's. Before I could remark on it, he was on top of me, kissing the nightmare away.

"Earth to Cordelia, heeeeeelloooooooo?" My thoughts snap back to reality.

Today was my day off from the hospital and Hannah and I had spent the morning doing some cleaning in my mother's house and had decided to go out for lunch. Josh and the others had finished up yesterday with the remediation and everything looked the same as I remembered. When I told Josh that, he beamed and said that was the highest compliment I could have given him. The next day I had been surprised when Fletcher, another of Liam's employees, had showed up to do a security system install. Fletcher had worked quickly and quietly, completing the work in a couple of days before showing me how to use the system. I had told Liam it was too much, but he had pushed back, giving a huge list of reasons why it was a good idea. His points had been valid, so I didn't fight him.

This was the first day that I finally felt safe to bring Hannah over, now that all of Liam's guys were out of the house. I was convinced that she wouldn't be able to keep her hands to herself if she had occupied the same space as them. She would blame the pregnancy hormones, but I knew her overactive imagination would get her riled up enough to do something regretful. I knew she loved Shane and she would be gutted if she hurt him by being stupid.

"What?" I asked taking a sip of my water. She looked up at our waiter expectantly. "Oh, sorry! I'll have the chicken bacon club sandwich, chips not fries." The waiter jotted it down and took our menus. Hannah turned her attention to me.

"The sex must be incredible if you can't even pull it together long enough to make it through lunch."

"Shut up," I groaned, closing my eyes and tilting my head up to the ceiling. I had finally told Hannah about Liam right before coming to lunch. She of course demanded me recount everything in excruciating detail, which I refused to do. "But it is pretty damn fantastic."

"Knew it!" she said triumphantly, before dropping her voice and running through a litany of salacious possibilities that had me shaking my head. I distracted her with talk of her baby shower that was coming up when my phone buzzed across the tabletop. I picked it up and unable to hide my goofy grin when I saw it was Liam's name on the text.

"Oh, is that him?! I hope it's a dick pic."

"For chrissakes, Nah-nah," I said using the nickname she hated, "you're married."

"But I'm not dead." I rolled my eyes at her and unlocked my phone.

Cordi, where are you?

Out to lunch with Hannah at Giodorno's, why?

Ah...Frank has some papers for you to sign regarding your mother's estate. He's at your house now, and your car is there but no one answered.

We took Hannah's car. Shoot I didn't think he'd have anything more for me after the million papers and forms he had me sign last night.

Don't fret, he's on his way to you now. Hate to interrupt your lunch, but he says this one is time sensitive. He's kicking himself for forgetting it last night. He's been under a lot of stress and doesn't have to deal with probate often. Are we still on for dinner tonight?

Absolutely :-)

I'll pick you up at 6.

Can't wait!

"God you love keeping a girl in suspense! What is with the shit eating grin?"

"Sorry," I said while feeling my cheeks heat up, "Apparently I have some more paperwork to sign, Liam's brother Franklin is on his way here."

"Is he as hot as his brother?"

"Hannah!"

"Again, I'm not dead, I can appreciate a good-looking man, if he is one."

I laughed at her and rolled my eyes. The front door swinging open drew my attention and I stiffened when I saw several police officers come into the restaurant. I felt like a lead weight had dropped in my stomach when I saw Jack was with them.

"Shit," I swore keeping my head down. Hannah looked behind her towards the door.

"What is…oh," she said when she saw Jack. He was caught up in a conversation with the other officers and hadn't noticed us. I was thankful as the hostess sat the group of five on the opposite side of the restaurant from us. Jack sat with his back to us, none the wiser. Hannah eyed me as I relaxed a little bit knowing he hadn't seen us yet. "You still haven't talked to him then, huh?"

Among the things that we had discussed in the car on the way here after the 'Liam bomb', I had told her about Jack's snit and immature behavior when my mother's house had been released. She had been appalled that he wanted me to clean up the crime scene with him.

"No," I muttered, taking another sip of my water and shifting in my seat, "I haven't had anything to say to him.

Because I'm certainly not apologizing for getting help with the house and cleanup."

"I would beat you up if you tried to apologize to him," she said, "Heck I would beat the living crap out of him if he demanded an apology from you. I know he's Shane's best friend and he's been your friend for a long time, but screw that. He was an insensitive asshole. Stay strong. If he wants to throw away your friendship because he was being an ass, that's on him not you."

Our waiter returned, setting down our food in front of us. When we had come here, I was ravenous. Now, after talking about Jack, I had lost my appetite. Hannah started in on her soup, salad, and half sandwich combo, before pointing at my sandwich.

"Eat," she commanded. I wanted to protest when my stomach made a loud gurgling noise and she gave me the haughty mom eyebrow that she'd been working on.

"I hate you sometimes," I said as I took a bite of my sandwich. She snatched a chip off my plate and popped it in her mouth.

"You know the rule," she said, "Bitch chip tax." Looking down at my plate and food, I wanted to correct her that it was 'bitch fry tax' not chip when she made a pleased sound at the back of her throat. "If I wasn't convinced before, I am now: a well-tailored three-piece suit is the sexiest thing a man can wear."

"What?" I asked, looking up to see that she was turned in her chair as she nodded in the direction of a man crossing the restaurant towards us. A familiar man, with a knowing smirk on his face, as if he could hear Hannah's whispered comment through the din of conversation the permeated the restaurant.

"Oh, you are in for a treat," I teased Hannah as Franklin got closer. Hannah's eyes nearly popped out of her head when she realized he was heading directly toward us. "That's Liam's brother."

"Damn, those are some fine genes that family has," Hannah murmured. The smile on Franklin's face got wider. I didn't doubt that he had heard Hannah, now for a second time, which meant his hearing was impressive.

"I don't think I've had anyone compliment my familial genes before," he said as he stopped at the end of our table, "Thank you?" I shook my head as Hannah's face turned bright red. I couldn't help but think that it served her right.

"You're welcome," she choked out as Franklin chuckled with a shake of his head.

"May I have a seat?" I nodded while laughing at how flustered Hannah was. I didn't miss the mischievous glint in his eye as he pulled out the chair next to her and sat down. As Franklin rifled through the documents in the slim leather padholder that he brought with him, I took a moment to really look at him.

His hair was a light shade of brown, several shades darker than Liam's, and he kept his much shorter than Liam and much more tamed, styled even. They were both clean shaven, showing off their square jaws, they had the same straight nose and eye shape, but that was where the similarities ended. Franklin's eyes were a dark forest green rather than Liam's hazel green. The more that I sat and thought about it, I realized that their body types were the main difference between the two brothers.

Liam's physicality was broad and packed with muscle; Franklin reminded me of a runner or a fencer – thin with a distinct elegance about everything he did. Even as he pulled out the papers for me to sign, he did so with a slight flourish. I pushed my plate to the side so he could lay the pages in front of me. I skimmed them as he pulled a pen out from the inside pocket of his jacket.

"I thought I had included these forms last night, but when reviewing all of the signed documentation I found that I hadn't included them," he closed his eyes and pinched the bridge of his nose.

"Liam mentioned that you were dealing with a lot of stress and deadlines, so I'm sorry that I've piled more work onto you." Franklin sighed and dropped his hand, his deep green eyes tired and almost looking through me rather than at me.

"Don't worry about it, Cordelia," he said with a smile, "I am happy to help you out."

"I hate to take you away if you have more pressing deals to oversee," I knew that Volsung did security, but didn't know much more than that. With his law background, I was certain that Franklin oversaw all of the contracts and more. As if he could hear my thoughts he replied.

"There is only one that I'm dealing with but it's…" he hesitated a moment before continuing, "it's a bit of a bitch. It's over a thousand pages that I have to comb through in less than a week."

"Jeez-us," Hannah piped in, "isn't that more than a little excessive." Franklin chuckled.

"More than a little," he agreed, "and we're realizing that it was a mistake and we're in over our heads. Unfortunately, I can't say much more than that." Both Hannah and I nodded in understanding. Even though he was Liam's brother, I didn't want him to get into trouble for talking about something confidential. He cleared his throat and pointed to the forms, "These are crucial because they're consent forms, allowing me to file and put in requests on your behalf."

"Alright," I said continuing to skim them before taking the pen he held out to me and signing on the highlighted lines. Once I was done, I handed them back to him and he tucked them back into the padfolio. He had just started to stand when he stopped suddenly, glaring at something over my shoulder.

"Cordi," Jack's voice sent a shiver down my spine, and not in a good way. I didn't miss the way that Franklin planted himself back in the seat, his entire body tensed. If his glare was anything to go by, Liam had told him about the altercation I had with him outside of my house.

"What do you want, Jack?"

Chapter 16

Liam

The damn cop showed up as I was getting ready to leave," Franklin groused as he collapsed into one of the chairs in front of my desk after I asked him what had taken so long. He was supposed to 'be right back' by his own admission, but he had been gone for nearly an hour. "I figured after him being an ass at Cordelia's home, you wouldn't want your mate to be alone with him." I gripped the stack of proposals in my hand a little bit tighter, ruining the pristine pages. I kept my eyes diverted and on the pages, rather than looking at my brother.

"What did he want?" I asked trying to keep my anger in check.

"To apologize," Franklin answered relaxing further into the chair with a tired sigh. "I think he was expecting her to apologize as well, but she held her ground. Your mate has a spine of steel. He also…"

Frank was silent for far too long and I looked up at him. He was regarding me carefully and I could tell he was contemplating if he should finish his sentence. I growled at him.

"My mate. Tell me."

"You don't have to be so dramatic," he said with an eyeroll, "He invited her out this evening to make it up to her. She of course turned him down, Jack was appropriately put out and tried to get her to agree to another night. She rebuffed him though, something that he was exceedingly not happy about. It's been a while since I've seen someone that angry and smelled a rage like his. I know you don't need me to tell you what to do but be careful with that one."

I grunted and turned back to the proposals for security contracts. He was correct that he didn't have to tell me that Jack was trouble. An officer of the law who had a long-time infatuation with my mate that had been shot down now repeatedly – it was a recipe for petty vengeances. It was one less thing I needed right now, but for Cordelia I would endure anything.

There was a knock on the door frame of my open office door and both Franklin and I looked. Fletcher was there with a frown on his face.

"Am I interrupting?"

Franklin stood, straightening his jacket as he did.

"No, I was just getting ready to leave. I still have nearly three hundred pages of contract to get through with regards to the agreement with the fae."

"Any luck?" my voice filled with hope that was dashed when Franklin shook his head.

"Not yet, but most of the details of the marriage were towards the end of the contract. But I had to go through the full thing just to be safe."

"There's only four days until the wedding," Fletcher said. Franklin rounded on him.

"Yes. Fletcher. I am well aware of that!" he snapped at our Beta with a snarl.

"Franklin," I barked coming to my feet. Franklin immediately backed down, scrubbing his hand across his face. Tense silence hung in the air of my office for a minute, before my brother sighed tiredly. His gaze swung between me and Fletcher. For the first time, I felt like I was seeing the dark circles under his eyes. I felt a sudden pang of guilt and concern in my chest. Franklin must have felt it too because he waved me off.

"I'm sorry, Fletcher. I will touch base with you in the morning, Liam." His voice was quiet and sincere before leaving the room. My wolf wanted me to follow him, to snarl and snap and tell him to pull himself together, but I forced him back. My brother had dealt with enough snarling and snapping from our father, I wasn't about to lay into him as well. I would give him the space he needed, but I wouldn't forget this.

"I didn't mean to intrude and cause problems." Fletcher stood, head bowed, pulled into himself making him seem small and unthreatening. Seeing him like that was a punch to the gut for me.

Betas were a bit of an anomaly amongst werewolves. They lacked the authoritative dominance that most werewolves had, and most found their presence soothing because they knew they wouldn't have to jockey for dominance with a Beta. There were others, packs and individual werewolves, who thought Betas were of better use dead than alive. Their thought process: a dead Beta shows other werewolves the cost of being 'weak'. It was complete bull. If you pushed them far enough, they would fight and could be more vicious than the most dominant Alpha because they never fought for themselves; they always fought for the good of the pack. The handful that I had known during my lifetime, however, had usually wilted under direct attack in an attempt at self-preservation.

It's not that they were sensitive or emotional, but there was something hardwired into Betas to yield. Normally it wasn't a problem. Fletcher never had to tip toe around us like I've seen other Betas do in different packs. He was valuable, not just to help keep the group calm, but his prowess with technology was second to none.

"Come in," I beckoned and motioned for him to take a seat as I poured two fingers of bourbon and handed the glass to him. It wasn't that the alcohol would calm him, once through the first transformation, werewolves developed a certain tolerance or immunity to the effects of nearly all alcohol, a perk of the higher metabolism.

The offer was a show of respect and apology for the way Franklin had behaved. It was my responsibility to keep the peace within the pack and it was currently my fault that Franklin was in the position that he was in and the cause of him lashing out at Fletcher. I knew others might not see it in the same light, that Franklin was the only one responsible for his actions, but they were wrong. Fletcher took the glass and sipped before setting it down on the edge of my desk. Acceptance and understanding. I doubted he would drink the rest.

"I wanted to report what David and I found from the police station."

"It took you longer than anticipated," I remarked. He had asked for infiltration permission before Loretta's funeral over a week ago.

"There was a complication, nothing to be concerned about, but there was a system security upgrade that I hadn't realized they had implemented. I did get in and found some information.

"They currently have a suspect that they are looking for, Loretta's ex-husband and Cordelia's father, Luis Hernandez. They had reports from a couple of pawn shops in town of someone matching his description selling lady's jewelry. They're beginning to think that it was a robbery gone wrong: Luis breaks into his ex-wife's home looking for some goods to pawn, she comes in, catches him, threatens to call the police, and he gets violent."

"What do we know about him?"

"He's got a rap sheet filled mostly with misdemeanors and petty crimes. Lots of pick-ups for drugs and a couple of felony identity thefts. He's been serving a jail sentence for the last three years and got out about a month ago."

"Sounds like they have a good lead for once," I replied and immediately noticed Fletcher's frown. "You don't think so."

"I talked about the details I found with Noah and David, and it just seems too convenient. Of all the charges against Luis, none of them are violent crimes. Sure, he got picked up in a couple of bar brawls, but nothing this extreme. Loretta was stabbed sixty-seven times. According to Noah, that indicates either an incredible amount of rage or lots of violence in the past. Noah noted that there's no escalation up to this, so the level of violence doesn't jive with his history. There are other things that don't make sense either."

"Like what?"

"Do you know how long it takes to stab someone that many times? How exhausting it is?"

"Do you?" I asked the mild-mannered Fletcher raising my eyebrows in disbelief. He shook his head.

"Not firsthand, but David was able to enlighten me. It would take time, between two and five minutes, and a lot of energy to commit that kind of crime. According to information that I have on Luis, he's pushing fifty and is overweight and out of shape. I doubt he would have had the time and energy to stab her and make a clean get away before the responding units made it to the house. Plus, robbery doesn't jive because there were no signs of forced entry."

The more Fletcher explained, the more likely it seemed that the police were chasing down a dead end.

"You said that you were going to compare the written reports with the digital and look at the signatures on everything. Were you able to do that?"

Fletcher coughed nervously as his face turned red.

"No, I---there was another---complication?"

"Is that a question or a statement?"

"It's nothing."

I stared at Fletcher. Patient. Expectant. He fidgeted in his seat.

"You know it's unnerving when you do that," he groaned picking the glass back up from my desk and draining the rest of the amber liquid. "I got caught."

"You—I'm sorry, what?"

"It's fine, I talked my way out of it, but I got caught before I was able to compare the hard copies."

"This sounds like the opposite of fine to me," I replied, keeping my voice level and even, trying not to betray the frustration that I was feeling. The last thing I needed was Jack and the rest of the police department knowing that one of the men I employed had gotten caught breaking into and hacking the police database.

"Look it's under control, she's not going to tell anyone." Fletcher's voice was defensive and ardent, and I could see in his eye something powerful and intense.

"She?" I asked oscillating from angry and curious.

"They hired a new database administrator after firing the old one. She was working late. She doesn't drive a car and was working in the dark so we missed her until it was too late. She only caught me; Dave was able to hide and I was able to message him to tell him to get out."

I leaned forward, looking intently at Fletcher. There was no trace of a lie in his words, but this was not a development that the pack needed right now.

"Liam, I know you're pissed, but we, she and I, came to a…mutually beneficial agreement…on her end she is helping me back door into the database and feeding me information."

"And what are you doing for her?"

"She has unique extra-curriculars that I am assisting with…"

"Simple, Fletcher. Spell. It. Out. For. Me."

Fletcher huffed out a breath and refused to look me in the eye.

"I'm helping her hack some gang's network out of Seattle."

"Fletcher—!"

"I know, Liam, I know! But just think of it as one of my independent contracts."

"She is blackmailing you!"

"It's only *really* blackmail if I'm not getting something out of the deal! Look, that's how I have the information on Luis, alright? She's looking for her kid sister who started hanging around some gang loser. She's worried about her and hasn't heard from her in a couple of weeks. She was telling me the truth."

There was something else that he wasn't saying. At first, I thought it might be something that he was trying to hide. But the longer I considered it, the more I began to suspect that the was something that Fletcher didn't realize himself.

"What is her name?"

"No."

"Her name is No?"

"It's not," Fletcher's voice was filled with indignation, "That was a 'No' as in 'No, I don't want to tell you.' She's done nothing wrong and she is helping us. I don't need or want you sticking one of the others on her and tailing her."

I noticed and immediate change in Fletcher's demeanor: Arms crossed, head up defiantly. This suddenly assertive and demanding demeanor wasn't like him at all. He was driven to protect this woman---his woman I realized. I didn't think his human head had figured it out yet, but I was certain his wolf had staked his claim.

"And you just trust her so easily?" I asked gently, trying to prod him to a realization.

Fletcher opened his mouth and closed it almost immediately. As he wrestled with his answer, I had to suppress a chuckle. Fletcher was always analytical, statistics and numbers, driven by hard and fast data which seemed to fly in the face of everything that he was and the magic of being born a werewolf. It was amusing to see him struggle with what was standing right in front of him. Looking at Fletcher's face, I could see that he was working through it as well and trying to come up with something that he could tell me.

"I do."

"Then you are taking her as a ward? You understand what that means?" I asked in complete seriousness.

Wards were individuals associated with the werewolf community that were normal mortals that knew to some extent about what we were and what we did.

After the incident with Cordelia in her youth, Loretta had been filled in about our world and made into a ward of the pack, and through that connection a ward of mine. Wards were expected to uphold the secrecy of the packs and of the rules of the council. Betrayal meant serious consequences, not just for the ward, but for their werewolf protectorate as well.

Fletcher gulped but nodded his head.

"I understand and I accept the burden of that responsibility, Alpha. But she doesn't know about us. She just knows that I work for a private security firm that's also looking into Loretta's murder."

"Good. Keep it need to know," I instructed, putting on a serious face and tone, "Don't let her side project distract you from the work you are getting paid to do."

"Yes, sir."

"Did you have anything else that you needed to report on then?"

"No, sir."

"Then you are free to go," I said turning back to my computer. "If you see Rich send him my way. I have a couple of proposals to review with him."

"He's downstairs, I'll grab him," Fletcher replied, the relief in his voice palpable.

Once he was out of my office, I stopped holding back my chuckle and allowed myself to laugh. I was almost certain Fletcher's ward wouldn't be one for long. His emotions had been all over the place when talking about her, and though he tried to convey a distant and disinterested vibe with regards to her, he couldn't hide how she had him tied up in knots through our pack bond.

"When it rains it pours," I muttered to myself as Rich came through the office door. Dressed in boots, black cargo pants and a gray tee, he looked like he was ready to run drills. His signature black colored dreads were tied back away from his angular face and well-groomed goatee were the only things that belied his past as a soldier.

"Are we finally going to get back out in the field instead of this pussyfooting around?" He asked, his voice amused and gray eyes searching, as he sat in one of the chairs in front of my desk. Rich was a man of action, so the inaction of the last few weeks, between Loretta's death and the wedding had him on edge. I was unphased by his attitude, he was a former special operations soldier and damn good at what he did. Even though he pretty much headed up all our field operations, he was only fourth in rank within the pack.

"Yes," I said giving him the answer that he wanted to hear, "but it won't be until after the wedding." Rich chuckled and shook his head.

"God save me from ever having to deal with being fucking pussy whipped." I looked at him and shook my head.

"You don't want to find a mate?"

"Honestly, hell no," Rich said with a chuckle, "who wants that kind of drama and headache. No offense meant."

"None taken," I replied after thinking about everything that had happened since Cordelia had come into my life. I would never even think of her as a headache, but the last couple of weeks were certainly 'eventful.' "But what happens if you find the one?" At that Rich guffawed outright.

"That's a good one, Liam, but let's be honest for a second. A woman would have to be a bat-shit crazy adrenaline junkie to put up with me, and frankly I don't think she exists." It was my turn to laugh.

"You say that now, Rich, but mark my words, you're going to find her when you least expect it."

"Doubtful, Liam, incredibly doubtful. Now let's look at these potential contracts and see about getting the pack back to work."

Chapter 17
Cordelia

"Can I ask you a question?"

Liam and I had just finished dinner at a quaint restaurant called The Sandpiper and were leaving the restaurant and heading for his car, a sleek, gunmetal gray Lexus RC F.

"You just did, but I suppose you can ask a second," he winked at me before pulling open the passenger side door for me and offering a hand to help me get in. As he shut me in, I rolled my eyes and muttered to myself under my breath about smartasses and not putting up with their antics. Liam slid into the driver's seat and started the car. It purred to life, near silent, I couldn't help but think about how this car cost almost as much as my entire college tuition. When I had told Hannah what car Liam drove, she had insisted on looking it up.

I wish that she hadn't.

All it did was accentuate the gap between Liam and I; I was beginning to realize just how out of my depth I was.

But that doesn't matter. This is short-term…*remember?* A small voice tried to convince me. However, the more time that I spent with Liam, the harder it became to imagine leaving Coeur d'Alene and moving on to Atlanta. I had started to imagine what it would be like to have a serious relationship with him, to take things to the next level. But I couldn't. I wouldn't. I just had to complete two more comps and I was done. There was no sense in getting attached now.

"What was your question?" Liam asked, sounding genuinely curious as he put the car into drive and pulled out of the parking lot. I closed my eyes and settled into the seat; I wasn't sure how this was going to go over.

I wanted to ask him what we were doing, what was this between us, and was it something that was going to go anywhere.

"What exactly is it that your company does?" I asked instead, completely balking on what I really wanted to ask. Liam didn't say anything immediately instead waiting until we stopped at a red light. He turned his eyes on me, and he looked at me like I was a puzzle that he didn't know how to solve. I felt a shiver race down my spine, I hadn't ever seen such a cold calculating look before from him.

"I'm sorry if you can't talk about it," I said immediately backing down and looking down at my fingers in my lap, "you know what, just forget I said anything."

"No, it's alright," Liam replied, "It's just…some of the clients and jobs that we deal with are sensitive and demand a certain amount of secrecy and discretion. I don't want you thinking that I'm not telling you everything because I don't want to, some of it I honestly can't tell you."

My mind immediately flew to crazy government conspiracies and international espionage. Strange though it was, imagining Liam in a tuxedo in some James Bond type scenario really didn't seem like a stretch to me. And I bet he would look incredible in a tailored tuxedo. Incredible and totally panty-meltingly hot. Liam's warm chuckle drew my attention and I turned to look at him. His eyes were on the road but the knowing smirk and glimmer in his eye sent a delighted thrill through me.

"I assure you it's nothing that glamorous. More often than not, the jobs that we take are low key and, to be honest, a little boring."

Had I said something out loud? I didn't think I had but I had been in dreamland, so I might have said something.

"We do a bit of everything," Liam said cutting into my thoughts again, "We offer a guard services related to asset protection along with executive and close protection, which makes up most of our business, but we also do surveillance and technical security – alarms and the like. Occasionally we'll consult on physical security, and we're starting to expand more into cybersecurity. Even more infrequent are the times that we are called to help with extractions of hostages or kidnapped individuals."

"That does sound kind of boring," I teased, thinking the exact opposite. It sounded dangerous, and exciting and so completely removed from anything that I had ever done or experienced. I suddenly felt like my chest was in a vice at the thought of Liam putting himself in harm's way. I took a deep breath, clenching and unclenching my fists to shake the feeling. It helped but there was still something tight in my chest.

"Don't worry," Liam murmured with a soothing chuckle, breaking the silence between us, "I mostly sit behind a desk and meet with clients. Unless we are on a job that requires all hands on deck, I rarely do fieldwork anymore." Again, in a short span of minutes I wondered how he seemed to know what I was thinking, was my tension and anxiety that apparent? Liam smiled at me when I looked at him, but it seemed tight, almost forced, as he steered the car through the early evening traffic.

As we pulled into the lot of the movie theatre, I heard Liam's phone buzz twice as it danced in the center console. He glanced down at it with a frown once the car was parked and the engine shut off before scooping it up and unlocking the screen. I tried not to look, giving him some privacy, just in case it was related to his work. Our time together had always felt like it was in a bubble, it was only a matter of time before the outside world made itself known. When I felt Liam tense up beside me, I suspected that our night was about to be cut short.

"Is something wrong? Do you need to take me home?" I asked, while Liam angrily tapped out a text message.

"No," he growled, "I can't take you home."

The hair on the back of my neck immediately stood on end, I felt overcome with the need to run. I needed to get out of the car, I needed to flee. The feeling of the gentle weight of a hand on my thigh made me jump, but then I immediately felt a wave of ease wash over me.

"I'm sorry, Cordelia," Liam's voice was soft and sincere, "I didn't mean to startle you."

"But is there something wrong?" I continued to press. I had never seen Liam's mood shift as quickly or as many times as it had this evening. There was something more intense about him – not to say that he wasn't usually intense to be around – but tonight that intensity had taken on an edge that I hadn't seen from him yet and it was beginning to worry me.

"Yes, something is wrong, but we don't need to let it ruin our evening. My team has it under control." A thought punched me in the gut from out of nowhere.

"Why did you say that you couldn't take me home? Liam, what's going on?" Liam didn't respond immediately. For a moment he just sat there, glaring out the front window, his left hand gripping the wheel like he wanted to strangle it, his right was still gently resting on my leg, like touching me was grounding him against whatever was going on in his head. After what seemed like an eternity of silence, Liam sighed.

"I can't lie to you, Cordelia," he said with a sorrowful and bitter tone, "The alarm at your house tripped about ten minutes ago. Someone is in your house right now."

"What?!" I was bewildered by his statement, "We have to go…we have to call the police…"

"Cordi, love, calm down," Liam's voice was soft but commanding, "My pack is already there. They're going to secure your house before we go back. This is what we do. I will make sure that it is safe." Liam's phone buzzed again and we both looked at it before he picked it up, unlocking the screen and reading the message that just came in.

"Who is it? What are they telling you?" I asked, both wanting and fearing Liam's answer. His brow was pinched, mouth frowning, like he really didn't want to tell me. So, when the words came out of his mouth, I think we're both surprised.

"Your father."

The world came to a screeching halt. My father? The man had never been a part of my life. He was always an annoyance for my mother on the periphery of our world and what was going on. I knew that he had spent time in jail and that my mother always referred to him as a criminal, so I had never purposely sought him out. But if he was at my mother's house—my house—did that mean that he could have had something to do with my mother's death?

When I was able to refocus my eyes on Liam, I saw a look of guarded concern on his face, like he was waiting for my reactions. When his gaze held mine, however, I saw something much more terrifying there. Rage.

I had seen people all manner of angry before, from miffed to furious (it was a side effect from working in the healthcare field), but what I saw in Liam's eyes transcended everything I had ever seen before.

"Do they have him in custody? Did they capture him?"

Liam jerked his head once, nodding. "The police are on their way."

"Take me home, Liam."

"Cordi—" his voice was rough, strained like he was barely holding on. That made two of us then.

"Now. Liam."

Without a word, he turned over the engine and tore out of the movie theater parking lot. I was amazed that he didn't get pulled over as he sped through the streets, swerving through traffic like it was standing still, and making it to my street in under five minutes. What I saw turned my stomach.

There were three large black SUV's parked haphazardly along the street and in the driveway of my house. The doors on the vehicles were thrown open as though the occupants had jumped out of them the minute they were moving slow enough, not caring about closing the doors. There were also three police cruisers in the street, red and blue lights flashing ominously in the early evening.

The house was lit up as if someone had turned on every light, and I noticed that all of the neighbors' houses were lit up as well, shadowy figures looking out to see what all of the commotion was about. There were two groups congregated, one next to an SUV and one next to the cruisers. I recognized several of the men next to the SUV's: Silas, Franklin, Josh, and Fletcher; the rest were unfamiliar to me but I assumed that they were all employees of Liam. Of course, next to the squad cars I recognized Chief Nelson, Detective Riley, and Jack.

Liam pulled his car to a stop and I was out and running towards my home, which had once again been violated. I knew that I should have been feeling fear and uncertainty, but the only emotion bubbling to the surface was a red, hot anger.

"Where. Is. He?" I snapped, venom dripping from each word as my anger and adrenaline rode hot through my veins. Every head in the vicinity whipped around to look at me.

"Miss Ramos," Detective Riley said holding his hands up and moving towards me speaking in a low, warning voice, "I'm going to need you to remain calm—"

"Calm? Calm!" I shrieked, my voice cracking, "He broke into my house! If I had been home, he could have…"

He could have killed me, too.

The words refused to leave my mouth, sticking in my throat and the haunting realization dawned upon me. The detective's caution about my father, Liam's same worry. I didn't want to believe it, but I knew he was trouble. My mother had told me enough stories to make me glad he wasn't an active figure in my life. I knew that he had been in and out of jail, always seeking my mother out when he was released, begging for more chances which she always refused him.

"Cordi," Liam's voice was soft and soothing, but I couldn't handle that right now. Soft would break me.

There was a commotion by one of the squad cars, and I saw him struggling with and officer and refusing to get into the back of a cruiser. I was moving before I realized it, ignoring everything but that bastard.

"*¡Hijo de puta! ¿Lo has hecho? ¿Mataste a mi madre?*" I demanded, shouting at him in the Spanish my mother had taught me, knowing his English was broken at best.

"*¡Mija! ¡No!*"

I don't know what came over me, but my arm swung wide, my palm connecting with the side of his face with a resounding crack the seemed to echo in the relative quiet that blanketed the street. Strong arms wrapped around my midsection and pulled me back harshly as my father was stuffed into the cruiser ungently and the door slammed closed. A warmth and familiar scent enveloped me as I fought back my tears.

"Cordi, calm down, love," Liam's voice had taken on a strange deep quality that I felt down to my toes. Firm. Powerful. It wasn't the same as the low, seductive tone he used when we were together and intimate. This was something completely different and I felt my anger start to bleed away. Much like in the kitchen on the day of my mother's funeral, Liam's breaths were slow and deep and I found my own matching his.

Detective Riley walked up, blocking my view of the cruiser as it pulled away from the curb. He talked to me, but only a few of the words penetrated: *questioning, evidence, motive, probable cause. Unsafe.*

"I'm sorry?" I said as the last word sunk in.

"I was just saying that it's probably unsafe for you to stay in the home tonight until the front and backdoors are repaired," he shot a look over my shoulder, "Seems like your men were a little overzealous when making entry." Liam's arms dropped from around me and he moved in front of me.

"They were doing what they've been trained to do. Something the men in your department should take notes on," Liam growled, staring down the detective. Riley stood a little bit straighter and I watched as his features hardened at Liam's slight. Neither man moved for over a full minute before Riley backed down, turning his gaze to me.

"Do you have somewhere to stay this evening."

"Yes," Liam and I both replied at the same time. I threw him a curious look as he turned back to me.

"You can stay at the estate—"

"No." I interrupted, my voice flat and firm. Suddenly I was tired: tired of everything that had been happening in my life and feeling like nothing was in my control. My mother's home, my home, had been my last safe haven and I felt like it was taken from me. I wanted to break down, but I wasn't about to do it in front of Liam, his employees, and a healthy portion of the police department. "I'll stay with Hannah. She still has her guest room made up for me," I supplied not looking at Liam and taking a step towards the house. "Is it alright to go in, Detective? I need to grab a bag."

"Yes, Miss Ramos," he responded, "The uniforms inside will direct you." For a moment it seemed like a weird statement, but then I realized, they would direct me away from the parts of the house that were an active crime scene. I gave him a tight nod and went towards the house, I could feel Liam shadowing me and it was all too much. I stopped in front of the steps.

"Just give me a minute," I say sharply over my shoulder.

"Cordelia." Even though there was a plea in his tone, Liam's voice washed over me like a caress. But there was something else there that grated on me: pity. I couldn't do this. He had watched my life fall apart time after time these last couple of weeks and I couldn't deal with him tonight.

"Sorry to cut our evening short," I said keeping my voice firm and refusing to look at him. I didn't want to see those gorgeous eyes filled with pity for me. "I'll text you when I get to Hannah's."

"Cordelia," he tried again, his voice firmer. I forced my feet to continue forward progress and moved up the steps.

"Good night, Liam," I said, dismissal in my tone clear. I made it up to my room before I completely broke down.

Chapter 18

Liam

"Sir?" Fletcher's voice pulled me from my dark, turbulent thoughts, jerking me fully awake and aware. It had been sixteen hours since I last spoke with Cordelia, sixteen hours since she dismissed me from her side when she needed me the most. I had felt her tumultuous emotions on the edge of my consciousness all night: rage, pain, embarrassment. But I had gotten nothing from her, truly from her, aside from a quick message that she had made it to Hannah's.

"Yes?" My voice was tired, with a strange mixture of defeated and frustrated. I raked my hand down my face as Fletcher hovered by my office door.

"I…can come back later?" Fletcher suggested, I could feel his uncertainty when it came to my mental state. I sighed.

"It's fine Fletcher. I'm fine. Come in."

He snorted at my remark but came in any way.

"You're a mess," he commented without any heat.

"You're blunt," I retorted and he shrugged.

"She'll come around," Fletcher's voice was soft but certain. I couldn't say I held that same certainty. Last night had been shaping up so well before Cordelia's father had ruined everything. But when the detective asked her if she had somewhere else to stay last night, I was suddenly thankful for her father's intrusion, because all of the pieces fell into place for the briefest of moments. She would come to the estate, the heart and home of our pack, and she would be safe. I could reveal everything about me, about the pack, about the world that she had no clue existed. I could show her that I could care for her and that the estate was the best place for her. But she shot it all to hell when she insisted on going to her friend's house. Realistically, I knew she was safe there, but I wanted her—no needed her here with me.

"I assume you have an update?" I knew Fletcher had been in contact with his source at the police station, his mystery woman.

"Jess told me they booked Luis on breaking and entering charges, enough to hold him for twenty-four hours and to question him about Loretta."

"Jess?" I homed in on. Fletcher cleared his throat and rubbed the back of his neck.

"She's the DBA," he explained seeming to realize his slip up, "From what she heard in the break room this morning though, it sounds like Luis is going to alibi out for the murder."

"Shit," I swore, feeling my frustration well back up. Based on the information Fletcher had given me before, I knew it was a long shot that Luis was Loretta's killer, but I had hoped, for Cordelia's sake, that things would be wrapped up sooner rather than later.

"What about her other research? Comparing the physical and digital reports," I asked, searching for any good news I could get.

"The detective and our friend Officer Miller are giving her the Blues Traveler treatment." Fletcher replied with a growl. I wanted to rage out and flip my desk but held onto my composure by a thread. If they were giving one of their own the run around, it meant the police had put all their eggs into the 'Luis is guilty' basket and were scrambling for answers.

"Keep on it," I instructed, "But I'm getting to the point where we're going to intervene regardless as to what they find out."

"Of course, I've already started working our own investigation with Noah. He's just waiting for the word and he'll find the murderer," Fletch replied. I gave him an incredulous look. It wasn't like our Beta to take charge and defy my direct order to not investigate. Seeing the look on my face, Fletcher merely shrugged. "There's something going on here, and I think we can all agree that it goes beyond the abilities and resources of the Coeur d'Alene police department."

I opened my mouth to agree when my cell buzzed on my desk. Seeing it was Rich, who was currently watching over Cordelia and Hannah, I didn't want the call to go to voicemail. Holding a finger up to Fletcher I answered my phone.

"They're leaving Silver Lake Mall now," Rich said by way of greeting, "You're going to owe Hannah one helluva gift once she pops her young one out."

"What do you mean?"

"That woman has badgered your mate all day about reaching out to you. She's on your side, for whatever reason, and is trying to cajole your mate into calling to you. She's really damn persuasive, I think she's missed her calling as a lawyer. She plays a mean devil's advocate." I mentally made a note to see if Hannah had registered anywhere yet for a baby shower. If she got Cordelia to talk to me, I'd buy her the whole damn list.

"Where are they heading now?"

"Mi Jalisco Taqueria on Dalton," Rich replied, "Apparently, and this is a direct quote, 'the parasite is craving chimichangas.'"

I chuckled. Hannah was a unique individual and from the way Cordelia talked about her, I knew she was a good friend.

"Uh-oh, boss," Rich said, smile in his voice, "I've been made."

"What are you doing? Are you following me? Did Liam send you?" The sound of Cordelia's voice sent a shiver of relief through him.

"Miss Ramos—"

"Is that him? Are you talking to him now? Give me the phone," I could hear her command softly. There was a rustling sound, "Liam? You have someone following me! Seriously? What the hell?"

I dialed in on her tone, she didn't sound angry. Without seeing her body language, however, it was hard to be certain.

"You realize protection details are what we do, right?" Rich chuckled and I could hear a smack. My best guess was that either Hannah or Cordelia had hit him on the arm.

"I don't need a protection detail," Cordelia exclaimed. I wasn't sure if she was talking to Rich or me.

"Cordelia, love," I said, calmly, trying to draw her back to me, "You were so upset last night, I didn't want to leave you alone. But I knew that if I forced the issue, I would only push you away. So, I gave you what you wanted, what you needed: space from me. But with the break in, your father being arrested, and the uncertainty about his guilt, I couldn't leave you entirely unprotected. Rich is discreet…usually. I'm not going to apologize for having him keep watch over you, but I do apologize for not telling you about it."

Cordelia sighed.

"I don't want to argue with you over the phone, and I can understand the thought behind it, but this is…" She trailed off, looking for the word.

"Overbearing?"

"Yes," she agreed emphatically. There was no way I could be mad at her.

"If I call him off, will you agree to meet me later?"

Cordelia fell silent. I could tell she was trying to pull away from me, but we both knew that wasn't what she truly wanted. She was my mate, and even though I hadn't told her that yet, I knew that she felt the pull between us, like two magnets. Her silence stretched on and I couldn't take it.

"Cordi, love, are you there?"

"I'm here," she replied, her voice small, "Tubbs Hill Trailhead, I'll meet you there at four. Mama and I used to walk it all the time, I like to go there and walk the trail when I need to clear my head."

I knew the trail she was talking about and it was close the where the fae lands started. The fae court dwelled in the lands beneath Coeur d'Alene Lake. It wasn't dangerously close to the trail head, but it was closer than I would normally be comfortable with, especially since we hadn't found an out yet. But I needed Cordelia and I could feel that she needed me as well.

"Four it is then. I'll meet you there?"

"I'll have Hannah drop me off."

"See you then, love."

"Bye," her voice was soft before the line clicked off. I looked up to Fletcher who had a sly grin on his face.

"Tell Noah to start his investigation," I said, picking up our conversation where we had left it.

"Of course," Fletcher said standing and heading towards the door of my office. He paused. "She's the soft you need." He didn't elaborate before leaving and heading down the hall. As I sat, musing about the conversation, I realized he was absolutely correct.

As Cordelia instructed, I was waiting for her at the trailhead at ten minutes to four. The late May weather was still mild enough that the afternoon sun didn't heat the air to blistering temperatures. There were still hours before the sun would truly set, but it was hanging low in the sky. I watched as another couple packed up bikes, having just returned from a ride and heading out, leaving me completely by myself as I waited for Cordelia and Hannah to arrive. With only the sounds of nature around me, I let my thoughts drift to Cordelia and what I felt for her.

For the last couple of weeks, I had been living in the moment, merely counting down the hours until I saw her again. I thought that finding my mate wouldn't have a major effect on me, but I had been incredibly wrong. I had thought my life had been full before, I had my pack and Volsung, defending the Ley, and dealing with the Council. I was busy from the time I woke up until I went to bed and I had been satisfied with that, I had felt fulfilled, accomplished. I was living a lie.

I had been ignoring the hollow feeling in my chest, believing that I could easily fill it with anything and everything else. I had even been on the precipice of losing the chance at happiness by an arranged marriage. Sure, with time I was sure that my wolf and I would feel some affection for Lord Alderkin's daughter, but it never would have been close to what we felt for Cordelia. We loved her passion, her drive, her humor, and her easy affection and understanding.

When it came right down to it, both my wolf and I loved Cordelia. Completely. Unconditionally.

I watched eagerly as Hannah's vehicle pulled into the parking lot for the trailhead. She pulled into a space close to my vehicle but not directly beside mine.

I could feel Cordelia's wariness faintly through our one-way connection. She was still upset about last night, and on unsure footing and overwhelmed. I was determined to do whatever I needed to ease her worries and fears. To show her that I could take care of her and still let her have her freedom.

And most importantly I wanted to help her realize that she loved me just as much as I loved her.

Chapter 19

Liam

I watched as both women got out of the car and approached. Knowing Hannah's insistence, I was curious to see what she had to say. There was a look on her face that could only be described as starry-eyed amusement. Before meeting Cordi, romantic notions and gestures had never been something that I had concerned myself with, and I often found them annoying. Sure, when I was young I had bought flowers or small presents for girlfriends, but at that time I was more concerned about whether those gestures would lead to getting laid than anything else. After, well, they certainly weren't annoying and more. I found myself frequently getting caught up in thoughts and daydreams where Cordi was concerned. Shifting my attention from her friend to her, I examined Cordi.

Her hair was loose, the slight breeze teasing it and making the long strands dance about her. I hated to see the dark smudges under her eyes, knowing that it meant she hadn't slept well. She was dressed in a worn pair of jeans that looked soft and hugged her legs like a second skin, she had on a loose gray top that hung off one shoulder. Aside from her eyes, she looked comfortable and at ease. It was a good look on her and I was determined to do whatever it took to keep her looking as relaxed as she was now. When she finally looked up at me, she smiled but her eyes were guarded.

"Hey, love, how are you doing?" I asked when they finally reached me. I had to bite back a smile at Hannah's sigh.

"Better than last night," she replied, and I watched as her shoulders took on a defeated slump. Silence hung between us, awkward and heavy. I wanted her to say more, to explain so I could understand what she was feeling.

"Well," Hannah interjected, "I'm going to head on out. Do you want me to wait for you, Cordi?"

"I'll be fine."

"I can drop her back off at her house when we're done," I interjected, holding a hand out to Cordelia, "Josh replaced the doors at your house this morning. It's safe to go back."

Cordelia looked at my hand, as though it might bite her before looking back at her friend.

"Go Hannah," Cordelia implored, "Shane had planned a date night for you two, I don't want you to miss it."

"Fine, but I'll text you later and you better respond. Take care of her, Liam." With that final parting shot, Hannah went back to her car, climbed in, and pulled out of the lot. Once Hannah was gone, I twined my fingers with Cordi's and pulled her to my chest and wrapped my free arm around her waist.

"What's going on? What are you thinking?" I implored. Cordi sighed deeply before taking a step back from me and tugging my hand. She didn't untangle her fingers from mine but tugged me along with her.

"Let's walk and talk," she said and moved toward the shaded path. We wandered along the dirt path in silence at a sedate pace for several minutes before she finally spoke.

"What are we doing, Liam?"

"Walking," I replied with a smile. She scoffed and I didn't have to look to know that she was rolling her eyes.

"Liam," she groaned, drawing out my name. I couldn't help but chuckle.

"What do you want me to say here, Cordelia?" I asked seriously, attempting to ease her into the confession that danced on the tip of my tongue, "What I said before still holds true: you and I are exploring the attraction and chemistry that there is between us. Taking it one day at a time to see where it leads."

"It can't lead anywhere," she mumbled, thinking I couldn't hear her. I stopped short, tugging on our joined hands to turn her toward me. Her eyes were downcast and I could smell a salty sorrow clinging to her. Raising my free hand and tucking it under her chin, I lifted her gaze to mine. There was something in her eyes that I couldn't quite read. My wolf immediately started to panic. Was she breaking up with us? With me?

"What do you mean? Please, Cordelia, speak plainly."

"I just…" she began, struggling with her words, "My life is a mess. My mother's death nearly wrecked me and now my father's a suspect. I'm on the verge of graduating from college and moving to start my career. And things between us…" She trailed off again, biting her lip.

"I think things between us are pretty good." I was desperately trying not to concentrate on her talking about moving to start her career. This wasn't the first time she had mentioned it, and depending on where she was looking to move to, it would very seriously change my approach if she was planning on leaving.

"And moving fast," she added, "Really fast."

"We can slow down," I replied back, even though my wolf was howling at me to shut up. "You have all the power here, Cordi. We can go as fast or slow as we need to for you to be comfortable. I don't ever want to push you."

"You overwhelm me, and it scares the hell out of me." Her voice was soft, insecure.

"That is never my intention," I told her honestly, looking deeply into her eyes. I could see what I felt for her reflected back at me. I knew in my heart that she felt the same way I did, but instead of giving into it, she feared it.

"Cordelia, you have nothing to fear from me. I swear to you."

The breeze suddenly picked up and changed directions. In that single moment, as I looked down at the woman I loved, everything changed.

I smelled the vampire before I saw him. I barely managed to push Cordelia behind me before he attacked. With an amazing amount of power, he collided into me after charging through the spot where my mate had been standing. I stood my ground, digging my heels into the ground and refusing to be pushed back. Using every ounce of strength I had, I grabbed the creature by the shoulders and hurled him into a mature tree, which snapped and fell at the point of impact. That should have put him down for the count. But I was alarmed to see him bounce back up onto his feet, hunched and snarling.

"Shit," I swore as I took in the gaunt features and glowing red eyes. The creature looked more like a prop or set piece from a bad horror movie, not an actual living being. "Feral." The word left my lips as a snarl as I let my wolf rise to the surface.

The Vampire Coteries had two weapons: Bloodstarved and Ferals. Bloodstarved were their elite warriors, abstaining from glutting on blood. The lack of sustenance made them sharper, stronger, and more than a little insane. Well-fed vampires were slower, sluggish in their movements but with sharp minds and powers of mental manipulation. The Bloodstarved walked the fine line between feeding and starvation. It was worth it for them to have those enhancements to their natural predatory abilities. I knew that there were families that prided themselves on their Bloodstarved status, for the amount of discipline that it took to manage the condition, and they bred other Bloodstarved.

But to become Feral was a shame or reserved for vampire criminals.

They were Bloodstarved that had gone too far, went a little too long without blood, and driven to the point of being insane with thirst. They were the strongest and the most brutal of the coteries' brawlers, kept in chains and only sent out when their nobility wanted someone dead. In a strange way it was an honor to be hated enough to have a Feral sent after you. One that I'm sure I would appreciate later, once my mate was no longer in danger.

"Cordelia. Run!" I commanded as my form started to contort with change. I didn't hear any movement from behind me and I suspected she was frozen in fear. My change wasn't going to help matters, but at the moment all I was consumed with was protecting her and my wolf was inclined to agree. I felt his anger bubble up as the Feral let out a guttural snicker.

"Prince Sebastian sends his regards for your pending nuptials with the glamoured ones," His eyes flicked to Cordelia, "Sowing wild oats then? Let's have a taste." He bared his fangs and charged towards her. Before I hadn't been prepared for him, now I was in my hybrid form – half-wolf, half-man – standing well over eight feet tall and nothing but solid muscle.

My wolf and I were now of one mind, the familiar, unified feeling settling in, and I couldn't tell where I began and he ended. We moved fast, tackling the Feral in the middle of his lunge towards Cordelia. We heard an audible crack as we connected with him and in an instant, we were rolling across the ground.

We could feel him attempt to bite into our shoulder, but the fur around our neck was too thick for him to penetrate. What we could feel were his claws, digging and tearing into the less protected flesh of our biceps. We then rolled with him across the hardened dirt path and into the underbrush at the side of the trail and down a small embankment where there was a mossy, muddy creek bed. We dug our heels and claws into the soft earth, slowing us down.

When we finally stopped rolling, the Feral was on top, salivating and his grip on our arms tightening. We snarled at him and brought our arms up between us and, with a howl, flung our arms to the sides. This broke his hold on us. Before we could grab him, he planted his feet and jumped backwards, away from us. We rolled up into a crouch, keeping our weight on the balls of our feet. We wanted to pounce, but he was faster than us. We had to be patient and wait. We watched with disgust as he sniffed at our blood on his talon like nails, his body quaked with ecstasy. He looked back at us. He let out another guttural chuckle.

"Wait until his lordship finds out that the mutt has found a mate. He will happily skip to the glamours and tell them of your betrayal. Even better is that now there is a way for him to control you."

The bastard's words sent us into a rage, and we bull rushed the monstrosity, crashing through the trees, back up the embankment, and towards the path. We felt satisfaction as the Feral's body cracked and snapped against the sizable trees and the underbrush tore at his gaunt flesh. Ferals were the strongest of the vampire kin, and we remembered needing the pack to help take one down.

Apparently, Ferals were no match for a raging werewolf whose mate was in danger.

Back on the path we slammed him into the ground and began to tear into his flesh. It was then that I started to pull back my consciousness from my wolf's to find myself again. As I did so, he reveled in the pitch-black blood and gore he was flinging across the path. To be fair, it did appeal to my baser side, but by higher functioning brain was stuck on the feral's words.

Unlike werewolves, who shared a pack bonds and a collective consciousness, vampires were mostly independent creatures, the only link existing between a master and their children. And my understanding was that their link was an open book in one direction. Children could not read the mind of their master, but masters knew everything that their child did. Ferals tended to be the outcasts of vampire society, but that didn't mean this one hadn't created children or had a master. But, with all vampires, when their master, their parent, died in combat, the children knew and it sent many into a downward spiral.

If he was truly an outcast, I was in the clear.

If his master was alive or if he had children, I was about to have a whole lot of explaining to do to the Fae.

The other thing that he had mentioned also set the hair on the back of my neck on end: that having a mate meant that I could be controlled. I had heard stories about mates that had been kidnapped and held hostage to weaken members of a pack. Never had anyone ever told me that a mate could control a werewolf, especially an Alpha. My thoughts went back to my office, the day that Cordelia had come to tell me that she didn't want my help in paying for her mother's funeral, and how quickly my wolf had forced me to my knees. That knowledge made the notion not seem nearly as far-fetched.

My wolf continued to rip and shred at the thing on the ground until it finally stopped twitching. He was convinced that we weren't going to have to worry about it telling Sebastian, or anyone else for that matter, about our mate. She was safe, because we did our job. My wolf was satisfied and started to slip back into his cave in my mind, but not before letting out a satisfied howl. I started to relax and shift back into a human. It was at that time that I looked back and saw Cordelia.

Her coppery colored skin was washed out and pale, her smoky, chocolate eyes were widened in absolute terror. She trembled like a leaf in a cold autumn breeze clinging to a bare branch, I could almost see the fear rolling off her. And I could certainly smell it. I cursed at myself, because I couldn't speak with my face still shaped as a canine-like muzzle. I couldn't calm her or reassure her. All she could see was the monster in front of her. This wasn't supposed to happen this way, and I could only hope that she would allow me the chance to explain.

Chapter 20

Cordelia

You—you…what are you?" I backed away from Liam – or rather the hulking, looming creature that had been Liam. I had just seen the creature in front of me literally rip another man to shreds. I tried hard not to look at the bloody mess on the ground but the coppery scent in the air made my stomach roil as I resisted the urge to throw up. There was something in the back of my mind that poked at me and told me that the man that attacked us, that had come after me, wasn't human.

Just like how Liam wasn't human either.

The dark coarse fur that had covered his skin slowly receded, the canine like facial features retracted as his face morphed back to the familiar square shape and angular jaw. My eyes were locked on his and that was the only feature that didn't change. I demanded again, "What are you!"

"I am a werewolf," Liam's voice sounded rough and aggressive. I took a step backwards my body tensed and ready to flee. He threw up his hands in a desperate plea. "If you run, my wolf will insist that I chase you. We both know that I will catch you."

"Werewolves aren't real," I snapped, choosing to ignore the veiled threat of his words, "That's the stuff of movies and old stories. They can't be real." He arched an eyebrow at me, and I silently cursed his disarming good looks.

"Then how, exactly would you explain what just happened?"

"I—I---don't..." I stammered shaking my head disbelievingly. This couldn't be happening. The thought was beyond insane: Liam was a werewolf. Had I slept with a monster? I felt disgusted with myself: disgusted with the fact that I didn't care what he was that I just wanted him to be mine.

"I know it's all a bit shocking, but I am telling the truth." He looked mournful for a moment before continuing, "This is – this is not how I wanted to tell you." He looked down at his hands and I followed his stare. His hands were coated in a thick, dark red almost black liquid: the life blood and guts of whatever had attacked us. This time I didn't hesitate. I turned placing a hand on the nearest tree and emptied the contents of my stomach onto the ground. I retched until I had nothing left and my midsection was cramping, all the while hearing Liam moving around behind me, and the water splashing in the brook that ran alongside the trail.

Finished, I wiped my mouth with the back of my hand and stood up before looking over my shoulder. Liam was there, with a look on his face that reminded me of a sad puppy – which I suppose made more sense now. He had discarded the shredded remains of his shirt and washed the gore from his hands. Even after what I had seen, seeing him shirtless released another slew of inappropriate thoughts.

"Cordelia," he said softly, reverently, "if you'll allow me, I will take you back to your house and explain everything to you. Once I am done explaining, the decision is yours if you want to continue our relationship or not." I was surprised to hear him say that last part, especially since it looked like it pained him to say it. I should have been running away from him screaming. I should have been calling the cops and reporting a murder. Jack should be carting him off in a sheriff's cruiser. But there was something about that look and the sincerity in his voice struck me to my core and I found myself nodding and agreeing.

When he moved, he kept his movement slow and obvious as if he was afraid of frightening me. Which, if I was being honest, he probably wasn't wrong. As he went to remove the remains from the trail, I looked away and focused on my breathing. In through my nose. Out through my mouth. When a hand came down on my shoulder I jumped.

"It's just me," Liam's voice whispered into my ear, "Come on let's get you home." Gingerly, timidly he wrapped a strong arm around my shoulders and guided me back down the short path to his car. I stared at the ground the entire time, the long shadows on the ground seeming darker and more ominous as the sun lingered on the edge of the horizon.

He opened the passenger side door for me, like he had always did, but now his head swiveled around surveying everything. I didn't immediately get in the car, fearful of what might happen in the small, enclosed space. As if he could sense my hesitation, Liam swept me off my feet and carefully deposited me into the passenger seat and fastened my seatbelt. Before I even had time to protest my door was shut and he was coming around the front of the to the driver's side. He slid in, tensed, and turned over the engine. I hazarded a look back, expecting our car to be chased by more of whatever attacked us. But there was nothing but an empty parking lot.

"Lots of families walk that trail," I said, trying to keep silence from building, "What if some kid finds ... that thing?"

"My pack is already on their way to deal with disposing the body." Liam answered twisting his grip on the steering wheel. "No one will ever have a clue about what happened on that trail."

Part of me wanted to point out the fact that I would always know. That the encounter, fight, and terror would never leave my memory. There was part of me that wondered how his...pack...knew what had happened, he hadn't used a phone to call anyone. I jumped as Liam's large rough hand covered my own, gripping mine tight, but his eyes never wavered from the road.

"So long as I am breathing, you will never have to endure that kind of fear again." His voice was angry and solemn. And I instinctively knew that it was a promise that he would die to keep.

That thought terrified me.

And made me feel shamefully aroused.

We spent the rest of the fifteen-minute drive in silence. Neither one of us speaking. I wondered what would happen next. But more than anything, I wanted to know what that thing was and if there was more of them. As my thoughts spiraled and drifted, slowly coming out of my frightened daze, I began putting the pieces together. When that happened, I could feel my anger once again stir up. because soon my thoughts were consumed by a single, serious question:

Did my father (or someone else) murder my mother? Or was Liam and 'his pack' the reason why my mother was dead? Was it something from their world that had murdered her because of her connection to them?

Anger welled up inside me, a red hot and bitter feeling that turned my stomach and made me see red. 'What if's' consumed my thoughts, so much so to that I began to tremble and feel my hands shake where they were tightly clenched in my lap. How could they pull my mother into whatever they're doing? Werewolves and monsters? How could they think that she wouldn't be hurt? Were they so selfish? Did they even care to protect her?

By the time we pulled into the driveway of my house, I was seeing red and couldn't stand to be around Liam. Before the car had fully come to a stop I was out and moving to my front door. Liam shouted at me, but I didn't heed him or really care. I was furious. I wrenched the new front door open, wanting the satisfaction of slamming it shut behind me, but it stopped halfway. I spun to look, and Liam was there in all his shirtless glory holding the door. I then did something I had only done once before to someone.

I hauled back and slapped him across the face with all the strength I had.

"¡Mierda!" I shouted, clutching my hand that now felt like ten-thousand needles has been poked into it. When I saw him at the estate weeks ago, I had jokingly thought that his face looked like it had been chiseled from granite. I was beginning to suspect that I wasn't too far off the mark.

"Not granite," Liam said out loud as he shut the door behind him. He leaned back against it, his arms crossed and an amused smile on his too-damn-handsome face. It pissed me off that he didn't even have the decency to look chagrined or contrite.

"What?"

"I am flesh and bone, not granite," he explained, "Typically speaking only preternaturals made or crafted from stone are the fae race, gargoyles, and golems that are crafted by witches."

I was sure that I hadn't said anything out loud. Could werewolves read thoughts? A panic washed over me as I tried to clear my mind, but he was so distracting. Standing shirtless. In my mother's foyer. I felt like I was a teenager, breaking the house rules. If my mother could see me now, she would be having an absolute fit. She would have been mortified to know that I had slept with her boss.

The corner of Liam's mouth quirked up and I just knew the bastard could read my thoughts. I don't know how I knew but something in my gut told me it was true. My anger which had been red quickly was stoked white hot and I immediately lashed out at Liam.

"You have two fucking minutes to explain yourself," I snapped, my fingernails digging into my palms to keep my hands restrained, "Then I call the cops." My words immediately wiped the smirk from his face. He pushed himself off the door with predatory grace. He closed the gap between us, his large frame completely filling my vision. Everything about his presence – the heat from his body, his distinct mixture of cologne and musk – overwhelmed my senses. But I did not back away from him, he was on my turf and I would not be bullied. Instead, I looked up at him and locked my gaze on his, feeling defiant and angry.

He slowly lifted a hand, cupping my face and stroking my cheek with his thumb, just like he had before he first kissed me. I immediately felt like I was going to melt through the floor. I took a steadying breath and refused to back down from his stare.

"Since the dawn of mankind, we have existed: preternaturals. Werewolves, witches, vampires, and fae. Beings that wear the masks of their mortal counterparts, but we're far, far from normal and mortal. Some decided to take the mantle of predator, preying on the weaker, defenseless mortals – vampires and witches," his other hand came up to stroke my hair, his eyes darting from mine to where his fingers wove into my hair and back again.

I gulped and suddenly the monster's papery, gaunt skin came to mind. Its blood red eyes, gnarled claws, and fangs replaced the vision of the man in front of me. A vampire? Had we really been attacked by a vampire? I feel my pulse race as fear clouds my vision. But Liam's rich voice pulled me from the waking nightmare.

"Then others of us took on the mantle of protector. Werewolves are protectors," he said caressing me, "We are protectors. My pack defends the Ley here. We keep ourselves separate from the mortals because we don't want to endanger them." I shook my head; I had no clue what a Ley was and why it needed to be defended. If they were meant to defend mortal, normal people like me, had the vampire come for me?

"What about my mother? What about me?" the words slipped out of my mouth before I could stop them. Liam gave me a sheepish grin and I could see worry in his eyes.

"Your mother was a ward of the pack, she knew of us and what we did, and we protected her from supernatural threats. I know you're thinking that her death had to do with us, but I promise you it didn't. As for you, Cordelia," Liam rolled his lips, his eyes heating, "You're different. Special..."

"I'm nothing special," I chimed in when he fell silent. He shook his head.

"No, you are special to *me*," he hesitated, absently stroking my cheek with his thumb, "I don't want to scare you, but there's not an easy way to explain this." I felt like I was about to jump off a cliff. That same gut instinct told me that if Liam explained things to me surfaced again, there would be no going back to life as I knew it. I had my eyes opened, which meant that the things that went bump in the night would hunt me, chase me down and it would be up to Liam and his pack to keep me safe. Could I do this? Was I strong enough?

To hell with it.

"Tell me," I pressed him, "Tell me everything."

Chapter 21

Cordelia

Liam looked relieved and suddenly I was swept off the ground and his lips were crushed to mine. I wanted to kiss him back, but he pulled away, his breathing shallow and sharp.

"Cordelia, you deserve something more romantic than this, and I promise you that I will make it up to you," Liam's voice was filled with excitement that made me laugh, "I know that this will be overwhelming but I will answer any questions that you have."

"I'm sure you will," I deadpanned as I took his hand and led him into the living room. I went to sit on the sofa but once again felt myself get swept up into Liam's arms. He sat causing the old sofa to creak dangerously, depositing me onto his lap, his arms secured around my waist and his face nestled close to the crook of my neck. His breath was warm and soothing, I felt myself relaxing and I thought about how easy and natural this felt. "What is the Ley?"

"The Ley is a collection of spiritual force and energy that certain immortal creatures can tap into. There are Ley Lines all over the world. Coeur d'Alene sits where a number of Ley Lines meet, forming a Ley Well. We, my pack, protect it from those that would use it to hurt mortals or use the power for the purpose of destruction."

Hearing him talk about his pack again, caused my curiosity to surface, "Is everyone at the estate…everyone who works for you…are they all werewolves?"

"Yes," Liam replied without hesitation, "There are fifteen of us in the pack, that is the maximum number of wolves in a pack."

"How long have you been here?"

He hesitated, but only for a moment.

"Our specific pack has been here for close to fifty years," he said the words slowly. I quickly tried to do the math.

"So, your father started the pack here and you took over for him?"

"Not exactly," he murmured into my neck, causing me to pull back and look at him. He looked guilty.

"Liam?" I was now genuinely curious about what seemed so bad. Liam looked me in the eye and sighed.

"When the last pack needed to move, the council, who oversee all the packs, selected me to be Alpha for this pack and I was able to cherry pick members from other packs. In the time that our pack has been here, I've always been Alpha."

"Wait…so…how old are you exactly?"

"A lot older than I look," Liam chuckled darkly. I looked at him, arching an eyebrow and crossing my arms. He huffed out a breath, "Two hundred and forty-four." My jaw dropped open.

"All those stories you told me about growing up—"

"Were one hundred percent true," Liam interrupted me before I could get upset, "They just didn't happen in the time frame that you thought they did." His voice trailed off and I stood abruptly, moving away from him and pacing the length of the room.

"The 'guard dogs?'" I demanded. He sighed sitting forward and resting his forearms on his knees, running a hand down his face.

"You had stumbled across two of my wolves, Eddie and Gus, who had decided to throwdown in a dominance fight. They're very close in terms of who is more dominant, and they've been jockeying back and forth since they joined the pack. It's a fairly regular occurrence. I didn't know your mother had brought you that day, otherwise I would have put a stop to the whole thing before it started," he explained looking chagrined and guilty. I stopped my pacing to look at him.

"Why can't I remember it clearly? Why do I think it was your dad who talked to me and not you?"

"Shit," he muttered running a frustrated hand through his hair, "Alphas have a little bit of magic they can use on mortals to alter memories. Not completely remove them, but to blur the details. Think of it like hypnotic suggestion."

"You hypnotized me to forget!" I cried out and Liam was immediately on his feet.

"You were seven, Cordelia! You were scared out of your mind and had just had a full-grown werewolf nearly rip out your throat for accidentally interfering in a dominance match. All I did was dull your memory enough to ensure you weren't absolutely terrified and wouldn't jeopardize the pack. It was after that incident that I was forced to tell your mother what we were and made her a ward of the pack." I stood there glaring at him as the ember of my anger resurfaced for a moment.

If I hadn't stumbled in that day…if my mother had never been told the truth about the men at the Benson Estate…would she still be alive today? Before I could even think of asking the question out loud, Liam interjected, "I swear to you, your mother's death is not related to anything that we do."

"Do you know who killed her?"

Liam faltered as he sank back down onto the sofa his head in his hands. For a moment he looked utterly defeated. I took cautious steps towards him until I was standing in front of him. He lifted his head to look at me and slid his hand up my thighs to rest on my hips, gently caressing up and down. The touch wasn't sexual, it was…comforting.

"No," he admitted, the shame and anger in his voice palpable, "Our council has very strict laws about interfering with mortals, so I told the pack to not look into it once we were certain it had nothing to do with us. I regret that now. After your father was pulled in,

Fletcher convinced me that we needed to conduct our own investigation. If the police fail, I promise you, we will find who killed your mother."

The conviction in his voice sent a shiver down my spine. I was certain that he would find the person that did it. My thoughts flashed back to the beast Liam was that had torn into another being, spreading gore everywhere. For a moment I thought my mother's murderer deserved nothing less. I was pulled from my dark thought by Liam's forehead resting against my belly right above the waistband of my jeans. I ran my fingers through his soft hair, both of us silent and contemplative for several minutes.

"Tell me more about werewolves," I asked, breaking the silence. With a sudden tug, I found myself, once again sitting on his lap.

"The first thing that you need to know about werewolves is that they are only ever born," he explained nuzzling my neck, "They are not 'made.' Our bites don't carry any kind of curse like they do in books and movies. Second, there is no such thing as a female werewolf. All werewolves born are male."

"That's a statistical impossibility," I huffed indignantly, "There has to be girls born to werewolves."

"You misunderstand, Cordi. A werewolf can have a daughter, but she won't possess the magic to shape shift. The gene or magic is always a recessive trait for females. The daughter of a werewolf could potentially bear a son who is a wolf, but she herself will never be able to access that ability."

"Alright. If there are no female werewolves…how are more werewolves born? Can only a woman who had a werewolf lineage have a child that could be a werewolf? God, is inbreeding a problem?" I asked and Liam let out a sharp bark of laughter. My breath hitched as one of his hands moved from my waist to my thigh, his touch light and teasing.

"No, inbreeding is not a problem. We mate with mortals or fae," he explained, his touch slowly danced towards the apex of my thighs.

"What are fae?" I didn't like how high-pitched and squeaky my voice sounded. Liam's chuckle was rich and dark like expensive hot chocolate.

"The fair folk, the Sidhe, fairies," he replied. I heard a twinge of something in his voice that sounded like regret.

"Like Tinkerbell?"

"Much more terrifying than Tinkerbell," he said with a dark chuckle, "The fae don't operate as werewolves or vampires do, being wholly a protector or wholly a predator. They live in groups call courts, tied to a natural power of the earth. Their king or queen, lord or lady determines where their court stands: on the side of humanity or against it. A very small number pick an actual side, most of them are entertained by mortal antics and suffering so they remain mostly neutral to conflict. They abide by their own laws which are convoluted at best, downright idiotic and contradictory at worst." As Liam spoke his hands took to wandering over my body, appreciatively caressing my curves and making me squirm in his lap.

Before I could ask him more about the fae, werewolves, or this whole secret world that I never knew existed, his lips were on mine again. The kiss started of sweet and chaste before slowly devolving into needy and hungry. His hand caressed my core through the layers of clothing. I squirmed in his lap thinking about how this wasn't enough for me. That I needed to feel his skin on mine, I needed him to chase the nightmare and worry away.

"As my mate desires," Liam mumbled, breaking our kiss long enough to give my thought an audible response. I wanted to ask him what he meant by calling me his mate. But as our kiss deepened, his tongue tangling with mine, all thoughts flew out of my mind. Whimpering and clutching his arms, I gave myself over to him, surrendering completely. For the third time in the last hour, I was swept up into Liam's arms, feeling a whole host of feelings: relief, protected, relaxed, and of course aroused. I knew I would get my answers and I certainly wanted them. But for the moment I was completely fine with getting lost in Liam's embrace.

He stared at the car in the driveway parked next to Cordelia's. It belonged to that recluse her mother had worked for -- Benson. Why was he at Cordelia's house again? He didn't like the idea of that shut in getting too close to his woman, especially after everything he had gone through to bring her back home and back to him. As far as he was concerned, the two of them had already spent too much time together. Benson was pathetic: hanging around her, clinging to her, attempting to win her over.

Attempting to corrupt her.

Cordelia was pure and sweet as newly fallen snow and Benson sought to warp and ruin that, he just knew it. The image of Benson attempting to force himself upon Cordelia filled his mind, and he was horrified by the thought. His grip on the steering wheel tightened as he felt bile creep up his throat. He wanted to vomit or charge in there and murder the man so he could never touch what was his again.

But surely his sweet Cordelia was in the house now, spurning Benson's advances and telling him to get lost. He hated that Benson had beaten him to the punch so often. His pathetic clinging meant that he was always around her, stepping in to help whenever he could, and taking up her time.

Time that she should have been spending with him.

She was meant to come to him for help, not Benson.

He knew that Benson wasn't the man for her.

She wouldn't betray him like this.

She had to know that they were meant to be together.

Still, he would hang around, keep an eye on things and make sure that the interloper left. He had worked too hard and come too far to have someone fuck up his plans at this point.

He was still a patient man.

He would wait, for now. If Cordelia betrayed him though, he shuddered at the thought, then he might have to go to extremes. But all he could do now was wait.

And watch.

Chapter 22

Liam

Cordelia was sound asleep curled up next to me, I nudged at her tired thoughts to make sure that she wasn't having nightmares about the vampire. I was relieved to sense that she was in a comfortable void, blissed out and satisfied. I couldn't help but take pride in making her feel that way. It had been four hours since the attack, and we had spent most of that time tangled in the sheets of the bed in her childhood room. I felt a little dirty about having only taken her in the bed she had slept in growing up, but my wolf was sated and gave no care to where we rutted our mate. I immediately felt more guilt.

I had distracted her with sex because I wasn't truly prepared for the conversation that waited for us when she woke up. I had dropped quite the bomb on her about what I truly was and the secret machinations of the supernatural world, which she had surprisingly taken in stride. She had asked question and I had told her a fair bit of information about our pack, but there was still more that she needed to know. Specifically, I still had to explain to her that she was my mate and what that meant because I was Alpha of a pack. I felt a sinking in my stomach.

I also had to explain that I was supposed to be getting married in just a few short days.

I rubbed my forehead willing away the headache that was starting to throb behind my eyes. I heard a muffled buzz at the foot of the bed. I carefully rose to my feet, making sure that I did not move the bed too much and wake Cordelia. I watched as she stirred reaching out in her sleep to the side of the bed I had occupied. I fought the urge to crawl back into bed with her and set about finding the remains of pants, which was the source of the buzzing. I fished my phone out of my pocket and connected the call.

"We've disposed of the Feral. How is your mate?" Silas's voice was firm and in control, and I thanked my stars for the thousandth time since meeting Cordelia that he was my second in command.

"Sleeping," I replied walking into the hallway and pulling the door almost closed behind me. I did not wish to wake Cordelia. "She's handling things surprisingly well, considering." Silas grunted into the receiver on his end.

"How much have you told her?"

"Basics – what I am, what we are, what else is out there."

"Did you tell her that she is your mate?"

I hesitated before responding, "I briefly mentioned it before we got distracted."

"You're stalling," Silas accused me angrily. I was taken aback by it.

"Excuse me?"

"The longer you draw out telling her, the more danger she is in from the covens and coteries," Silas' voice had calmed from his previous statement, but I could still hear the familiar ring of anger in it, "The pack will help you protect her, but you have to do your part. You need to quit being so damn selfish, William."

Now I was pissed.

"It is not as easy as that, Silas, and you fucking know it," I snarled, "If I declare that I have found a mate before Franklin finds a loophole or something we can exploit in the treaty, we run the real risk of disrespecting and pissing off Lord Alderkin and fae court. You know what happens when the fae feel that they've been wronged: bloodshed. And lots of it. With potentially a coven and coterie breathing down our necks, the last thing we need to do is piss off our only ally. So, this selfishness that you perceive me to have is really self-preservation for not just myself and the pack, but for the entire damn town and all the mortals here. Now, put my damn brother on the phone."

I heard Silas let out an angry snarl, but I didn't much care. He would obey or I would end his life. That was the advantage of pack life sometimes, everything was straight forward and easily solved if it escalated to violence.

"Well," my brother's voice was now in my ear and sounding amused, "I'm not quite sure what you said, but you sure pissed him off. How are you, brother? Do I need to send Ephraim over to Miss Ramos' house?" Franklin tried to tease, but I could hear the underlying concern in his voice.

Ephraim was of middle standing and served as our pack medic. He had served in the military for many years and had obtained his knowledge and training for triage and critical wound care from that. I appreciated that my brother had not outright asked or implied that I was in a weakened state. The wounds on my arms from the Feral's claws had healed quickly as I had driven Cordelia to her home.

"I am fine," my response was curt, "No need for Ephraim to cross town. However, my dear brother, I hope, for your sake, you have good news. I'm not about to tell my mate that I'm supposed to be getting married in three days."

Franklin chuckled but it was a mixture of tired and strained.

"I will say that I have news, I'll let you determine if it is good or bad. The Lord's son and lawyers are good, but I think I may have found something that we could exploit."

"That sounds like good news to me."

"Yes," the way my brother drew out the word made me suspect that it was not as good as I had hoped, "Ultimately the Lord's love of flowery language and superlatives is what is going to get you out of the predicament that you're currently in. In the terms and conditions of the treaty, subsection D outlines all of the details of the matrimony, and there is a specific clause that states, 'He who possesses the blood of an Alpha, that which flows through his veins providing him the vigor of his office, shall serve to represent the Pack within the bonds of matrimony and reflect the strength of the accord which has been agreed upon, et cetera, et cetera.'"

"English. Franklin."

"The language does not *specifically* state that our representative in the marriage must be the Alpha; just that the blood of an Alpha flows through his veins. They will surely attempt to argue it, but I have precedent from the Black Forest Accords of 751."

For just a moment, I felt hope flare in my chest. Franklin and I were true brothers beyond the pack. Our father had been an influential Alpha and helped to establish the various territories in the United States. We both shared Alpha blood.

"You could--" I began excitedly before he interrupted me.

"I can't. There is another clause: 'The bride and groom shall their eyes avert before the ceremony. Their gaze to meet only at the appointed hour.' Translation, the groom and bride can't see each other any time before the wedding. And unfortunately, part of the ritual of this whole thing, as your best man, was that I meet the bride to be and determine if she was acceptable."

"Why the hell did you even bother to tell me about it?" I snapped. I wanted to scream in frustration.

"Because, my dumb older brother, you and I aren't the only ones in the pack that have the bloodline of an Alpha." The realization hit me like a fucking Mac truck.

"Jason." Our young 'pup', fresh to the pack because his aggressive Alpha father could not handle the fact that his own son might, someday, challenge him for control. The young man had been a werewolf for just over five years and still learning the limits of his abilities and how to harness the wolf. Could I do this: saddle this young man with a burden and responsibility that was supposed to be my own? Silas would use that word again: selfish.

But Cordelia was my true mate, and frankly my loyalty to her surpassed my loyalty to the pack. I was certain that there would be push back, but I didn't care.

Cordelia was mine and nothing, *nothing* would stand between us.

"Make it happen," I told my brother.

"As you command." He disconnected the call and for the first time in weeks I felt able to breathe a sigh of relief. I turned to go back into Cordelia's bedroom and stopped short immediately. She was standing in the doorway, sheet wrapped around her curvy frame and tears running down her cheeks. I had been so preoccupied with the conversation with my brother that I hadn't sensed her approach at all. I swore.

"How much of that did you hear?"

"Enough." Her voice was strained and her grip on the sheet tightened, her knuckles turning white.

"I can—"

"—explain?" She interrupted with a snarl that rivaled my own, "I don't fucking think so. You're getting married in three fucking days! So, what was I, some kind of final conquest? One last roll in the hay before you get saddled with the old ball and chain?" The vitriol in her voice and her accusation cut both me and my wolf deep. He demanded I fix this, but if I were being honest, I had no clue how to even start going about it.

"It's not like that at all," I said taking a step towards her. She took a step back.

"I don't care," she spat, "I trusted you and you've done nothing but lie to me! I want you to get the fuck out of my house and never contact me again."

"Cordi…love…no…" I begged, feeling utterly pathetic and terrified at the thought of losing her. I took a step towards her, and she took a step back. She was hurt and wouldn't let me comfort her.

"Don't call me that," she sobbed, her voice filled with rage and pain, "And I suppose that it's too fucking bad for you. Get out of my house, now. Before I call the cops. I never want to talk to you again."

I wanted to resist her direct command. I wanted to stay and explain everything to her. That she only heard the half the conversation with my brother. That I was not getting married. That I was hers forever.

But it was like a heavy gate had slammed down on connection that existed between us. One moment she was there and the next moment I couldn't feel that tug that I had gotten so used to. She had made her decision and I found that I could not fight the command that I heard in her voice. My wolf had no choice but to follow it and mourn the loss. She had no clue what she had done, what she had asked of me. The Feral's words came back to me, mockingly:

Even better than that is that now there is a way to control you.

I hadn't believed the stories about mates and their power before now. That was my folly. I understood the true power of wolf's mate, an Alpha's mate now. It wasn't a myth that they were the only ones that held sway over an Alpha. The reality was sinking in that an Alpha's mate's word was law. She told me to leave and to never contact her again and as much as it pained me and my wolf, I couldn't not help but comply.

I felt like my mouth had been filled with cotton as I brushed past her and gathered up my boxers, jeans, and shoes. I quickly pulled them on, unable to bring my eyes up to hers, and headed towards the front door. As I exited, the door slammed shut behind me, and I heard the deadbolt slide into place. Even through the door I could heard her let out a gut-wrenching sob. Every fiber of my being wanted to go back and hold her, wipe away her tears, and tell her that everything would be alright. I wanted the chance to explain everything to her, but she had determined that I didn't deserve it.

And frankly, I didn't think she had been entirely wrong about that decision.

I hopped into my Lexus and quickly reversed out of the drive. As Cordelia's house vanished from my review mirror, I dialed my brother back.

"Disregard my orders about Jason, I'll go through with it," I couldn't keep the sadness from my voice, and I heard my brother's breath hitch in the car speakers.

"What happened?"

"She dismissed me," I explained, attempting to sound more unaffected, but I knew I was failing at that, "Make the appropriate preparations. We need to be ready to ensure that this wedding goes off without a hitch." I did not veil the order.

"As you command," my brother responded, and I hated the pity I heard in his voice. Angrily I ended the call right before a baleful howl escaped my lips. As I drove back to the pack's manor the void where she had resided in my mind felt like a gaping chasm. I felt empty. Hollow. Incomplete.

I would mourn her loss, but I had to move on because that's all that I could do.

Chapter 23
Cordelia

Hey, is everything alright Cordelia?"

I jerked my head up from the patient file on the computer I had been looking at to the person that had spoken to me. My site supervisor, Barbara, looked as tired as I felt. Which made sense because it was just after midnight and we were both at the hospital. I had requested extra shifts, including this overnight shift for the emergency room, to try and get my last comps done for my externship. I was one away from being completely done. Which meant that I could leave this God-forsaken town and never look back.

And hopefully stop thinking about him.

"I'm fine," I replied, plastering a fake smile on my face. "Just tired. I'm beginning regret requesting the overnight shift."

"Well, I've got good news," she smiled, "Just had a sixteen-year-old check in with abdominal swelling and acute pain in their lower right abdomen, fever, and nausea. I'm going to have you do your last comp on him."

The symptoms sounded like appendicitis, which would be an easy final comp.

"Sounds great!" I feigned excitement. I felt a pit in my stomach. When I finished this, I would be able to graduate and take the job in Atlanta. Which meant I could move on and never see Liam again, the thought of which made me want to throw up.

"Good, they're headed to exam two. Grab a cart and I will see you over there."

As I began to gather up the things that I would need, my thoughts drifted to Liam. I had spent the last two days in a sad, manic state. Hannah, her mother, and I had been working double time on cleaning out my mother's house. Hannah of course had been my first call after I kicked Liam out of my house. She had showed up with her mother and a bottle of wine as I bitched about how dumb and sleazy men were. I realized that they were both happily married, but it helped to have someone to vent and rant at.

Hannah's mother made sure that I wasn't drinking alone as we went room by room and started to button things up. We finished the upstairs this morning, leaving the downstairs living spaces which would be easy. I was keeping some of the furniture for my move to Atlanta and Hannah's mother offered to store the items I was keeping until I was settled in my new job.

Keeping myself busy over the last two days, I was doing everything I could not to think about him, and then crying myself to sleep every night. I couldn't wrap my head around why I felt like my heart had been ripped out. I had only known him for two weeks! It was a whirlwind romance that I needed to get through the death of my mother. Right?

As I wheeled the cart with the ultrasound equipment towards the exam room, I tried not to think about the other things he had revealed to me. Werewolves, witches, fae, and vampires. It sounded like it was ripped from the pages of a bad fantasy novel. If I hadn't seen the demonic red eyes of the vampire or watched Liam transform into a giant half-man, half-wolf I would never have believed it. Now I jumped at shadows and strange noises in the night, wondering if because I knew, I was now being hunted. My mind and overactive imagination had taken what they were given and were running amok.

None of it mattered though, as I knocked on the door to check if they were ready for me to come into the room. In just a few short hours, my externship would be complete. I would pack everything I owned and leave this town behind me…

…and never look back.

The constant dull throbbing in my head was what woke me. I wondered for a moment if I had drunk myself to sleep after my shift again. I opened my eyes, blinking and squinting, as I tried to focus on anything around me.

It was dark and I was laying on a concrete floor of a room that smelled like dust, damp, and spray paint. I could just barely make out vague shapes of unmoving human forms looming around me. As my eyes adjusted to the darkness, I figured out that the shapes were mannequins dressed like classic movie monsters. Where was I? How did I even get here?

I tried to remember what I was doing before, but my memories were wispy and confused.

I had been at the hospital, half-way into an overnight emergency room shift. I had just completed my last comp for externship.

From there things were fuzzy.

I had asked if I could take a break and grab a coffee and then…darkness. I could only remember bits and pieces. Starbucks had been closed, same with the cafeteria, so I was stuck with vending machine coffee. I could literally remember the burnt smell and taste of the acrid black liquid, but there was something else there. I had been talking to someone, but I couldn't remember their face.

Then I tried to sit up and realized that my hands and feet were joined together at the wrist and ankle with a thick bands of duct tape wrapped around them. I felt twin waves of panic and nausea wash over me as I began to struggle to sit up. I scooched and inched across the floor, looking for a wall, a box, or anything that I could use to help me sit up and get to my feet.

"Help!" I cried out. "Please, is anybody there?" My voice was rough and panicked, but a little muted. The drapery, mannequins, and other items seemed to be muffling my cries for help. I eventually found a crate that I could use to get sit up. I tried to calm myself by slowing my breathing. I had to keep calm to figure out how to get out of this situation and what happened.

Something had happened after I got coffee, I was positive about it.

I didn't want to waste much time trying to remember. I looked around for something to cut the tape and didn't see anything immediately useful. I began to bite and tug at it with my teeth. I immediately tasted dirt and adhesive, but it didn't matter to me. My only thought was to get out of here. Focused on my task, my mind began to relax. Shadowy, fuzzy images started to come back to me, slowly solidifying but I still felt groggy and struggled to focus. Had I been drugged? Knocked out? Flashes of memory started coming back to me.

I had my coffee and was in the break room with my phone. I had been thinking about Liam all day and I had decided to text him. Even though I knew he was supposed to be getting married, I couldn't shake him or the desire that was slowly consuming me from the inside out. I was going to text him. To tell him to hell with everything and that I didn't care who or what he was or that he was getting married, but that I needed him on a primal level. But maybe putting some distance between us and trying again we could do things right this time.

I knew that I had typed out a message asking if he was around and then...

I remembered.

I remembered every horrifying, gut-wrenching detail.

A door slammed somewhere above, and panic set in. I pulled, tugging and biting, to get the tape off my wrists. I heard slow, creaking footsteps across the floor, moving closer and more ominous with each step.

I had just finished typing out the text Liam when Jack had popped his head into the break room. I was tired but I had been excited to see him, to hopefully make amends since I knew I was going to be leaving soon. He and his partner had apparently escorted a suspect to the hospital, and he was popping his head in to check on me. He had asked me about the externship. He asked me if I was excited to be back home.

There was the sound of a door opening and a pale beam of light illuminated the stairs leading to the basement that I was in. I had a tear through the many layers of tape, but I knew it wasn't going to be enough. I tried to pull my wrists apart, I tried twisting them, I tried anything that might tear the tape. Heavy booted steps work their way down the stairs and into the darkness I had been stored in.

I was honest with Jack. I didn't really want to be back in Coeur d'Alene, that I wasn't happy here, and that once I had finished dealing with my mother's estate I was going to be leaving.

"Wait?" He seemed confused, "Leaving? But you just got here."

"Once I graduate though, there will be nothing to keep me here. My mom is dead, Jack, why would I want to stay in a place that only serves as a constant painful reminder of her. Besides, I already have a job lined up, it's not an opportunity that I want to pass up." I was also thinking about a potential long-distance relationship with Liam that would allow us to take things slow, take our time.

"But what about Hannah? She said you were going to be the godmother for her daughter! You were going to help her out!"

"She has her family and Shane's family. She doesn't need me. She and I have already talked about it, and I can be the fairy godmother from afar."

"But, what about your position here? The hospital could hire you."

"Jack, I don't want—"

He had slammed his fists on the table. The outburst of anger was unlike him or at least how I had known him before going off to college.

"Jack?" For the first time ever, I was afraid of my friend.

A shadowy form moved through the boxes and crates to where I was sitting, shining a light in my eyes, blinding me even as I continue to fight with my restraints.

"Cordi…" Jack's voice was sad. I felt the urge to vomit.

"It's not all about you," Jack snarled, "Why are you being so selfish. You can't go to Atlanta and leave me again."

"How did you know about Atlanta? I only ever told my mother about Atlanta before today." Hannah and her mother had both been surprised by my news, and neither of them had a reason to talk to Jack let alone tell him about it.

I grabbed my phone and went to leave, the sinking feeling in my stomach grew rapidly. Jack grabbed my wrist, jerking me away from the door. I dropped my phone when he wrapped a strong arm around me, pinning my arms to my sides. I felt a sharp pain in my neck, things started to get fuzzy.

"I was patient enough, Cordelia," Jack's voice was seething, distorting in my ears. "The lengths I took to get you back here. You're not going to leave me again."

Jack knelt in front of me, still dressed in his uniform, and set the flashlight on end so it was pointing up at the ceiling. It cast frightening shadows across his face as he grabbed my forearms. There was no smile on his face.

"I told you, you're not going to leave me again."

Panic gripped my chest; I felt a cold sweat break out at his stony words. There wasn't a doubt in my mind that Jack had killed my mother to bring me back to town. My fear was of what he was going to do to me now that he had me.

"You're right," I said, crying and trying to keep myself together, "I'm going to stay here. With you." Jack reached out his hand and stroked my hair and face. I tried to keep still, but I flinched away from him. His frown deepened and he shook his head.

"Cordi, you had your chance. You wasted it." Jack pulled out a knife and cut up through the tape before bringing the blade to my throat. "Hands behind your back." He applied pressure and I tried not to gulp.

Obediently, I put my hands behind me. He used his one free hand to reach behind him and I could hear the clink of metal on metal. Before I could even think of bolting to the stairs, I felt hard metal wrap around my wrist. The ratcheting sound and the bite of the cuff into my wrist caused my panic to skyrocket. I went to pull my other wrist away, but the blade against my throat kept me from moving it too far. Once the other cuff clicked into place, Jack pulled back from me and stood up, brushing off his uniform pants.

"I want you to think about what you've done to us…to me. When you're truly ready to apologize, we'll see where I stand."

"Please," I sobbed. Jack didn't say anything, he just turned and walked away. Stomping back up the stairs. He was acting in a way that I had never seen before: cold, mechanical, and deadly serious. When I heard the door slam, I immediately started tugging at the cuffs. He had looped them through an exposed pipe. I leaned forward, pulling against the pipe with all of my weight but it refused to budge. I could feel the tears running down my face and I realized that someone was screaming.

Me. I was screaming.

I thrashed about, trying every angle and using all of the strength I could muster to get free. But in the end, I sunk to the floor, sobbing, wondering how long it would take someone to notice I was gone. I don't know how Jack took me from the hospital. He was a cop, trustworthy and believable, no one would suspect a thing. I had told Hannah so many times about just up and leaving once my externship was done. Would she realize that I was missing and not just gone? My site supervisor might realize something was up, or Rhonda. My thoughts drifted to Liam and I let out another miserable sob.

I wanted to apologize to him. I should have given him a chance to explain. If I had, I probably wouldn't be in the situation I was in now. I wish I could tell him.

The reason I had been so mad about everything was because I was madly in love with him.

But I would never get the chance to tell him now.

But you could.

There was still some rational part of my brain not completely consumed by panic. I could?

I could!

He had never said it out loud, but Liam always seemed to know what I was thinking. He had hinted about some special connection between us. I didn't know how far this connection stretched, but I knew that I had to try. But what and how? He hadn't given me any instructions or explanation of how it worked.

I thought back to all the instances where he seemed to know what I was thinking or feeling. Usually, I was thinking about him. My breath was still short, hitching every two or three gulping breaths because I was trying to stop crying. I closed my eyes and blocked out everything that was happening, as best I could, focusing on clearing my mind and thinking about him.

I focused on what I could remember about him: his eyes, his scent, the feel of his strong arms around me. I felt like I was chasing the memory of him down a long, endless hall, trailing behind his image but reaching for him. He always seemed to be just barely out of reach, like he was dodging me on purpose. Every time I tried to get his attention, he would speed up or take a larger step from me. I knew it was all in my head, but I was feeling physically exhausted with chasing him. I couldn't keep this up forever. I wasn't even sure that I could keep it up for another minute.

With a final tired lunge, I grabbed his arm which felt frighteningly real. He stopped and turned to look at me, his handsome features contorting into a look of shock and horror. I felt like I was about to collapse, but I managed to croak out two words.

"Liam. Help."

Chapter 24

Liam

I opened my eyes and stared at the faces of Silas, Franklin, and Jason. They had been with me in my suite as I prepared for my wedding. All three of them were still trying to convince me to let Jason go through with the whole affair and that I should be chasing Cordelia down. While I was telling them off, my vision was consumed by static and my head erupted in the most blistering white-hot agony I have ever felt. Cordelia had kicked down the gate that had closed off our connection. She then reached out to me through our bond and full on blasted me with emotion.

Pain.

Remorse.

Panic.

Love.

Fear.

Everything that I felt from her was completely raw and unfiltered. It physically pained me and made me feel sick. But it wasn't just the emotions that I got from her.

Liam. Help.

She was in pain and in danger. All my Alpha instincts kicked in immediately. I had to save her. I had to protect what was mine.

"Liam, what is it?" Jason asked, not knowing any better, not realizing I barely had the beast under control. I was immediately on my feet and had him pinned against a wall. My hand tightened around his neck and there was something primal, something satisfying in hearing him struggle for air.

"My mate is in danger," I growled, dangerously close to losing my cool, "She is in pain. She needs me and I am not there to protect her."

"Easy there, Liam, don't kill the only person that can spare you from this marriage," my brother's voice was steady and calm. There was a faint hint of command in Franklin's voice which made my hair stand on end. I released Jason, who slumped to the floor and gasped for air, and turned to my brother. He didn't back down from my glare, but there was a nervous tremor in his voice as he started to speak. "Jason is the only one that could possibly take your place at this point, William. I am not going to tell you what you need to do."

"Your brother is right," Silas chimed in from my flank, "Take a step back and tell us what happened."

My heart continued to race and I could feel the adrenaline burning through me but I managed to take a deep breath. The room was silent except for Jason's coughing.

"She reached out to me, through our bond," I said beginning to pace, "She is scared and in pain and she…"

Love.

She loved me.

My anger quickly gave way to panic. I had to save her.

"I need to find her."

"We know," Silas said in the most calming voice I had ever heard him use, "Did she tell you where she was?"

"No, all I got was emotions mostly," I said shaking my head. I concentrated on Cordelia, but the connection felt like it was full of static. I didn't know what that meant. Was she hurt? Unconscious? The connection hadn't ever felt like this before. "I can only feel static. I can't feel her." I didn't like the look that Silas and Franklin shared with each other.

"Lorelei."

We all turned to Jason.

"What?" Silas asked. Jason pushed himself up from the floor, his tuxedo completely disheveled. He brushed himself off.

"Lorelei will be able to find her." I looked from Jason to my brother, whose eyes had lit up.

"Yes! Yes of course she will!" My brother darted out of the room.

"Would you explain what the hell you're talking about?" I demanded from Jason.

"Lorelei's title in the fae court is The Keeper of Tethers and Lost Things. It was one of the reasons why

Lord Alderkin suggested her as part of the treaty. She can see and follow the connections between people and places, which would be handy with the some of the work that we do. Did you read any of Franklin's briefings?"

"I skimmed them," I admitted sheepishly.

A few moments later, my brother returned with a woman with pale blue skin in a long, flowing white, green, and blue marbled dress that was evocative of wave crashing on the shore. Jason immediately yelped and turned to face the wall, head bowed, eyes closed. I wondered why because to say that she was breathtaking would have been a gross understatement.

Her heart shaped face was a combination of childish and womanly. Her hair was a rich green color that had streaks of blue running through it. Most of her locks been twisted and pulled into a complicated up-do; the strands that had been left loose were curled to form perfect ringlets to frame her face. Her rounded cheeks, dewy skin, and button nose were dainty and contributed to a youthful look. Her sparking eyes were an intense shade of emerald, surrounded by thick lashes and accented with dramatic makeup. They were currently narrowed with her brow furrowed in a look of concern. Her full lips were turned down into a frown.

She was undeniably gorgeous, this fae woman. But for me she didn't hold a candle to Cordelia.

"That is not necessary, Jason. We are going to need your help so you're going to have to look at her."

I remembered the clause in the treaty, about the groom not laying eyes on the bride before the wedding. Jason very carefully turned around. I watched the young wolf's face flush with color and his jaw drop as he saw his future bride to be.

"Don't worry about the Lord or the treaty," she chimed in, her voice an interesting combination of soft and forceful, "I have enough leverage on him that he will sign the treaty, if only to keep me quiet."

"Why help us?" Silas asked, suspicious. Lorelei gave us a brittle smile.

"He is a bastard," she said without hesitation, "And has made most of my life a living hell. Your pack, this marriage to a pack member, is my escape." There was a painful truth in her words and expression. I immediately felt bad for her. I had never considered that she would only see the arrangement as a positive. Jason growled beside me which caused her to blush. "I-I understand that time is of the essence," she stammered before extending out her hand to me, "I need to see something that belongs to her."

My heart sunk to my feet.

"I don't have anything of hers."

My anger surged when Lorelei rolled her eyes and shook her head in disbelief. Before I could snap at her she grabbed my hand. The moment that there was contact between us, I felt like I had been hit by a surging wave. It took me a moment to realize that sensation was the force of her magic working. Lorelei's eyes had gone completely white and her mouth moved without sound. A strange feeling came over me and set my teeth on edge. I was overcome with the sensation that I had walked through a massive spider web and was standing in the middle of it.

Dozens of threads clung to me and extended out, some incredibly thin and fine like gossamer, other looking more like braided cables, and one looked to be made of platinum and gold and much stronger than the rest. I could see that one was linked to each of the others in the room, Silas, Franklin, and Jason, but most of them went beyond the room vanishing into the walls. Lorelei let go of my hand and the vision of that web began to fade from my eyes.

When I looked up at her, Lorelei's appearance had returned to what it had been before, except that her skin was several shades lighter. She swayed on her feet for a moment, but Jason materialized next to her, helping her steady herself.

"I know what direction we need to go," she said rubbing her temple.

"Good. Where is she?" I asked taking off my suit jacket and rolling up my sleeves. She shook her head.

"That's not exactly how this works. I can see the strand and where it leads, but I can't see the end destination. I will have to lead you there."

The four of us exchanged a look. Judging from the protective arm Jason had around her, he wasn't about to leave her side. I sighed, I didn't have the time to argue.

"Franklin, bring the car around, we'll head out immediately. Silas, round up the other members of the pack." They both nodded and headed towards the door, but it opened before either of them made it to it. Fletcher walked in, phone in hand and wearing his most formal set of cargo pants. He had mentioned in passing before we headed to the venue that his contact at the police station had information for him.

"Apologies for the intrusion," he said moving past the two at the door and heading straight to me. "Sir, I needed to tell you about this immediately. The reports were all changed."

"What?" I shook my head, confused and lost as to his meaning.

"The reports on Loretta's murder. I finally convinced Jess to pull up the edit details on the individual records. She went to compare the digital files to the hard copies, and she discovered that they had all been destroyed and where they should have been there was only an empty box. When she found that she went into the edit details and discovered that the digital files were all altered by the same user."

"What does that mean?"

"I believe that the person making the changes was involved in the murder and has been covering it up. Someone that has access to all of the information and systems."

My mind immediately flew to one person.

Cordelia's friend.

"Jack Miller."

"Y-Yeah, Jackson Miller's ID was the one that made all of the changes," Fletcher replied, puzzled, "How did you know?"

His attraction. His territoriality. His frustration.

Motive.

His history and connection with the Ramos family.

Means.

My wolf howled inside my head. He wanted blood. He wanted vengeance.

"Find him and bring him to me," I snarled looking at Silas, "I want him alive. Take the pack." Silas's eyebrows shot up.

"The whole pack?"

"I will take Franklin and Jason with me," I ordered, "I am trusting you to bring him back to me in one piece."

"As you command," Silas replied stoically. I turned my gaze to Fletcher.

"You can find him." Even though I didn't phrase it as a question, the Beta responded with a nod.

"Yeah…of course. I should be able track his phone, or find him through social media, or something." It was the least sure Fletcher had ever sounded, but he immediately started tapping away on his phone. I could hear it ringing twice before it picked up and he softly spoke, "Hey Jess, I'm going to need another favor." He followed Silas out of the room to get the rest of the pack. They could sense my deadly intent and there was a ripple through our bonds: the thrill of the hunt.

"Alpha," my brother addressed me, "we are sure of this course?"

I knew what my brother was really asking. I turned to Lorelei and Jason. He had her seated and was offering her a small plastic bottle of water from the side bar of the suite. Lorelei seemed to have regained some color high in her cheeks, but it might be her blushing at the attention she was receiving from Jason. Perhaps it was a lingering effect of her magic, but I could see that there was a connection between them. Not as strong as what existed between Cordelia and I, but their bond was certainly that of mates. All it needed was time and I was certain that it had the potential to grow into something strong and unshakable.

"Yes," I replied before turning back to my brother. "I think this is the only course of action we have at this point. Damn the treaty and consequences. We will deal with things as they come."

He nodded in agreement.

"I'm sure that we will persevere. We always have," he replied gripping my shoulder, "But we need to find your mate first."

I nodded at him before I approached Jason and Lorelei. Jason stood to face me, and it didn't escape my notice that he stood directly between me and Lorelei, completely blocking her from my view.

"We need to go," I told him. He looked like he wanted to argue, but Lorelei stood drawing his attention. She looped her arm with his and looked up at me. In that instant, her youthful gleam left her eyes for a moment and I swear I saw the wisdom of ages in her.

"I know what she said, what you felt. We will find her. I always find what I set my sights on."

"Thank you." I had never meant anything more in my life. Because of her I was going to be able to rescue my mate. And she didn't have to help, especially because the whole situation could be views as a slight to her, but she was anyway. I knew that the fae typically dealt in subterfuge and subtle displays of power—wheeling and dealing for advantages, but I sensed none of that from Lorelei. She nodded and started to move towards the door, pulling Jason along beside her.

"All I know now is that she is to the north," she explained, "She feels far, but I'm hoping she's just outside of town. I'll know as I get closer."

The four of us exited the venue quickly, skirting around the various hangers-on, well-wishers, and, most importantly, her father and family. Lorelei led us down a back staircase and through the back ways of the venue until we came out on a loading dock. The rest of the pack had gathered, still in their suits and loading into several trucks and SUV's. Seeing us emerge, Silas approached and tossed a set of keys to Franklin.

"We haven't told the fae anything. His highness seemed upset that we were all leaving."

"You should have told him to get bent," Lorelei replied stepping away from Jason to take the keys from Franklin. Hitching up her skirts, she headed towards the one SUV without anyone in it. Jason immediately followed her and Franklin trailed behind attempting to get the keys from her. Silas chuckled.

"She's a pistol."

"I feel equal parts relieved and worried for Jason," I chuckled before looking at him deadly serious, "Remember: I want him alive. He must pay for the crimes he's committed."

"As you command."

I clapped him on the shoulder and jogged to our transport. I climbed into back seat with Franklin and closed my eyes. Without hesitation, Lorelei took off, peeling out of the parking lot. I blocked out my brother's loud protests, closing my eyes and concentrating on Cordelia. Immediately all of the thoughts and memories about her that I had suppressed came flooding back. Focusing on her opened up my link to her, but it was weak and strained. The only things I could feel were her fear and panic. Through our fragile link, I reached out and tried to comfort her.

"I'm coming, Cordelia."

Chapter 25
Cordelia

For the second time I woke up confused and disoriented. I took a deep breath, inhaling dust and everything came back to me in a rush. Jack had murdered my mother, kidnapped me, and my only hope of rescue was Liam, a werewolf, my mother's former employer, and the love of my life that I had tossed to the curb like last week's trash. I took another deep breath and the dust caused me to start coughing. Immediately my head because to throb, like it had just registered that I was awake and it was okay to start transmitting pain signals.

"Fuck," I groaned, trying to figure out why my head hurt so much. I didn't remember Jack striking me to knock me out.

Cordelia?

I jumped at the sound of someone whispering my name. I felt panic grip my chest as I looked around the room, frightened that Jack had returned. But it was empty, except for the lifeless mannequins.

"Hello?" I called, attempting to ignore the migraine of the century that was pounding in my temples in time with my quickening heartbeat. "Is there someone there?"

Cordelia calm down...

The voice tickled at the back of my mind, it was familiar and strange at the same time. Taking slow, deep breaths I looked around the room, but there was no sign of anyone else. Had Jack left me alone long enough for me to be hearing things? A low, vicious growl made me flinch as it reverberated in my head.

We will feast on his flesh; he will never touch you again.

This voice was different than the first. The first had been soothing and familiar, this one was primal and dark. I still didn't know where either were coming from.

You're. Not. Helping.

The first voice returned, chiding the second in a firm, dismissive manner. *You're just confusing her. Cordelia I need you to focus...*

By this point I had moved beyond panicked. I had just accepted that I had lost my damn mind and I was hearing things.

Close your eyes, love, and relax...

With nothing to lose, I did what the ghost voice instructed. I leaned my head back against the pipe and closed my eyes. Relaxing was harder to do because the cuffs kept biting into my wrists and shooting pain up my arms. I shifted and fidgeted until I found a comfortable position. My breathing became steady and even, somewhere between awake and dozing.

"Open your eyes, Cordi." Liam's voice was right next to me, and I was startled at the sudden closeness. When I opened my eyes, I felt disoriented immediately. Gone was the dark, musty basement that I had just been in. Instead, I was in Liam's office with its large desk, filled bookshelves, and massive window that looked out into the woods.

Laying in front of the desk was a massive black wolf that was bigger than any canine I had ever seen. It lay with its head on its front paws, yellow eyes trained on me. Taking in more of the surroundings, I realized that I was laid out on a rich leather sofa that hadn't been in his office the last time I had been in there. The brush of fingertips on my cheek felt too real and I flinched, unprepared for the contact. The wolf let out a low rumbling growl.

"Hush you," Liam scolded and shot a glare at the wolf.

Liam?

Liam!

As if hearing my thoughts Liam looked back at me as he knelt on the floor next to the sofa. It had been nearly three days since I kicked him out of my house, but his beauty struck me dumb once again. But it had lost some of its edge: his skin was a few shades paler and his cheeks seemed sallow. His eyes had dark circles under them and they didn't have the sharpness I was used to seeing in them. I tried to sit up to touch him.

"Relax Cordelia," Liam murmured moving closer so that I could touch him, "Our connection is still fragile. I've never heard of a mate bond being overloaded like that. When you reached out to me, you didn't hold back and it caused our bond to short out for a while. I don't think bonds were meant to handle that much…"

Mate bond? Overload? My mind was trying to process what he was talking about. My confusion must have been evident because he began to explain as he stroked my hair.

"This space, this room is…not real," he said regret heavy in his voice. "We are communicating through our mate bond. Since you've never done it before, I thought it best to give you some place that you were at least familiar with."

I could feel tears start to well up at the corners of my mind. This was just an illusion. I was still trapped. I felt despair wash over me like a tidal wave.

"No, no, no darling," Liam cooed wiping away the tears as they spilled over onto my cheeks, "Cordi, love, we are coming for you. We're going to get you and then we're going to deal with Jack."

"He killed my mother," my voice sounded strange to my ears: reedy and weak. Liam immediately shushed me and placed his fingers against my lips.

"Try not to speak," Liam cautioned me, "Your end of the connection is still a little burnt out from before. Try not to strain yourself. Just think, I can hear your thoughts just fine here."

There was so much I wanted to tell him, I couldn't even imagine where to begin:

I'm sorry.

I was wrong.

I missed you.

I love you.

Liam went still after the last thought, his eyes suddenly filled with cold determination.

"I should be the one apologizing. I should have been honest from the start about the marriage contract which has been voided. You did nothing wrong, Cordelia, know that. I missed you too and..." he paused, like the words had gotten stuck in his throat, "And for the last...I...I thought I knew love and what it meant with the brotherhood of my pack and that packs I've been in before. You have opened my eyes and I realized that I was missing all the facets that love could contain. You are my all, my everything, Cordelia. I love you."

The wolf lifted it head and tilted it to one side, as if it were listening to something.

The fae is still having problems. Ask her.

Liam looked between the wolf and I, his expression grim.

"Cordi, love, can you tell me anything about where you are at? Lorelei is tracking you but something is interfering. We'll know what it is once we find you, but we are so close."

I didn't know who Lorelei was, or how she could track me, but I could tell him about where I was. Images of what I could see flashed through my mind.

Basement.

Mannequins dressed as movie monsters.

Haunted House, maybe?

Jack was here maybe an hour ago, wearing his uniform.

Can't be far from town. Liam nodded, recognition lighting up in his eyes.

"Yes, alright, that should be enough to find you," Liam sounded excited, "I'm coming, sweetheart. Rest now, we'll be together before you know it."

My eyes felt heavy and I closed them unwillingly, fighting to stay awake, but I couldn't help the long blink. When I opened my eyes, I was back in the basement. It was hard to not sob in despair, but my chest felt light and warm. Liam seemed to know where I was, and he was coming to save me. That little bit of light and little bit of hope was enough to keep me quiet and relaxed.

Soon I would be back in his arms.

And soon this whole nightmare would be over.

I just had to hold on a little bit longer.

Chapter 26

Liam

I opened my eyes and I was in the backseat of the SUV as Lorelei drove through the woods that surrounded town. It was a little disorienting and I hated leaving Cordelia alone, but I could still feel her through our bond. I could feel her hope and it made my chest ache. I needed to get her back. I needed her to be safe in my arms again, and this time nothing would drive us apart.

"Anything?" Franklin asked cautiously, "Were you able to reach her?"

"She's in a basement where there are a bunch of props stored along with mannequins that are dressed like monsters." I pulled up my web browser on my phone. "She seemed to think that she was in a haunted house of some sort. There can't be too many of those in this area of town."

"Let's be real, we're not in town anymore," Lorelei commented as she stopped the car at a four way stop. She had driven us this far before she started having problems following the thread the connected me to Cordelia. She was frustrated and felt terrible, but she was certain that something was running interference with her magic. Which could mean a lot of things: a coven had warded the place where Cordelia was stashed or it could have been as simple as she was in a building that was constructed out of metal that had a little bit too much iron in it.

"In the fall there's one of those forest maze things that has a haunted house along side it," Franklin said aloud looking up from his phone, "It's maybe five minutes from here. That could be where she is."

"You're navigating," Lorelei said, and Franklin sat forward and directing her in his calm steady manner. I glanced back down at my screen, relief slowly flooding through me. A message came in from Silas.

> **Still looking. Reported for work but has failed to respond to two different calls. Noah had ears on the police scanner, Fletcher is doing the techie thing. Rest are in teams of two searching his normal haunts and beat. Will update in ten.**

I quickly texted him back that we were on our way to where we believed Cordelia to be. Once we had her the plan was to return to the pack's estate, secure her and Lorelei, and then hunt Jack down. I dropped my phone into my pocket, not expecting a response. Silas knew what it meant if we were forced to hunt Jack down. I hoped the man tried to run from us.

The thrill of the chase was the best part of hunting as far as my wolf and I were concerned.

"There." Franklin said pointing to the right. A sprawling, dark building loomed casting long shadows in the setting sun. Everything about the house screamed manufactured horror, the type of horror that you find at the seasonal stores that pop up every fall. The building's façade was designed to look like a stereotypical haunted house that you might see in a movie or television show: something vaguely Victorian with its wrap around porch and high peaked eaves and towers.

The vehicle hadn't stopped moving before I jumped out. Taking a cursory glance around, there were no signs of other vehicles. The dirt and grass looked like it had been torn up by a truck, but I wasn't well versed enough to know if it was recent or older. Without waiting for the others, I charged up to the entrance. I barely broke my stride when I shouldered the door open with more force than needed, a loud bang echoing through the building.

"Cordelia!" I shouted, moving through the space, looking for anything that might be stairs down. I felt a warm tingle through our mate bond. She had heard me, she was here.

"Liam! Liam, I'm down here!" Cordelia's voice was faint and coming from under my feet. The relief in her sobs made my heart wrench in my chest. I would never let this happen to her ever again. Franklin suddenly at my side moving further into the house and we looked for the stairs that would lead to the basement.

"Jason and Lorelei are outside. The place is warded, but I don't know if it is intentional or not." His voice was wary and I grunted, wrenching doors open looking for a way to my mate. It wouldn't be the first time a mundane human pulled scary looking runes out of an old book for a haunted house, but the thought of covens was still at the front of my brain.

"When we find Cordi, see if you can find them and break the enchantment." I wasn't taking any risks. As it was, it was taking all my self-control to not start ripping up floorboards to get to Cordelia. The owners would be lucky if I didn't burn this place down once I got her out.

"Here!" Franklin shouted from a room away. I raced over to him brushing past him into the basement. He headed off to search for the enchantment. I cautiously made my way down the stairs. Not because of the darkness though. To a normal human, like Cordelia, this basement was pitch black. To a werewolf, with enhanced sight in darkness, everything was just in muted shades of gray. I was cautious just in case Jack had set any traps.

"Liam!" Cordelia sobbed from the wall opposite of the stairs. Hearing her voice, chased all thoughts of traps from my mind. I just needed to get to her.

"I'm here, love," I said shoving past boxes and poorly dressed mannequins. When I found Cordelia, I could barely keep my wolf's murderous desires a bay. Cordelia was sitting awkwardly on the floor, arms pinned behind her by a pair of handcuffs that were threaded through a pipe in the wall. She had on a pair of light-colored scrubs that were covered in dirt and dust. I immediately went to her, wrapping her up in my arms, and held her for a moment as she sobbed into my chest.

"Hold on, baby, I'm going to get you out of here." I said stroking her hair and trying to soothe her. One arm around her, I reached up with the other, grabbed the pipe, and with a strong jerk pulled it completely from the wall. I stood her up carefully, her sobs dissolved into a gasping laugh.

"I pulled on that for half an hour," she groused as I carefully spun her around and tugged the links of the cuffs apart like they were a toy, giving her back the ability to use her arms.

"You must have loosened it for me—*oof!*" She knocked the wind and my smartass response out of me as she flung herself at me, her arms around my neck, her trembling body flush with mine. Immediately my arms wrapped around her waist and I was happy to hold her as she cried into my tux. I murmured soothing words as I stroked her back and held her until her sobs subsided.

"I thought I was never going to see you again…I thought…"

"It's okay, love," I crooned, kissing her forehead, "Don't think about the what-if's. I'm here, you're safe now. Let's get you out of here." With her arms still around my neck, I bent down, hooking one arm behind her knees and the other around the middle of her back, and lifted her into my arms. She shifted enough to bury her face into the crook of my neck. I was relieved that she was no longer crying but was now worried that she might be suffering from shock.

"Liam! Problem!" my brother's voice rang out through the quiet house. With Cordelia safely nestled against me I climbed the stairs up from the basement two at a time. Frank was waiting at the top of the stairs, phone in hand, and a scowl on his face.

"Repeat what you just told me, Fletcher."

"I had Jess patch me into the department's system and traced the LoJack on Jack's squad vehicle trying to find his patrol route. He took off for the northside, in your direction, like a bat out of hell ten minutes ago. Last ping was on the edge of town about three minutes ago. I'm guessing he remembered to disable the tracking device then. We're all on our way to you, but I got a feeling he's heading back for Cordelia. Something spooked him." Cordelia began to tremble in my arms, short shallow breaths betrayed the panic she was trying to hide.

"How far out is the pack?"

"Ten minutes—"

Lorelei's scream interrupted Fletcher. Followed by several gunshots and a rage filled howl. Then pain reverberated through the pack bonds to me and the others. Jason had been injured, shot. Franklin bolted for the front door. I took shelter behind a wall with Cordelia gently setting her down on the floor.

"Stay low, stay hidden," I commanded, my voice a growl as I began to change from human to wolf. Between my own wolf's rage and my pack mate's pain my transformation was happening fast, my wolf knew its prey was at hand and it was ready for the kill. "I will be right back." Cordelia nodded.

"I love you," she whispered.

I love you, too. I pushed the thought through our bond. My transformation was nearly complete and a wolf's muzzle doesn't lend itself to talking very well. I raced for the front door as a wolf, my senses sharper and my anger stood on the edge of a blade. There was no doubt in my mind that I was going to kill Jack. Silently slipping through the splinters that remained of the front door I took in the scene.

Dusk had settled in, the light from the sun dim as it had nearly sunk behind the horizon and the shadows were dark and deep, perfect for hiding the black fur of my wolf form. From my position I could easily see our vehicle. Between the front of the vehicle and the haunted house, Franklin was crouched, using the mass of metal for cover. He glanced in my direction and gave a shake of his head. While Franklin didn't usually carry a weapon with him, aside from his smart mouth, we knew there were a couple of handguns stored under the seats of the vehicle. He apparently hadn't been able to get to one.

My eyes moved down the vehicle to the rear passenger side. Jason in his half lupine form was sprawled out, face down in the dirt. The ground beneath him was dark with blood. My hackles raised in a silent growl when the coppery scent hit my nose. I knew that he had only been shot three times, but I could feel his pain almost as if it were my own: one bullet in the right arm, a second grazed his thigh, and the third was a through and through in his right shoulder. Nothing fatal, but he had lost a significant amount of blood that was disconcerting.

Kneeling next to him with her arms raised to the sides with hands up and palms out was Lorelei. She was chanting something in the strange language of the fae as magic flowed from her hands to form an iridescent bubble around both her and Jason.

About twenty feet in front of her was an all too familiar truck with the driver's side door open, like a shield. I started to slink through the shadows making my way around to Jack's position, when things took a turn towards the strange.

"Let Cordelia go, Benson!" Jack hollered from behind the door of his truck, "I know what you did! You murdered Loretta Ramos." I stopped in my tracks and tilted my head in confusion. What angle was Jack trying to work?

"I don't know what you're talking about, Jack. I had nothing to do with Loretta's murder," my brother called out, doing a spot-on imitation of my voice. For once I was thankful for all of the trouble he had gotten me into growing up by imitating me. There was also true confusion in his voice, mirroring what I felt.

"You're a sick, sick man Benson. You are obsessed with Cordelia, you killed her mother to bring her back to town and then swoop in like the hero to snatch her up. You stalked her and she never knew because she believed you were a nice guy. Well, I see right through your bullshit. I caught you here with your mobbed-up crew and whatever the hell *that* is. Did you stash her away in there?"

His intent dawned on me and if I were human and not wolf, I probably would have laughed at the sheer audacity of it all. My wolf was not nearly as amused and goaded me into continuing to slink along. Jack meant to pin the blame on me for Loretta's murder and Cordelia's kidnapping. He would come out looking like the hero cop, I would be the evil, obsessed millionaire, and Cordelia would be trapped with him. I had apparently underestimated his intelligence, something that would not happen a second time.

"Cordelia will tell the truth," Franklin shouted the line I fed to him through our bond, keeping Jack distracted, "She already told me that you confessed to the murder."

"She's been through a lot and post-traumatic stress disorder isn't uncommon in the families of murder victims and people who have been abducted."

Son of a bitch, he was going to convince everyone that she was crazy. His word against hers, with no other witnesses, he was sure to be believed.

"You son of a bitch," Franklin swore. "Hey are you there?" From his tone, I could tell that Franklin was talking to me.

Nearly. Keep him angry, keep him distracted.

I pushed the command through my bond to him. I had to stick to the shadows, and there wasn't much cover around the house. I had to move very carefully to not draw Jack's attention my way.

"It's almost a perfect plan," Franklin taunted, "but even if you kill me, you're going to go to jail, you dumbass." There was the smartass mouth of my brother that I was looking for. "I run a security company for chrissake! My team of hackers was already on to you changing the digital reports! We have enough evidence to prove you did it, and if I wind up dead, my men know to turn it over to the police immediately."

"What!?" Jack shrieked.

As I circled around the back of the truck, my mouth started to water. His back was to me, gun at his side. He had no clue I was here, and I knew I had to be quick to keep my advantage. He had no clue that he was about to die in a flurry of fangs, claws, and fur. I leapt at him. My bulk forced him painfully into the door, my claws shredded right through his vest, shirt, and the flesh of his back as I dug in, and my jaws clamped down on his neck. The satisfying taste of copper on my tongue and the thick crunch of his neck snapping were enough to satisfy my wolf. As I tore into him rending his flesh, like the animal I was, I was filled with several moments of regret.

Regret that it was all over so quickly.

Regret that he hadn't suffered more.

Regret that I hadn't inflicted upon him the pain he had put Cordelia through. I rolled his body to his back before tearing out his throat with my powerful jaws. As I reveled in his blood, I could hear several vehicles pull up behind me, the pack bonds lighting up as my men spilled out of the cars and started securing the area. Franklin filled everyone in on the situation before he and Silas started barking orders. I could hear Ephraim talking to Lorelei to get to Jason and start working on his injuries. When Noah said he would get Cordelia out of the house, the corpse was no longer of interest to me. In a blink I was standing in front of the door, staring down Noah and keeping myself between the pack and Cordelia.

"Fuck me," Noah breathed, taking a step back and off the porch, "I didn't even see him move."

I took a menacing step forward towards him. When Cordelia's soft, firm voice made me stop in my tracks.

"Liam, that's enough."

Chapter 27

Cordelia

I'm sure it was probably breaking some werewolf protocol giving Liam a direct order like that, but I suspected he wouldn't forgive himself for attacking one of his employees…pack mates…friends. I had come to the front door after hearing multiple different voices and someone shout that Jack was down. Standing there in the doorway, I could feel everyone's eyes on me, I could feel the disbelief in the air and almost laughed as it turned into astonishment when the massive black wolf that I knew was Liam huffed out a breath and lay at my feet. I reached down to scratch behind his ears when Franklin stopped me.

"That might not be such a good idea right now," he said risking Liam's wrath. "He needs to be cleaned up and so does the area. We're working with borrowed time. I know that my brother would feel much better with you safely back at the estate." Liam chuffed a breath at him and Franklin glared before muttering, "You know I'm right."

What came after was a blur, but there were a few things that stood out. A young man who had been shot by Jack was triaged and loaded up into the back of one of the SUV's while I was ushered into the passenger seat of the same vehicle. Climbing into the seat behind me was a beautiful woman wearing what I assumed had been a lovely wedding dress at some point.

The strapless gown was torn and stained with dirt and blood. I felt guilty that it was my fault her dress had been destroyed, but she didn't even seem to notice. Her attention was on the injured man in the back of the car. She was on edge, but in control of herself. As I stared at her it dawned on me that her skin was tinted a pale shade of blue and her hair was a deep shade of green that was simultaneously natural and unnatural. Once I got over the shock of her strange coloring and remembered my manners, I introduced myself and drew her attention. She shook my hand with a shy, sweet smile.

"Nice to meet you Cordelia, I'm Lorelei, but you can call me Lore," she replied her inflection emphasizing the last syllable of her name and making it sound like 'Laura'. Her voice reminded me of a bubbling brook and there a soothing and familiar quality about it. I found myself relaxing into the seat as activity whirled around us. Lore was torn between being polite to me and glancing over her should to the injured young man in the back seat. I nudged her knee and nodded towards the back.

"Is he your mate?" I asked since it was just Lore, the injured man, and me in the car. Lore gave me a bittersweet smile.

"Yes…no…I mean…he will be," she said haltingly before sighing and finally settling on, "It's complicated."

I looked at her quizzically but didn't press for more information as the back hatch opened and yet another man climbed in and closed the hatch. I couldn't see him well from my seat, but I could see the man that then opened the driver's side door and slid into the seat. My brain screamed *'Danger!'* at the sight of him. Everything about him was hard edges and severe, from the defined, sculpted muscles of his tattoo covered arms to the fierce features of his face. A nasty looking scar ran down the right side of his face, bisecting his lips that were turned down into a frown. I gulped as I noticed the scars also ringed around his throat. I found myself involuntarily shrinking back from him. As if sensing my fear, he turned his coal black eyes to me, his stare critical before it flicked up to the review mirror.

"I'm Dave," his voice was rough and filled with gravel, like it caused him physical pain to talk, but there was the hint of something lighter, a lilting accent of some sort that he fought, "Back there is Ephraim, the injured one is Jason. Since you're Liam's mate, you probably ought to know 'is pack." He turned over the engine and pulled out of the lot, easily navigating the dark, wooded roads.

"Are we taking Jason to the hospital?" Lore asked about two seconds before me. Dave shook his head and hung a right a little faster than I would've liked.

"Can't. Gunshot wounds 'ave to be reported to the police…" he trailed off, but I picked up his meaning. With Jack being the culprit, taking Jason to the hospital would cause police to ask some uncomfortable questions and Liam's pack needed to keep a low profile since I assumed Jack was now dead.

"Don't you worry your pretty little heads about him," the man in the back, Ephraim, chimed in, "He's in good hands." I still couldn't see him, but Ephraim's voice was all South. His drawl was thick and his words unhurried. Dave let out a grunt that I think might have been a laugh.

"Ephraim back there 'as been patching up soldiers since the civil war—"

"World War one, asshole, I'm not that old."

"—'E's probably better than any doctor in Idaho or the surrounding states."

"Wait," I said craning around and looking into the back seat trying to get a better look at him, "That means you're over a hundred years old!" It really shouldn't have been a surprise since Liam had told me he was well over two hundred years old, but it was a fact that I still couldn't quite wrap my head around.

"Hundred and twenty-six actually," he said and his head popped up over the back of the middle row of seats. "But we usually stop counting after about seventy or seventy-five." Looking him, I would have pegged him somewhere around his early thirties with his mischievous blue-grey eyes and crew cut sandy blonde hair. There wasn't anything about him that screamed 'soldier' or 'I'm over one hundred years old.' My brain was having problems processing this information and it must have looked like it because Ephraim let out a gut laugh.

"Oh, darlin' it ain't nothing to freak out about," he laughed, "Trust me in the coming weeks you're going to learn about stuff more interestin' than our life expectancies."

"That's enough," Dave growled at Ephraim, "Liam wants to explain it to 'er when they get finished cleaning." Ephraim held up his hands in surrender.

"You're the one that brought it up," he said defensively before sinking back down to tend to Jason who started to cough and stir. The rest of the ride went by in silence. Dave drove around the town, down dark back roads until the estate appeared in the darkness. It was hard to believe that three weeks ago, I had barged in here wanting to give Liam a piece of my mind. My whole world had changed in such a short time. Everything that I knew had been turned onto its head, and I was finding that I was alright with it.

Dave stopped the car as close as he could get it to the front door. Immediately, he and Ephraim jumped into action. Dave was out of the car and had the tailgate open before I had even unbuckled my seat belt. Ephraim bundled up Jason and carried him like a sleeping toddler as Dave opened the front door for him. Lore and I got out of the car and headed up the steps. Dave jerked his chin towards Lore.

"Go on and follow," he instructed. "Jason will sleep it off, but if you want to stay with 'im, it should be fine. 'E's not likely to rage if you're nearby and 'e can scent you. If you don't want to stay with 'im, Ephraim can get you set up in one of the rooms near 'is. You," he said turning his attention to me, "follow me." Lore and I shared a look.

We had only just met, but I had felt an immediate kinship with her. We were both caught up in a whirlwind of dominant male personalities whether we liked it or not, but we were in it together. She shot me a brilliant smile, as if she understood what I was thinking, before taking off after Ephraim hitching up her ruined skirts to move quickly. I reluctantly followed Dave through the dining room and into a cavernous kitchen.

"Sit," he barked pointing to a chair at the breakfast bar. I did as I was told while he flipped on lights. He left the room, heading down a hall off the right of the kitchen. The instant I was off my feet and I realized that I was safe, I felt the exhaustion set in and my eyes began to droop. I leaned forward with my elbows on the gray marble countertop and held my head in my hands, the remains of the handcuffs jingling in the silence of the kitchen and closed my eyes.

Considering I had started my shift at nine the night before and, if the time on the oven was correct, the clock had nearly circled back around, I had been awake for nearly twenty-four hours. Not counting the parts where I had been unconscious, which I didn't count as real sleep. It was no wonder that I felt exhausted. And that didn't even factor in the stress and panic I had been through. Thudding footsteps coming down the hall made me jump and Dave was back in the kitchen, with a small, leather zippered pouch in his hand. He pulled out the stool next to mine.

"Give me your 'ands," he grumped opening the small case. It held at least a dozen thin metal rods. The end of each was twisted and contorted into a different shapes. I turned in my seat so I was facing him and held out my hands, trying very hard not to think about how much they were trembling. Dave pulled two of the rods out and looked at the cuffs. His face scrunched up and I just knew that it was because of my tremor. He let out a suffering sigh and took both of my hands in his, his hold was surprising gentle like I was made of glass and ready to shatter.

"Look at me, *chérie*," his voice had lost all the growl and anger that it had had up to this point, and I realized the accent that he was trying to hide was a French one, which stuck me as funny and strange considering his hard, intimidating looks. However, there was no mistaking the command in his voice even with the accent. My eyes flew up to his. They were still black at pitch, but I noticed the faintest ring of green around the edges. "You're alright now. Liam and the rest of us will make sure that *never* 'appens again, okay?"

"Okay," I replied while feeling about as far from that as possible. Dave didn't look like he believed me, but he took the two tools, lockpicks I realized belatedly, and with a couple of clicks got the cuff off my right hand and it fell to the floor with a clatter, which made me flinch.

He turned and repeated the process with the cuff on my left wrist, but caught the metal cuff before it had the chance to clatter to the floor loudly. I started to pull my hands back when Dave held my right forearm and began to turn my wrist and look at it. I looked down to see that both of my wrists were swollen, red, and laced with small abrasions that were bleeding. He grunted, displeased.

"He…Jack…he cuffed my hands behind me and looped the cuffs through a pipe on the wall," I said suddenly feeling embarrassed, "I pulled and struggled trying to break the pipe or the cuffs. I must have done most of the damage myself."

"Doesn't 'elp that asshole 'ad them on you about as tight as they could be. Ephraim will take a look at them." He stood to leave, but I grabbed his arm to stop him. At first, he tensed up, as if prepared to fight me, but then relaxed as he looked down at me.

"I don't want to take him away from Jason. These are just some scratches; he got shot. All I need is some Neosporin and some gauze and bandages."

"Liam will insist—"

"Liam is not here right now," I interjected, "Jason needs Ephraim, I don't. Honestly, I just want a shower, some aspirin, and some sleep." I knew I probably looked like hell. My scrubs wrinkled and covered in dirt and dust, stiff with old sweat, I didn't need a mirror to know that my hair was a mess and that my eyes were probably red and puffy from crying. For just a moment, Dave's hard expression softened.

"Fine," he said, gently pulling his arm from my grasp, "But if Ephraim says Jason is stable enough for 'im to walk away, 'e's going to want to look at your wrists. I'll get you set up with the bandages, ointment, and aspirin. Anything else?"

"I wouldn't say no to a shot of whiskey."

The bark of laughter that came out of Dave was unexpected and rusty. I had a feeling that it wasn't a sound he made often.

"I think that can be arranged. Just don't tell Liam."

Standing alone under the hot spray of the opulent glass shower, I finally allowed myself to break down. As the water sluiced over me, I sunk to my knees and cried with body wracking sobs. I cried for my mother, I cried for myself, I cried for Jason, and I even cried for Jack, the sweet boy that I had known, not the monster that he had revealed himself to be. What had gone so wrong since high school? What had happened to my kind, caring friend? I would never know. Sitting on the floor of the shower, watching the dirt rinse out of my hair, the murky brown water swirling around the drain, I tried to make peace with the fact that I would never know.

As much as I wanted to stay in the safe, warm cocoon of the shower, my wrists were stinging, the scabbed cuts having been reopened from the water and gently scrubbing the dirt out of them, and I knew I needed to tend to them. I stood, my legs shaky, and quickly went about cleaning my hair and scrubbing myself down with the body wash that was in the shower. Upon opening it, I realized it was a scent I was familiar with: Liam's crisp clean scent. I supposed it made sense that the third floor suite Dave had taken me to belonged to Liam. He had been anxious as he stood in the small sitting room pointing me to the bedroom and its bathroom. He hadn't followed me in, or even gotten close to me once we had entered through the solid wood double doors.

I scrubbed until my skin was nearly raw and the water had started to cool off. Stepping out into the steam filled bathroom I grabbed a fluffy black towel and dry off. With it wrapped around me I ventured into the bedroom. Everything was silent, and there was no sign of Liam yet. I took a moment to take in the whole room. I had been in such a rush to get to the shower that I hadn't hardly looked at anything else.

Like the bathroom, everything was in shades of black, white, and gray. I usually thought of those colors as cold and clinical, but there was something warm about the room. The walls were a gentle dove gray, the duvet and sheets on the bed were a warm inviting cream color. All the furniture was a matte black, softening the hard, modern lines of each piece. A lamp on the bedside table was on, it's light dimly lighting the room and casting long shadows on the walls.

I noticed a silver tray sitting on the end of the bed that hadn't been there when I first arrived in the room. I walked closer to get a good look at it and bit back a smile. On the tray was a tube of anti-bacterial gel, gauze, bandages, a couple of aspirin, a glass of water, and a shot glass of an amber colored liquid. Securing the towel around me I went to work, patching up my wrists as best I could. The gel stung as I rubbed it on, but I knew that it would help. I wrapped each wrist as best I could before taking the two aspirin with the water. I had been joking when I told Dave about the shot, but I figured I wouldn't hurt. I knocked back the shot, embracing the smooth burn of whiskey as I swallowed it. I then carefully moved the tray to the trunk that was at the foot of the bed.

Once I was patched up, I walked to a double set of doors next to the bathroom door, inside was a clean and highly organized closet. Suit jackets, pants, and shirts were hung with precision. Seeing his clothes, I thought about my pair of dirty scrubs on the bathroom floor. There was no way I was going to be putting those back on, but I didn't have anything else here. I looked around, I was sure that I could borrow something of Liam's but all the shirts hanging were designer brands and far too expensive to use as a night shirt. Not feeling comfortable with taking one of those I continued my search.

After I opened a couple of different drawers, I eventually found a pair of gym shorts and a soft, worn tee. I pulled the shirt over my head, its length coming down to mid-thigh and almost left it at that. However, my lack of underwear made me think twice. I pulled on the shorts and cinched the waist as tight as I could. I padded back to the bathroom, hanging the towel on a hook on the back of the door and tossing my scrubs next to the small trash can and headed back into the bedroom.

Looking at the inviting, king-sized bed, I knew that I wasn't going to be able to stay awake waiting for Liam. I couldn't help myself, I was so exhausted, so utterly and completely drained of energy. I figured it wouldn't hurt to just lay down for a little bit. If Liam or any of the others needed me, they could wake me up. I pulled back the covers and slipped in between the silky, cream-colored sheets. I groaned in satisfaction as I stretched out, it felt like I was sinking into a cloud. All of the aches, the bumps, and bruises didn't seem so bad as I sunk deeply into the cradling comfort of Liam's bed. I closed my eyes before my head even hit the pillow. Still warm from my shower, in the most comfortable bed I had ever known, and a dim light that was just enough to allow me to sleep while chasing away my nightmares, the lure of sleep was impossible to resist, and I let it pull me under.

I'd figure out everything else when I woke up.

Chapter 28

Cordelia

It was just after one in the morning when our caravan of vehicles pulled up to the estate. Dave was outside sitting on the front steps smoking a cigarette waiting for us. When I got out of the vehicle, he crushed the cigarette on the bottom of his boot and tucked the butt into the pocket of his signature leather jacket he always wore. He stood and approached me.

"Where is she?" I demanded, using more force than I needed in my voice. Dave couldn't hide his wince from me, and I should have apologized, but I was too tired and frustrated for that. The pack and I had spent the last four hours cleaning up the aftermath of Jack, Jason, and myself. Which included covering up the murder of a police officer and staging his home like he had run away while also leaving enough evidence to show that he was the one that had murdered Loretta. The police would hunt for him, but they would never find him. Jack's body was currently being spirited away to our secure site, where it would be cremated and reduced to nothing but ash.

"Your room," Dave replied, "she fell asleep a couple of 'ours or so ago." I started to stalk past him when he flung his arm out to stop me. The growl that emitted from me was enough to send any man or wolf running, I could see Dave's throat bob as he swallowed hard, reconsidering his attempt to stop me from seeing my mate. He found some reserve strength and met my gaze. "Not like this, Liam."

I didn't dignify him with a response.

"You're keyed up, angry, and smell of blood and death," Dave said, "This is no way to go to your mate. She deserves more than that." There was an anguish in his voice, and I paused to consider him, the situation, and myself. I was the only one that knew his deepest secret and darkest shame, and that knowledge made me pause.

I looked down at myself. I was in a set of spare clothes that we left in all the vehicles, a tattered pair of jeans and black shirt. I knew that beneath all that my skin was stained with Jack's blood, I had cleaned my hands and face so we could work without arousing or drawing attention to myself. But the man's blood was still under my fingernails and I could still taste the coppery tang in my mouth.

Dave was right and I hated that he was right.

"I will take it under advisement," I said, which was the closest thing to a thank you that I would allow myself. Dave nodded and lowered his arm. I started to move past him when I stopped and put my hand on his shoulder. As sign of understanding and solidarity.

"They make you crazy, sometimes," he said, softly, bitterly so only I could hear him, "'ave you acting in ways that you never thought possible. But a mate is the best damn thing that could ever 'appen to a wolf," He swallowed hard, "It's also the worst damn thing when you lose them." He reached up and patted my hand where it sat heavy on his shoulder before lifting it off and tilting his head up to expose his neck, a sign of submitting to me. "Go, the rest of us got this," he said, the volume of his voice slightly elevated.

I nodded, and immediately the rest of the pack behind me started to move, resuming the work they were doing before Dave had challenged me. I headed into the house and as much as I wanted to head up the stairs and to my room where Cordelia was sleeping, I headed down to the basement first. I headed straight for the industrial shower room we had there that was specifically for cleaning up after nights like tonight.

I wanted to take a quick shower, but forced myself to take my time, scouring and scrubbing my skin until it was nearly raw to get rid of every trace of blood. I brushed and scrubbed my teeth three times before gargling mouthwash twice. During my shower, I also took time to calm down. Dave was right, I was keyed up and ready for violence with the whole night putting me on edge when I didn't need to be.

Jack was dead.

Cordelia was in my den, my bed and safe.

We had done everything we needed to do to maintain the secrecy of the pack.

Anything else could be dealt with later.

Finally, out of the shower and toweled off, I grabbed a set of spare sweatpants and pulled them on before putting a towel around my neck to catch the water remnants as they dripped from my hair. After the longest night of my life, I was headed upstairs to my rooms. To my mate. My body and mind were both beyond a point of exhaustion as the adrenaline had finally bled from my system. Thankfully, I didn't see any of the rest of my pack on the way up, and I suspected it was on purpose. Going into my suite, I threw the towel on an armchair and headed for the bedroom. I opened the door quietly and felt my heart leap into my throat.

One of the bedside lamps was on, its soft glow gently illuminated the room, allowing me to see the most perfect sight. Cordelia lay on her back, her dark hair cascading over the cream-colored pillow like an inky waterfall, one hand above her head and another on her stomach. I frowned at the white bandages around her wrists and wished for a moment, and not for the first time that night, that I could kill Jack all over again, but I found the strength to calm myself, remembering Dave's words. Although her face was relaxed with the bliss of sleep, I could tell her sleep had been restless and troubled. The sheets were rumpled and pooled around her knees, allowing me to see the smooth skin of her legs and the tantalizing curve of her hip that was nearly hidden by the too boxy gym shorts and oversized shirt she was wearing.

My gym shorts and my shirt.

My chest swelled with a proud, possessive surge. Even in my clothes she looked sexy. Hell, she was probably sexier *because* she was wearing my clothes. I walked around to her side of the bed, pulling the sheets back up to cover her before switching off the light. I then made my way back around the bed and slid in next to her. My weight dipping the bed must have stirred her, because I heard her soft voice, filled with sleep.

"Liam?" she sounded so innocent, so hopeful, so scared just by saying my name. How could a single word, a single name, be loaded with so much weight?

"I'm here," I gently crooned to her, moving my body closer to hers as she rolled toward me, her head resting on my chest like a pillow, her right arm around my waist. I wrapped my arm around her as she drifted back to sleep. I lay there awake for a long time, savoring the feel of her skin on mine and running my fingers through her long dark hair. I kissed her forehead.

"I love you," she murmured, still asleep. I couldn't help the quiet chuckle that bubbled up.

"I love you, too, Cordelia." With my mate in my arms, I slept peacefully for the first time in decades.

When I woke up, it was to the sensation of light, feathery kisses and silky strands of hair moving down my chest towards the top of my sweatpants, which were now tented beneath the sheets. I lay there, pretending to be asleep, waiting to see just how far my mate would go. After everything that had happened the day before, I decided to cede control to her for the morning. We would only go as far and as fast as she wanted.

I could feel her pull down the top of my sweats just enough to free my now throbbing member. But what I wasn't prepared for was the wet hot feel of her mouth around the head of it.

"Fucking Christ!" I groaned, trying not to jackknife off the bed and slam myself down her throat. Her tongue circled once before she released me with a loud, wet pop.

"I wondered if that might wake you up," she teased, her voice still a little sleepy but sultry. With a playful growl, I flipped our positions so that she was underneath me on her back. I slowly ground my hips and erection against her as she squirmed under me.

"As far as I'm concerned, that's the only way you're allowed to wake me from now on," I said into her neck as I nuzzled and kissed her exposed skin there. Her gasping whimper let me know just how turned on she was.

We took our time, our love making unhurried and leisurely. Aside from my sudden move to pin her beneath me, I let her take the lead. We explored each other's bodies with languid curiosity we had never had before. Before everything had been so fast, harsh even, with the fervor of two people who couldn't keep their hands off each other. Now, the need and the desire were still front and center, but the urgency was gone. I wasn't scared of losing her now that I finally had Cordelia where I wanted her. She had finally made it to my bed, she was mine, and if I had my say she would never leave my bed.

When her stomach started to grumble after the fourth hour of our marathon sex session, and we were both sated on each other, I realized we were going to have to venture out for food. Mostly because there was no way in hell I was letting any of the pack into our bedroom.

"Let's go get you some food," I said kissing her forehead, nose, and lips before reluctantly rolling out of bed and pulling on my sweats. "Just let me hop in the shower real quick," she said snatching up her borrowed shirt and shorts and heading towards the bathroom, "I smell like sex."

"So?" I asked with a chuckle, "I like the smell of sex on you. It makes you smell like me, that you're marked as mine." She paused, looking back over her shoulder at me.

"I'm not sure if I should take that as a compliment or not. Besides not all of us can looked perfectly rumpled after sex," she gestured at me angrily before gesturing to her own mussed hair, "I'm not going out with this rat's nest." She vanished into the bathroom, leaving me standing there and shaking my head. I walked into my closet and pulled on a tee before barging into the bathroom after her. She let out a startled yip, but I kept my eyes averted as I brushed my teeth.

Settling into a natural morning rhythm was so easy with her. I couldn't imagine a time before I had her here, like all of that time before didn't matter. She just belonged. True to her word, her shower was quick, and she was out and dried off back in my clothes in no time flat. She was struggling with her hair, however, which was a tangled nightmare. I winced as she tugged and pulled on the knots.

"Doesn't that hurt," I asked coming up behind her and snatching the comb out of her hand. I sectioned her hair and began to comb through the knots, much more gently than she had been doing.

"Yes, but beauty is pain," she said with a snort, "Normally I have conditioner and a paddle brush to help with the tangles, but I'm making do with what you've got."

"I can send one of the guys over to your house to gather up some supplies and clothes for you." I felt her tense and I could see her eyes narrow in the mirror.

"No offense," Cordelia replied, "But I don't want your pack mates pawing through my things. I would much rather do it myself." Her chin jutted up and I knew this wasn't a fight I wanted to have or was going to win.

"We'll both head over this afternoon and gather your things," I said, combing out another knot, "I don't like you going over by yourself. I especially don't like the idea of you living in that house by yourself."

"But it has one of the best security systems installed by the best company in town," she said sweetly batting her eyes at me. I couldn't suppress my own snort of laughter.

"If you think I'm letting you out of my bed now that I've had you in it, you have another thing coming." I said combing through her dark tresses to make sure there were no more knots.

"Liam," she said with a glint in her eye and mischievous smile, "are you asking me to move in with you?"

"Less asking and more telling, if you want me to be completely honest," I said setting the comb down next to the sink and turning her to face me. Her eyes were wide with shock, and I cupped her cheeks with both hands, gently stroking her skin with my thumbs. "Cordelia, I haven't done anything right when it comes to you. So, I intend to make amends on that. As my mate, as my partner, you are going to be a target of some nasty individuals – Witches, vampires, and probably even some fae after yesterday. They will target you to get to me, and I would never be able to live with myself if something were to happen to you because you were at your house, away from the protection of the pack.

"Werewolves don't have magic that is flashy or showy, we can't cast spells and we can't manipulate nature, but what we lack in showmanship we make up for in power. Our home, this estate, is an extension of us, we know when something is wrong or if there is someone here that isn't supposed to be. Within our territory, we are faster, stronger, and more impervious. Jason's injuries, if they had happened on our grounds, wouldn't have been a fraction of what they are." Her face fell.

"Don't." I said forcing her to look at me, "You're blaming yourself for his injuries, but you didn't know. You had no idea because I didn't do my duty right. All the fault lies with me, Cordelia, not you. But now that I'm telling you, now that you know, do you see why it is so important to me?"

"Yes," she said before worrying her lip, "but I don't want to be trapped."

"You won't be," I assured her, "I know it may seem like house arrest, but you are still able to come and go freely. You can still travel and see friends, go to work at the hospital, go out and live life, but living with me is non-negotiable."

"What about the job that I accepted in Atlanta?" she asks her chin slightly up and defiant – a look that once frustrated me, I now found endearing and loved whenever it made an appearance. I knew how important this was to her, I knew that there was only one answer that I could give to her.

"If that is what you want, I will move the pack," I answered, "It's a lengthy process to move a pack's territory, details, council politics and legalities that I don't want to bore you with, but it's something that happens fairly regularly. The business that we operate can really be run from anywhere and because no one in the pack works outside of that company, it shouldn't take as long to get everyone settled."

"You'd do that for me?" her voice was filled with wonder. I leaned down and kissed her on the lips, pouring everything that I felt into our connection, physical and the strands of the mental connection that were beginning to settle in and awaken once more after she had blown them out. Every moment of our relationship played through my mind and through our connection. Every emotion I had felt I gave to her. I surrendered to her completely and held nothing back. When I pulled back her cheeks were flushed and her eyes a little dazed.

"I would move heaven and earth for you, Cordelia, if only to see you smile."

She was silent for a moment, her hands gripping my forearms. I could feel her indecision, chaotic and confused, at first. Then it slowly melted away.

"I want to stay."

"As my mate commands."

Chapter 29

Cordelia

I wasn't sure what to expect when Liam and I made our way downstairs and towards the kitchen. Knowing that the house was filled with guys, I worried about how all of them would react. While there had been no fraternities at small university I had attended, but I had plenty of friends at big schools who had told me tales of their walks of shame out of frat houses. Grown men cat calling, hooting, and hollering as they kept their heads down and tried to ignore the embarrassment and shame that welled up in them. All in all, it was not an experience I wanted. Ever.

When we entered the kitchen, I had expected a whole crowd of people, like when I had left the house after confronting Liam. I had been expecting to get roasted and teased for sleeping with their Alpha and boss. I was surprised when the only other person in the kitchen was Silas. He stood at the island, with a cup of coffee in his hand and a copy of the Idaho State Journal open out on the counter. Liam took a seat at the counter and nodded towards the newspaper as I slid onto the stool next to him.

"Report." He commanded. Silas took a long pull from his mug before shooting a glance at me. The growl that bubbled up from Liam should have frightened me at the savage, ferocious sound that wasn't human, but there was a comfort knowing that he would defend me and was ready to fight for me. I didn't like that he was ready to fight his own friends…his pack…

"Did you do it right this time?" Silas asked, completely disregarding Liam's command and growling. This lack of regard wasn't lost on Liam either. I felt a wave of energy pulse out from Liam, washing over me like a hot breeze in the summer. And while I felt mostly unaffected by it, looking at Silas I could see that the giant man had been Liam's intended target. Silas had gone pale, hunched over as if in pain, the now empty mug dangling from his fingers. The two glared at each other until Silas shrugged his wide shoulders and looked away. The tension and energy that radiated from Liam dissipated as quickly as it had manifested.

"Yes, I did. Now, report."

"Front page news, unfortunately," Silas replied this time, closing and spinning the paper to Liam, "but not entirely unexpected. A cop's apartment gets raided, revealing evidence that he was behind a recent, grisly murder coupled with the fact that he looks like he's on the run – that's going to be hard to keep under wraps in even the best circumstances."

"Blowback?"

"Minimal," Silas replied and pulled something from his pocket and slid it across the counter to me. I realized it was my cell phone. "People want to talk to Cordelia: police, reporters, Hannah and her parents. I've been screening the voicemails as they've come in. Hannah, in particular, has sent over a dozen messages since the story broke this morning."

"Shit," I said unlocking it and opening my messages. There was a whole string of conversation between Hannah and I that I know I didn't write, starting with the night right after Jack had knocked me out in the break room. I shivered, thinking about him sending messages as me from my phone.

"Apologies for invading your privacy, Cordelia," Silas said, sounding truly sincere, "Fletcher and I suspected you wouldn't want your friend to worry while you were indisposed. He brute forced the facial recognition so that he could continue to respond and not arouse suspicion that you had gone missing."

"Wait," I said looking between Liam and Silas, "so we're not telling the police Jack kidnapped me? We're just going to pretend that it didn't happen?" I tried to keep the disbelief and frustration out of my voice, but I could easily hear how incredibly sour and angry I sounded. Liam slid his arm around my waist and tugged me, stool and all, closer to him. His arm was tight around me while his other hand stroked my arm and he nuzzled against my neck, planting a kiss on my pulse point. He pulled back and looked me in the eyes.

"As far as the outside world is concerned, yes. Nothing happened last night aside from you having a case of food poisoning and having to duck out of work early. But the pack will always remember what happened and they will know the truth."

"We will," Silas said solemnly before Liam continued.

"If you were to go to the police to report that he had kidnapped you, that would lead to an investigation, you would have to be interviewed and interrogated," his voice dropped to a growl, "and you would have to relive that horrible experience over and over…and for what end? Jack is dead. He faced his judge, jury, and executioner last night and justice, as far as we are concerned, has been served. Not just for what he did to you, but for what he did to your mother as well. To report your kidnapping to them so that they could try to hunt a dead man would only wear upon you and I wish to spare you from that."

"Not to mention, there would be other questions asked: How did we find you? How did we know Jack wasn't there?" Silas added, "While I believe we would be able to convince the police that Jack was never there, if they look too closely, they could poke holes into the work that we did to cover up what really happened. We could risk exposure of our true nature, and that would be catastrophic."

As they explained it, they made complete sense. But it still didn't sit quite right with me. I had instilled in me a deep respect of the police, so it seemed foreign and wrong to cover it all up. When Silas mentioned it could expose them for what they really were, werewolves, it dawned on me that it was for the best.

"Alright," I agreed, "No telling anyone the truth. I wouldn't want to put the pack in danger. Especially considering everything you've done for me." I nuzzled in closer to Liam, "I couldn't do that to our pack." As soon as the words left my mouth, I felt a strange tingle go through me and my head began to pound, like a sudden sharp headache. After a moment, the pain subsided into a dull, distant throb, but I could tell that there was something there that hadn't been there before. Faint whispers in the back of my mind that nudged at my thoughts.

I knew that Liam was over the moon that I had called it 'our pack' and not 'his pack.'

I could also tell that Silas was equally impressed, and glad that I was accepting my role as den mother.

"What the hell?" I asked, panic in my voice, and shook my head before looking up at Liam and then at Silas, "Why do I know what you two thinking?"

It is our mate bond, I could hear Liam's voice, but his lips didn't move, *It is part of the magic that werewolves possess. Your acceptance as my mate and being part of the pack has opened your link to me and, in turn, the pack.*

"If you clear your mind," Liam continued out loud, "You'll be able to feel a connection to all of the members of the pack."

"Isn't that...invasive and rude?" Both Liam and Silas chuckled at my question.

"I forget how strange it is for non-werewolves. No, it's not," Silas replied before tapping his temple, "The pack can always sense the other's thoughts on a surface level — emotions mostly. Nearly all of us have been in a pack and have shared that connection since we were teenagers. To us, it's natural and something that we've grown accustom to."

"It's really not bad at all. But because you are my mate, you might experience a little more than emotions. My connection to the pack as Alpha means that my connection runs deeper to keep the pack in balance and to make sure that they are being taken care of."

"And everyone is just okay with you knowing all their thoughts all the time?"

"It's not like I spend my whole day reading their thoughts," Liam chuckled, "Think of it like background noise or chatter, it's there but indistinct unless I focus on it to hear what someone is thinking. Tell me, do you hear anyone now?" I sat for a moment not saying anything and listening. There was nothing, but it wasn't completely silent. I could hear a faint hum, nothing loud or overt, but it was there and with a little concentration I could tune it completely out. It wasn't that bad, if I was being completely honest.

"See, I told you it wasn't that bad," Liam said with a wink before sliding off his stool and heading toward the coffee maker. "Cream and two sugars," he commented as he set about making me a coffee. A realization settled upon me.

You mentioned before that you had accepted me as your mate the moment we met. If that's what it takes to open the connection: have you been able to read my thoughts this whole time?

I could visibly see Liam tense up and freeze.

Cordelia—

You have! I glared at his back as he continued to work on making a cup of coffee for me.

Not all of them, I promise! Strong emotions or pointed thoughts I could pick up, and sometimes your emotions bled into mine.

I sense there is a but coming…

But when you would sleep, and your guard be completely down. It was like a flood gate had opened.

Oh God! I was mortified. The number of explicit dreams I had had about him…

They were all very flattering, love, and left me incredibly turned on and frustrated most mornings.

Oh. I felt embarrassed thinking about what he would have done to deal with his frustration. *I would just like to say the reality is far better than anything I had dreamt or imagined.*

Silas' deep chuckle pulled me from my thoughts and conversation with Liam. I looked up to see him gathering the paper and shaking his head.

"I had forgotten what it was like to be around a newly mated couple."

"What do you mean?" I demanded. Silas gestured to my face.

"You need a better poker face when you're sharing dirty thoughts with Liam."

"What?!" I cried as Liam burst out laughing.

"Your emotions were all over your face, Cordelia. It's not hard to put two and two together." He turned to Liam who was trying hard not to spill coffee all over the place. "I'll leave the paper in your office. I'm going catch some sleep myself. I'll see you two in a few hours." Silas tucked the paper under his arm and headed out of the kitchen as Liam kissed my cheek and set a mug of steaming coffee in front of me before resuming his seat and wrapping his arms around me again.

"Don't worry, Cordi, I think you're sexy when you blush. Especially when that blush is caused by dirty thoughts about me."

"Oh, stop it!" I snapped at him while trying to push his arms away. Liam just laughed and pulled me closer.

"Oh!" a quiet startled voice from the doorway stopped our mock fight, "I'm sorry I didn't mean to interrupt." We both turned to look. Standing in the doorway was the familiar figure of Lore, dressed in blue sweatpants and black shirt that were about three sizes too big. Unlike the night before, when it was an ethereal shade of blue, her skin tone was now a pale, milky white. Her emerald colord locks were now blonde ringlets. Knowing how she had looked the night before, this change seemed off-putting and unnatural.

"I hope, eventually, you'll be comfortable enough to not need a glamour when you are in the pack's estate," Liam said to Lore, who blushed a bright red and looked like she wanted to run out of the room. I slid off the stool and out of Liam's arms, walking towards her. Taking both of her hands in mine, I pulled her attention to me and away from Liam.

"How are you, Lore? I know that I'm still trying to process everything that happened last night and I am feeling a bit overwhelmed." I said it all with an inviting smile, trying to help her become more at ease with everything that was going on. She seemed to latch onto the fact that I was giving her an outlet and a lifeline.

"I didn't sleep much to be quite honest with you. I slept curled up in a chair next to his bed. I was worried about him and afraid that if I—I closed my eyes, something would happen."

Him meaning Jason, the wolf in Liam's pack who was taking his place at the altar. The thought of an arranged marriage seemed barbaric to me, but I could hear and almost feel her concern for Jason in every word and move. I clasped her hands a little bit tighter.

"It's going to be alright. I know that you and I are both new to everything," I said gesturing a hand to the house around us, "but if you need anything at all, please don't hesitate to ask me. If I can't answer or can't do it, I'll force Liam to do it." There was a bark of laughter from Liam at the same time that Lore pulled back to give me a shocked look. The look was only on her face for a moment before a more mischievous look overtook her features.

"I like you," she said sounding surprised. Which I supposed the surprise made sense, since I ruined her wedding by being kidnapped and stole her future husband out from under her.

I don't like those thoughts, mate. Liam's voice chastened me through our bond. *I don't like you blaming yourself for something that was entirely out of your control. Besides, I wouldn't have been able to go through with it. When you reached out to me, Jason, Franklin, and Silas were already working on talking me out of it and letting Jason take my place.*

Shrugging off the thought for the moment, I responded to Lore, "I like you too. And if you help me keep everyone in line and from bossing us around too much, I think we're going to be excellent friends." This made Lore laugh, a soft sound that reminded me of a babbling brook.

"I make no promises—" she stopped, her eyes going distant for a moment, "I need to get back upstairs." Her words were hasty as she pulled her hands from mine and made for the kitchen's exit.

"I'll be up to check on the two of you soon," Liam said, but Lore was already gone. I turned back to him and he had a frown on his face. Before I could even ask, Liam was explaining.

"She's hiding something," his voice was soft and concerned.

"Do you think it's a dangerous secret?" I asked, moving back toward Liam so he could wrap me in his arms again.

"I don't know, but I do know that she threatened her father, a powerful lord of the Fae, with something and he immediately bent to her will after we had battled with him and his lawyers for six months. Whatever it is, it's enough to strike fear into him, which is enough to raise some concerns. I will have some of the pack look into it—"

"Don't," I interrupted, causing Liam to arch a skeptical eyebrow at me at my one-word command. "I know I'm new to all the supernatural stuff, but I'm not new to the inner workings of a woman. If she has a secret, having the pack dig for it is only going to push her away and strain any relationship she has with us. She's already so unsure and had everything she thought was going to happen be thrown right out the window. The icing on the cake was seeing Jason get hurt. You didn't see her in the car last night, Liam. She couldn't focus on anyone or anything but him. Give her time and I'm certain that she will open up to us. But you and the others can't treat her like an outsider."

"Beautiful and wise," Liam smiled before leaning down to kiss me on the lips gently. "I will take your counsel under advisement, however if there is a threat to the pack, I will be forced to push her."

I nodded; it was only fair. I opened my mouth to respond when I felt a tug in my head and the white noise from the pack got a little bit louder and I could feel a distinct emotion from the pack: curiosity. Liam chuckled.

"Everyone is waking up, are you ready for this?" he asked even as I could hear muffled voices and footsteps heading towards us in the kitchen. Standing there in his arms, I felt like I could take on the world.

"Absolutely. Let's go greet our pack."

The smile that lit up Liam's face was nearly blinding as the pack filed into the kitchen which quickly descended into chaos.

But I had never felt more at home.

Epilogue

Liam | Twenty-four hours later

What is it you wanted me to see?" I called out while coming down the stairs of the defunct machine tooling shop our pack owned and used for disposal. The massive furnace in the basement had once been used to heat metal to a near molten, malleable state, but Joshua had retrofitted it for the disposal of humanoid remains and it was impressively effective.

The room it was housed in served as a sometimes morgue complete with a handful of battered stainless-steel tables affixed with drains that fed into a communal drain on the floor. The space was a step above crude, but it didn't need to be fancy. It just needed to work for our purposes. Besides, the pack didn't need to arouse suspicion by moving in a bunch of brand-new autopsy equipment into a run down, seemingly abandoned building.

Reaching the bottom of the stairs, I could see Ephraim, Joshua, Daniel, and Fletcher gathered around one of the tables, upon which were the remains of Jack. Seeing his mauled body caused a spike of rage to flare up in my chest, remembering everything that he put Cordelia through made me want to kill him all over again. I let loose a growl which made the other four men jump to attention and immediately seek out the threat.

"My apologies," I said, breathing deeply to calm myself and I caught the scent of rot and decay coming from the body. "I am experiencing some regrets about killing him so quickly." Ephraim chuckled, it was a dark and bitter sound.

"I can understand that Liam," he said glaring at the remains, "But we might have a bigger problem on our hands." He beckoned me over to the table before lifting and rolling the shredded remains of Jack's torso to reveal his upper back. I immediately noticed the large star shaped brand on his shoulder, the symbols were intricate, but I did not know the specific meanings of each. But the pentagram shape could only mean one thing.

"He was bewitched?" I asked with a cold, hard voice looking to Daniel; the son of a werewolf and a witch, he was the pack's expert on all things related to witchcraft and a practitioner in his own right. A fact that had led him to be spurned by packs before. If it were true, it meant that Jack might not have been acting of his own volition, which meant that his death might have been needless.

A creeping doubt began in my gut and weighed down my shoulders. It wouldn't have been the first time I had unknowingly killed someone that had their free will stripped away by a bewitchment spell, but that didn't make it an easier pill to swallow.

"Yes and no," Daniel answered, leaving me on edge, but saying nothing more, his gaze glassy and intent on the body, as if looking for something beyond the physical. Fletcher picked up where he left off.

"I compared the components and markings to the council's database of known ritual symbols and sigils. Most of the brand indicates some kind of amplification spell work. Specifically, enhancing the target's feelings to the extreme and causing them to act out in extreme ways."

"The residue of the spell isn't very strong, Liam," Daniel chimed back in, his eyes regaining their focus, "It didn't take very much to push him to do what he did. He was nearly there already."

The news was a bit of a cold comfort to me. I always tried to be diplomatic in resolving conflict, using violence only as a last resort when all other options had been exhausted. When it had come to Jack and what he had done to Cordelia, diplomacy hadn't even been an option, I had gone straight to violence and murder. As much as I wanted to lean into the fact that Jack had already been obsessed with Cordelia, I knew that Jack's death was going to weigh on my conscience for a while. If we had known about the bewitchment, we might have been able to help him.

"Which of the covens are we looking at?" I asked, finding a distraction away from my bitter resentment towards my own guilt and Jack, and examining the markings closely. Universally speaking, all coven or witch magic worked on the same fundamental principle: balancing five elements within a sacred circle.

However, each coven and each witch had their own preferences and flavor of spell components that they liked to use. Once might use dirt or clay as a representation of earth, while another might use oak or redwood to accomplish a similar effect. Knowing the components of a spell often spoke volumes about the person who crafted the spell. So much so that in the tenth century, the Council of Wolves had started keeping a track of covens and their spells.

Fletcher and Daniel both had a sour looks on their faces that told me it was not good news.

"Sir, it has all the hallmarks of the Sallow coven but—" Fletcher began haltingly and hesitated.

"But they were supposed to have been eradicated in the 1690's by their own kind," I finished for him. I was familiar with the cautionary tale, every Alpha was.

"Why would witches take out other witches?" Joshua asked speaking up for the first time. Daniel let out a snort.

"There has always been infighting. Over secrets and spells, mostly," Daniel supplied, "But the Sallows were a special case and the covens agreed for a change and dismantled them piece by piece."

"Why?" Joshua persisted. "They created the most terrifying creature to ever roam the earth: A warlock," I answered. Daniel shifted from foot to foot uncomfortable.

"Aren't those just male witches?" Ephraim asked with snort.

"No, there are those that call themselves warlocks, but the males of witch families are always the weaker sex when it comes to magic. Most male witches can't cast a spell without help from another, they just don't conduct power in the same way. They use the name in the hope of inspiring fear," I replied feeling a headache start to come on.

"A true warlock is a demon possessed male witch," Daniel picked up where I left off, "Normally the demon calls the shots in a possession situation, but the Sallows had crafted a spell that would allow the possessed to control the demon and its power. The Sallow warlock had literally rained hellfire down upon a town where an opposing coven was living."

"There are some who say he could summon the souls of the damned to do his bidding," Fletcher said quietly, looking at his tablet. "They're the worst kind of news."

"So, someone is pretending to be a Sallow Witch," Ephraim said as he dropped the body back on the slab, "Doesn't mean that we're going to be overrun with warlocks."

"Except that we might," Fletcher said, "The mark on Jack is identical to a mark that was used by the Sallow

Warlock." Everyone went still at that, suddenly now regarding the body with more trepidation.

"Salt the body and burn it," I instructed Joshua, "Mix the ashes with lead and then bury them far away from town. I'll inform the council."

"It could be coincidence," Ephraim argued, "Somebody found a picture somewhere, or another coven had a copy."

"Could be," I soberly responded, "But I don't want to take any chances. With the Ley here, the last thing I want to do is pretend like there isn't a threat. I'll inform the council, and we will be on our guard." I stared at the body, wondering how a dead man could continue to cause trouble for me and my pack. A bitter laugh bubbled up from the dark pit that had formed in my stomach.

"What is it Liam?" Joshua asked.

"I can't help but think how crowded our town is becoming. Fae, vampires, a coven, and now potentially a warlock. I don't like it at all."

"But we'll overcome, right?" Joshua sounded so unsure. I looked at each of the men in turn, allowing my confidence to wash over them.

"Of course we will," I said, "We vowed to defend the Ley and the innocents inhabiting the land around it. We have everything to fight for, we will succeed." Each of my pack members nodded in solidarity and all was still for a moment. I knew that if a warlock had surfaced, it was going to be a fight. Thinking of Cordelia, I felt a small pang of anxiety. We did have the most to fight for, the most to spur us on.

But that also meant we had the most to lose.

Cordelia | Two Weeks Later

The city of sunshine didn't disappoint everyone attending the commencement ceremony. There was nothing but blue skies and puffy white clouds lazily drifting along. There was a breeze coming off the lake that helped keep everyone sitting on the track in black caps and gowns from completely burning up and sweating through their clothing underneath. While I tried to pay attention to the speeches that were handing out sage advice about our futures and how we could affect the world, I couldn't help but let my mind drift about how much my life and my future had suddenly taken a left turn.

During the last couple of weeks as I finished up my externship, the pack had stepped in and helped me wrap up my mother's estate, from sorting out the belongings I wanted to keep, to coordinating an estate sale, to getting the house sold and moving my belongings into the pack estate. David had even enlisted two of the other pack members, Daniel and Robert, to drive out to my apartment in Bend to clear it out. It was a little overwhelming, if I was being honest, to go from being completely on my own to suddenly having a massive support structure at my back.

Liam hadn't been stretching the truth when he said that werewolves were protective. Through my ties to Liam, I could feel how excited the pack was to have someone to protect and that their Alpha had a mate. More often than not, when I asked one of the guys for something or for help, I felt a warmth fill my chest through the pack ties: delight. They were ecstatic to help me and when they would say that it was their pleasure, they literally meant it. It was foreign to me at first, but it quickly became second nature and I rarely thought about it anymore.

"Oh my god, can you believe that?" Hailey Santas, a friend and classmate in my program, hissed as she elbowed me in the ribs and pulling me from my thoughts as she pointed towards a group of guys in the chairs across from us. I immediately noticed the silver flask being passed along their row.

"Unbelievable," Bailey Whitehead, another of our classmates, chuckled, "They couldn't at least wait until after the ceremony to get wasted?"

"Engineers," we all grumbled together as the commencement speaker wrapped up to polite applause and students started to file up to receive their degrees.

When it was finally our department's turn, our row and the one behind us stood and headed for the stage. As I moved with my fellow, soon to be graduates, I could feel Liam's gaze on me. Don't ask how, because I couldn't explain it, his gaze felt like a very physical thing and I felt surrounded by it, like he was right there with me.

I am always with you.

His thought made me smile and I had to blink back tears. Liam was constantly showing his support and proving to be an amazing partner. Even after telling him I wanted to stay in Idaho, he insisted that we had a discussion with the pack about potentially moving to Atlanta to allow me to pursue my dream of big city life. All of them were on board with a potential move and insisting that I at least consider it. I ended the meeting by telling them that I had already declined the position in Atlanta and accepted a job at the hospital where I was completing my externship. All of the pack had been a little stunned, and Liam asked me at least three times a day if that was what I truly wanted. He was supportive, considerate, and loved me with abandon.

Which was a good thing because I loved him with that same reckless abandon.

"Cordelia Elena Ramos, magna cum laude," Doctor Preston's voice called out and I walked across the stage to Doctor Gupta, the college's president, who handed me my diploma and shook my hand. I couldn't tamp down my ridiculous grin as the pack cheered and whistled from the stands. They had all come out for the ceremony, even Jason and his new wife Lorelei, who I had become immediate friends with. The newlyweds were still dancing around each other, unsure and timid, but I had a feeling once they settled, they would have a good thing going.

After what had felt like an eternity, the last of the degrees had been awarded, Dr. Gupta made his closing remarks, and the ceremony was officially done.

Head towards the fountain in the middle of campus. I directed Liam who, I knew, would tell the others. I listened to the 'Alieys excitedly chatter as we walked, arms linked to the fountain and caught up with several of our professors that we hadn't seen in the last year.

"Cordelia, I am so proud of you," Rhonda said, hugging me tightly while I waited for Liam and the others to make their way down from the stadium where the ceremony took place. When she released me so I could see her face, I could clearly see the pride and pain there. "How are you?"

"Good," I said, not missing her skeptical eyebrow raise, "I miss her every day and it hurts, but I'm not alone." I felt a familiar tingle on the back of my neck as I felt Liam's gaze hit me. I turned to see the pack approaching and didn't even try to fight my smile.

"Sweet Baby Jesus," Bailey murmured next to me. "That many good-looking guys in the same place should be illegal," Hailey concurred, fanning herself, as Lorelei darted forward to give me a hug, her glamour that made her appear human in place. It was weird seeing her with pale skin and blonde hair, when I was used to her blue hued complexion and deep emerald-green hair.

"Congratulations, Cordi," she said, a huge smile on her face. Over the past two weeks, she and I had become close as we were both adjusting to life in the pack's estate and commiserated about all the strong-willed personalities that surrounded us. I had even introduced her to Hannah and the three of us doing a weekly brunch on Saturdays, just us women and no men, much to their dismay and aggravation. The two, after some initial awkwardness, had hit it off and were fast friends.

Lore had also helped bring me up to speed on the new world I was finding myself in. Apparently in preparation for her arranged marriage to Liam, she had studied werewolf pack dynamics extensively and was fascinated by the links between everyone. That was her thing, though, seeing the web of how everyone and everything was connected.

And I would have thought there might be some residual awkwardness since she was supposed to marry Liam, but there was none to be found. In fact, she had just recently admitted to me how relieved she had been that she had finally gotten a say in the matter and had insisted that Jason was more than adequate for the treaty requirements. I had been surprised, because Liam had made it sound like she didn't have a say in the terms of the treaty, that it was all laid out by Lord Alderkin and his sons.

When Liam had explained to me that Jason was the only one that fit the qualifications in the original treaty that the fae had created, and that somehow Lore had overruled it all with a whispered word to her father, I knew for sure that my suspicions were right: that there was something more going on. Something that Lore was hiding, but for the moment I kept my suspicions to myself.

"Thanks, Lore," I said returning the hug. She released me and moved to Jason's side, who immediately wrapped a protective arm around her, but still held himself stiffly, as if he still wasn't quite comfortable with physical intimacy.

They'll get there. Liam's thought teased me and I turned my attention back to him. He approached holding a bouquet of flowers, a mix of daisies and carnations, which he gave to me before wrapping his arm around my center and kissing my temple.

"Congrats, love," Liam murmured, his lips brushing against my skin. I swear I could hear the 'Aliey's sigh and swoon behind me.

"It's finally done," I said, my words heavy with meaning that I knew he would understand. I knew he would know that I meant more than just the stress of school. That I meant the stress of what happened with my mother, with him, with Jack, and everything else over the last month. Liam's chuckle rolled through me, somehow putting me at ease and on edge at the same time.

"Not quite," he said. I took a step back to look at him critically. He just smiled, reached into his suit jacket pocket to pull out a small velvet box, and slowly lowered himself to one knee in front of me. I could feel the tears well up in my eyes. In one of our many talks, Lorelei had told me how the Alpha of a pack lowers himself to no one. She was gobsmacked when I told her how Liam had knelt in front of me the first day we had met. And here he was, again kneeling to me and the significance was not lost upon me.

"Cordelia—"

"Yes," I interrupted him. He smiled, opening the box.

"You need to let me ask the question first, love. I had a whole speech prepared, too."

"I'm sorry," I said, faking contrition, "By all means, please proceed." That got a rumble of laughter from his packmates. He shook his head.

"Cordelia, before you came into my life, I was content. And the fool that I was, I believed that being content was all I needed. You storming into the estate to argue with me, changed everything. It was like I was finally breathing for the first time in my life. I hadn't realized that I was holding my breath waiting for you. You breathed life into me. From your humor to your passion, and even your anger, you showed me that life is so much more than merely being content. I want to share all of that with you and so much more. Will you marry me?"

"Yes—" The word had barely left my lips before Liam had surged to his feet and wrapped his arms around me. Before I could even squeak out a protest, he had me dipped deeply and his lips sealed over mine. I paid no attention to the clapping, the cheers, or whistling from the people around us, everything just melted into white noise.

Was it going to be easy: being married to the Alpha of a werewolf pack that defended a huge source of magical power while somehow also running an impressive security firm?

Decidedly not.

But if anyone could do it, I knew I could.

Besides, now that Liam had me, I knew that it meant the other members of the pack could finally find their mates. And there was a small, somewhat sadistic part of me that couldn't wait to see what kind of women would bring this ridiculously dominant group of men to their knees.

Character Guide

A quick reference guide for the members of the pack

The Coeur d'Alene Pack (By Pack Rank):

William (Liam) Benson
> **Role:** Pack Alpha/CEO
> **Mate:** Cordelia Ramos

Silas Harper
> **Role:** Pack Second/Logistics

Franklin Benson
> **Role:** Pack Lawyer

Richard (Rich) DeLong
> **Role:** Operations Team Lead

Noah Fields
> **Role:** Investigator

Ephraim McDaniels
> **Role:** Medical Expert/Pack Doctor

Connor Payne
> **Role:** Negotiator/Fighting Instructor

Augustus (Gus) Grant
> **Role:** Range Master/Firearms Instructor

Edgar Reed
> **Role:** Enforcer

Joshua Thompkins
> **Role:** Remediation Specialist/"Cleaner"

David Clarke
> **Role:** Physical Security Specialist/Thief

Daniel Holmes
> **Role:** Occult specialist

Robert Kinglsey
> **Role:** Mechanic/Driver

Jason Walker
> **Role:** Undetermined

Fletcher Young
> **Role:** Beta/IT Specialist

Also by Addison Norris

The Hidden Preternaturals

The Coeur d'Alene Pack

Saved by the Pack

Married into the Pack

Hacking the Pack

Returned to the Pack

Shielded by the Pack

Serenading the Pack (November 2024)

Running with the Pack (May 2025)

Joining the Pack (November 2025)

Endangered by the Pack (TBD)

Hunting with the Pack (TBD)

Protected by the Pack (TBD)

Found by the Pack (TBD)

Hidden by the Pack (TBD)

Negotiating with the Pack (TBD)

Taking on the Pack (TBD)

The Court of Alderkin

The Magician (2024)

About the Author

Mother, wife, nerd, and writer Addison Norris is a brand new independent author who has been writing stories since she was in the 4th grade. When not writing (or reading) paranormal romance, she uses her nerdy know-how to oversee a donor database for a higher education non-profit and utilizes her convoluted thought process and impeccable plotting to run tabletop roleplaying games for her friends in person and online.

She also enjoys the peace and quiet of Southern Oregon and wrangling her husband and son.

For more information or updates on new releases follow Addison on Facebook.